THE WEIZMANN PROTOCOL

Ethan Paritzky

Order this book online at www.trafford.com
or email orders@trafford.com

Most Trafford titles are also available at major online book retailers.

Note for Librarians: A cataloguing record for this book is available from Library
and Archives Canada at www.collectionscanada.ca/amicus/index-e.html

Printed in Victoria, BC, Canada.

ISBN: 978-1-4269-1750-9 (Soft)
ISBN: 978-1-4269-1751-6 (Hard)

Library of Congress Control Number: 2009935801

*Our mission is to efficiently provide the world's finest, most comprehensive
book publishing service, enabling every author to experience success.
To find out how to publish your book, your way, and have it available
worldwide, visit us online at www.trafford.com*

Trafford rev. 9/18/2009

www.trafford.com

North America & international
toll-free: 1 888 232 4444 (USA & Canada)
phone: 250 383 6864 ♦ fax: 812 355 4082

FOR MY PARENTS, WHO KNEW I COULD
AND NEVER DOUBTED I WOULD

"The world is governed by far different personages from what is imagined by those who are not behind the scenes."

Benjamin Disraeli
British Prime Minister
1868-1880

"A man who does not trust himself can never really trust anyone else."

Cardinal De Retz

PROLOGUE

Jaffa—British Mandated Palestine—1936

Chaim Weizmann was petrified, certain his pounding heart would burst right through his chest. He knew holding the meeting in Jaffa was risky, but he hardly expected to be caught in the middle of an Arab riot. The anger and hatred hanging in the air was as suffocating as the mass of humanity jamming the tight confines of the old port city.

As men in *keffiyehs* and *dishdashas* rained sticks and stones on them, Weizmann regretted not opposing the Pact more forcefully. Yet David Ben Gurion had been persuasive, convincing Weizmann that he had to deal with Ibn Saud and Philby. Things in Germany—and all of Europe for that matter—looked bleak for the Jews; they needed a safe home and had few options left. The leader of the Saudi tribes and his British lackey made quite an offer, one Weizmann thought was suspect, but also believed was the lesser of possible evils.

He studied the brown leather satchel slung across the chest of his aide, Michael Freeman, gravely. The bag contained the Pact, the future. Weizmann fought off fear and focused on getting out of the cobblestone labyrinth and back to the landing craft. The undulating mass clogged the easiest path to the clock tower and the harbor.

Suddenly thrust forward, Weizmann's head snapped like a whip. One of the two bodyguards the Zionist Commission assigned to accompany him and Freeman to the clandestine meeting with Ibn Saud and Philby hustled him along. Veterans of the Jewish Legion that fought the Ottomans with the British in World War I, the bodyguards' roughness gave Weizmann hope that he and Freeman might get out with their skins, and return to London with the Pact.

The quartet moved rapidly through Kikar Kedumin's square and past the church and monastery of St. Peter. Weizmann's hat flew off and he grabbed at it. Instead, another push forward. "Leave it. You can get another," one of the guards barked.

The disrespectful tone didn't offend him, but Weizmann couldn't help feeling like a dog on a leash, his movement and path dependent on his master. And like a dog, Weizmann panted, sweating profusely, hot and tired. Shortly he'd be dehydrated.

One guard cursed as a stone tossed from the crowd split the skin on his calf, opening a deep cut and turning his cuff a deep crimson. Weizmann glanced at Freeman, hunched over, rounding his shoulders about the satchel, like a human umbrella, shielding it from the storm.

The four scuttled into Rehov Ruslan alley, and Weizmann saw the street was deserted. On a table to his right sat an abandoned game of backgammon and unfinished glasses of thick Turkish coffee; to his left two *hookas*, knocked over in a hurry. He smelled spices, a whiff of hashish, and saw a woman with chestnut eyes peering through the slats of a broken shutter. The city's Arab inhabitants had left in a hurry to join the riot or shut themselves in their homes.

The men moved down the street, but the swarm closed the distance, shouting *Allah uah akbar*—God is great!—and "Death to the Jews and British!" A rock struck Weizmann's bald dome. Blood trickled down his neck onto his collar. His thumping heart pulsed with the hideous shouts behind him. He began to panic, told himself to concentrate on the bag and the need to get it back to London and the Zionist Commission.

More of the mob rounded a corner, coming straight at them, stone and wood flying though the air.

Strong hands whipped Weizmann around again and pushed him down a different path. He felt like a whirling dervish, dizzy and spinning out of control. He had no idea where he was, no sense of direction, chaos. Yet he trusted the bodyguards and moved his legs as quickly as he could. He had no choice.

Freeman stumbled on the cobblestones. Pain twisted his face.

"Are you all right?" Weizmann gasped.

"Turned my ankle when I fell," he responded, unaware it was the size of a small pumpkin.

"Hold on tight to that bag. Don't let it go." Weizmann eyed the satchel, praying.

They reached another intersection, and Weizmann heard one guard yell, "Make a left. We'll try to double back to Kikar Kedumin. The square should be clear by now. The British should have the beaches cleared so we can get to the shuttle without having to circle the city walls."

Suddenly a loud pop. Freeman dropped the satchel and gripped his right arm, blood seeping though his fingers. Weizmann froze, then lunged for the bag, his knees scraping the ground. Another round and stone shards flew by Weizmann's head. One guard fell on top of him and knocked the wind out of him. A third shot rang, followed by a high pitched scream. A body topped by a red and white-checkered *keffiyeh* thudded next to Weizmann's face. One of the guards had picked off the sniper.

Weizmann almost choked when he was yanked up by his collar. "Keep moving! Don't stop!"

"Where's the Pact?" Weizmann screamed.

"Right here," Freeman shot back.

The grimy, bloody-faced aide had the brown bag tucked tightly under his good arm.

At the intersection Weizmann was shoved left while the limping Freeman was steered to the right directly into the third prong of the human trident. Stones and sticks ripped him and his bodyguard as the crowd converged on its prey.

Everything stopped. The loud screams fell silent, and Weizmann went limp. He could see only the mob swirling around Freeman like a whirlpool. He scanned the ground for the satchel. Nothing but sandals, brown feet, and dust. He thought the light of his soul was expiring, along long with any chance for the Jews.

"Freeman?" Weizmann yelled, groping for his aide.

The body guard grabbed him in a bear hug. "No! Let's go. We've got to get you out of here. We can't help them."

The last time Weizmann saw his aide, Freeman was trying to stand, clutching the brown bag in front of him, hugging it like a distraught child. The rioters beat his back with canes and clubs, and he went to the ground.

Weizmann moved around one corner, down a different alley, and then around another corner toward the square. Suddenly, gunshots and yelling men. He tensed, then deflated, imagining Freeman dead on the ground, his blood running in the street.

More importantly, he'd lost the satchel. It was the end of everything Weizmann and the Zionist Commission had worked for. It was quite possibly the end of an entire people.

CHAPTER 1

Philadelphia—the present

Jake Meyer zigzagged between the white lines, careful not to sideswipe a lamppost, never looking in the rear view mirror. Exhilarated and focused, he slowed to thirty-five miles an hour, did it by feel, his eyes on the pavement, so the speedometer actually read thirty- seven. In one fluid motion he turned the wheel hard to the right, yanked the parking brake up and took his foot off the pedal. Had he been traveling any faster he might have rolled the car.

It wasn't worth it. Before the car came to a complete stop he released the brake, stepped on the gas and sped off in the other direction.

Jake did that six times and then parked, his heart pounding. His hands ached from gripping the wheel so tightly. He uncurled his fingers and leaned against the headrest, steadied by the adrenaline rush and the fall weather. Vivaldi's *Four Seasons* rose from the Blaupunkt speakers, and an autumn breeze wandered through the cracked window. *Vivaldi got it right*, he thought. The music was perfect. The parking lot was perfect.

It was empty.

In front of him, paper pumpkins, turkeys and Pilgrim hats plastered the store windows, and an accordion of letters spelling "Happy Thanksgiving" hung from entrance to entrance. Not that he could see the decorations at that hour. He just knew they were there.

Jake stared at the storefront and thought how the period from Halloween to New Year's day was his favorite time of year. The air cooled, the leaves and the sky changed colors, even the scents grew sharper. Things got warm and cozy. Lately, though, the fall months seemed no different from the rest of the year. When did it all change?

When did fall feel like summer, which felt like winter and then spring? When did everything just run together? When was it that the only difference between the seasons was whether it was dark or light when he got home in the evening?

Jake Meyer wasn't sure, but he suspected it had something to do with age and work. Most likely work. He thought about the courtroom earlier that day. Opposing counsel made a ludicrous argument on his motion for summary judgment that the idiot judge actually bought. How could they be so stupid? Had they no sense of right and wrong? Of justice?

Jake's muscles tensed, and his serenity disappeared. Why did he get so agitated? Was he addicted to the anger?

"The *affair* and its aftermath triggers your rage," his therapist suggested. The *affair* was the reason Jake left his job with the United States Treasury Department and started his own legal and investigative practice. The shrink from the University of Pennsylvania opined further that Jake's hostility was the dormant effect of growing up in the household of a "good" cop where the world was black and white. When life's gray realities appeared and people didn't behave according to his childhood values, an internal conflict occurred, and his anger erupted like a volcano. So said the therapist, and over the years Jake let the anger define and consume him. That gave him an odd energy and purpose, but it was exhausting.

Initially Jake resisted the therapist's condescending psycho-babble. He hated being emotionally filleted in the office on Chestnut Street. Like most people, baring his soul to a stranger, even one educated at an Ivy League institution, was difficult. But after seven years Jake accepted the shrink's theories. The *affair* had rocked his world—made him feel helpless, solidified his cynicism and ignited his anger, which settled into ashes of frustration. He sensed that he lacked control and that a safe existence was a concept, not a reality. Jake responded to his emotions with semi-strenuous cardiovascular workouts or practicing j-turns and parallel stops in empty parking lots. All that released serotonin in his brain, provided temporary relief from his feelings, and gave him a fleeting illusion of control.

Jake took off his driving gloves, put them in the glove compartment and retrieved his cell phone. The yellow light was blinking. He flipped it open and found a text message: "In need of your services. Please call 41-43-255080 at your convenience."

That's interesting. Forty-one was the country code for Switzerland and forty-three for the Canton of Zurich. He hadn't seen such numbers in years, when the Treasury Department assigned him to the Alpine nation. He wasn't pleased to see them again.

He looked at the clock. Two in the morning, which meant eight a.m. in Zurich. He needed to get home and into bed. He had a client meeting later in the morning with a woman who suspected her lover of cheating. The lover was also a woman, which made the investigation more interesting but no less tedious. For Jake it was just a job.

He stared at the number on his phone. He pressed the *send* button but before the connection made, he pressed *end*. Who had called him? He still had some friends at the U.S. embassy in Zurich, but he didn't recognize the number. And even if he knew the caller, did he want to talk to anyone from Switzerland? Wouldn't it open old wounds from the affair? Like leaving a piece of shrapnel in the skin, removing it could cause more problems. But then again, he didn't know how to let things lie. He was the cat that curiosity hadn't killed.

Yet.

He pressed *send* again, the connection made, and after four buzzes someone answered.

"This is Henry Walsing." The voice was masculine but pleasant.

Jake dispensed with the preliminaries. "How did you get my cell number?"

"Your secretary."

Jake raised an eyebrow. He doubted that. His assistant Debbie had been a legal secretary for over twenty years. She knew better than to hand his cell phone number out to clients. For some reason, he decided not to call Walsing on the lie.

"I'd like to hire you," Walsing said.

"For litigation or transactional purposes?"

"Neither. Investigative."

Jake's P.I. license was more than a resumé filler. He earned it a few years before going to law school, and it helped land him the job with Treasury. Now the license allowed him to put another title on his office door and expand his potential client pool. Unfortunately, business

3

remained stagnant, and he spent too much time hounding clients to pay their fees, which only fueled his pessimistic feelings about people.

"What sort of investigation are we looking at?"

Walsing hesitated. "It's delicate, even complicated. I'd rather not talk about it over the phone."

Jake didn't like the response. He could have described the gist of the job without divulging anything particularly sensitive. Did the guy want him to look into some corporate impropriety? Or was it a personal matter? The lack of candor and the fib about the phone number didn't sit well. Jake's instinct told him to turn the case down.

"I'm sorry. I'm really busy these days, Mr. Walsing, but I can make a couple of recommendations."

Walsing sounded mad. "Mr. Meyer, three personal injury cases and two investigations into spousal infidelity do not qualify as busy. I could have called any number of private investigators. I don't need your referrals. I need you."

Jake was uneasy. Walsing knew his exact workload. How did he get that information? Moreover, Jake didn't like the hint of desperation in Walsing's tone. Nervous clients were always the most demanding and controlling. "I really don't think . . . "

"I'll quadruple your fees and cover all your expenses."

Jake was shocked. Eight hundred dollars an hour was unheard of. Not even senior partners in the biggest firms commanded that much. The too generous offer was suspicious. What did Walsing want for that? It almost didn't matter. Jake needed the money, and the outrageous offer outweighed most of his qualms.

"As far as payment goes . . ." Jake started but Walsing cut him off.

"Not a problem. I'll have your fee deposited into your account every three days. If I'm not happy with your work, I'll stop paying, and we'll be done."

He wouldn't have to fight to get paid. What a novelty. Walsing knew how to push the right buttons. "Okay, when are you coming to the States? We can schedule an appointment right now."

"The matter is here in Switzerland. Can you leave tomorrow?"

Walsing must have figured Jake could just drop his other cases. He'd have to rearrange his calendar and hire colleagues to make court appearances for him. It would be a hassle, but what really tumbled Jake's brain was the thought of returning to Zurich. The city hosted painful memories for him. Going back to the scene of the *affair* would be hard. He wanted more information. "Before I make the trek overseas, I'd like to have some idea of what's going on."

Walsing paused again. "I am with the Claims Resolution Tribunal here in Switzerland. Are you aware of our work?"

"Yes. You pass out funds to Holocaust victims." Jake knew the outfit. A few years earlier a New York federal judge approved a settlement in a case filed by Jewish families who lost money in Swiss banks. The CRT adjudicated individual claims and distributed the money.

"That's what we do, more or less," Walsing replied. "Anyway, I need your help tying up some loose ends."

Walsing was going to overpay him for tying up loose ends? "Can you tell me anything else?"

"As I said, I'd prefer to brief you in person."

Jake hesitated.

"It is fairly urgent, Mr. Meyer."

How urgent can it be? Jake wondered. Perhaps shaking things up would be good for him, give his car's transmission a rest.

"I haven't been to Zurich in some time."

"Yes, I know."

Jake bit his lower lip. "Okay, I'll be there tomorrow."

"See you then." Walsing hung up.

Jake stared at the phone, wondering what he had gotten himself into. He flipped it shut, reversed the car, turned the wheel hard and shifted into drive without stopping, heading home to pack.

CHAPTER 2

London

"**W**e'd like you to find your way into a colleague's home and obtain visual evidence of his deviant behavior," the stodgy, round-shouldered Member of Parliament said to The Merchant over a pint of ale in a Hyde Park pub.

The MP's Conservative Party was floundering at the polls, its efforts to take Parliament back from Labor stalled. Some senior members had determined that a well timed scandal, played out in the tabloids, would turn the voters around and kick start a drive back to power. So after some haggling over the price and the logistics of payment, The Merchant accepted the assignment.

The job should have been simple. Get in, snap a few photos of the target in compromising positions, drop them off at a designated location and reap a nice financial benefit. Retirement on an island in the Caribbean, daily golf or scuba diving, and long sunsets to calm the soul would only be a couple of additional assignments away.

Yet the first time The Merchant watched the fourteen-year-old street urchin scurry away from Edward Mulberry's door, he knew he'd disobey instructions. He'd never get paid, and he might even piss enough people off to screw himself out of the work he needed to leave his life behind. But the job struck a chord deep inside, more dissonant each time he watched the slim boy leave Edward Mulberry's home.

The Merchant tailed Mulberry for four weeks, which was not terribly difficult given his routine schedule. Mulberry was typically British—tall and thin with a pointy but straight aristocratic nose. His blue pinstriped three piece suits were undoubtedly Burberry. And he was despicable. Not because he lied to his constituents, every politician did that. And not because he drank too much. What made Edward Mulberry the lowest form of life in The Merchant's view was his affinity for young boys. Every Tuesday night Mulberry went through a side door of the Knight's Head pub in Soho and came out at one in the morning, well after the legal closing time. Once outside he pulled out a cell phone and dialed a phone number that he got in the pub.

Mulberry rushed home to his flat in St. James, and at around a quarter of two a boy about fourteen was dropped off on the corner. Mulberry stuck his head out the door and beckoned his prey. "Quickly! Come inside, you idiot. Do you want someone to see?"

Hidden in a park across the street, The Merchant tried not to imagine the abuse inside the house. He checked his watch every five minutes, and after an hour, the boy left Mulberry's flat. The Merchant unclenched his jaw, but as the boy walked under a street lamp, he noticed the child's red cheeks, bruised eyes, the bloody nose.

After another thirty minutes, The Merchant glided across the street, disarmed the alarm system and picked the lock. The Stasi taught him well, and he made his way silently through the devil's lair.

The flat was clean and orderly, but The Merchant knew that. He'd broken into the place a few times while Mulberry was out. He walked up the carpeted stairs to the second level into the comfortable den. Mulberry snored on a brown leather sofa, his legs stretched on a coffee table, covered by a blue plaid blanket. A half empty bottle of twenty year old Glenfiddich and a tumbler sat next to his feet.

The Merchant turned off the flat screen television tuned to BBC 1, pulled up a chair and nudged Mulberry's legs off the table. The blanket fell, revealing pale, skinny chicken legs.

Mulberry sat up, but his sodden face lacked the usual shock and surprise of one whose home and sanctuary are invaded. After a moment he posed the obvious question, "Who are you, and how did you get in here?"

The Merchant ran a hand over his bald head and crinkled his brow. He was confused. He always worked dispassionately, a practice his Stasi instructors drilled into him. He was neither sad nor glad to inflict damage or death. The profession required it, because emotion led to hesitation which often led to failure. But just then he felt emotion percolating in his gut. What was it? Would he hesitate?

Mulberry stood as if to walk out of the room. The Merchant quickly pulled out a silenced Makharov and fired a shot into the sofa.

"Sit down, Mr. Mulberry."

The MP returned to his seat. "Do you know who I am?" The Merchant had just called him by name.

More silence.

"Don't just sit there, tell me what you want?" Mulberry slobbered, his voice laced with drunken arrogance.

"I know you," The Merchant said softly.

"Well, I don't know you. I don't believe we've met. How could I know someone like you?"

"We haven't met. But I know you. I know you very well and not because I've watched you for the past few weeks."

Mulberry tilted his head, puzzled. Fear began to register on his face.

The Merchant's rage swelled, then settled. He stood and aimed the gun at Mulberry. Usually, he'd double tap quickly, end things fast for the victim. But this time he fired once into the MP's chest and watched for a moment as Mulberry suckled for air. The second round was to the head.

As he left the flat The Merchant realized he didn't regret disobeying instructions and forfeiting the fee. He hadn't killed Mulberry for the boy or any general sense of justice. Nothing like that. Rather he did it for himself. He shed some emotional fat. Not all of it, but enough to make him feel a bit lighter.

CHAPTER 3

Zurich, Switzerland

Jake didn't notice the pounding of the heavy rain or the streams of water that ran down the passenger window. He simply stared through the glass and the downpour. He never imagined he'd be back in Zurich; there hadn't been any reason to return. Things were still raw. Time really doesn't heal all wounds, he thought. They may appear to be closed, but they fester just beneath the surface. One simply learns to ignore the pain and discomfort. Leaving his former job and fleeing Europe had helped the process.

Yet, like picking at a scab, Jake reluctantly accepted Walsing's offer. As a result, he opened up these old lesions. It wasn't just for the money, though a cash infusion would certainly help his struggling practice. Rather, it seemed Walsing had handed Jake an opportunity to perform an exorcism, to cleanse his soul by returning to the scene of the possession. But could he perform the rites on himself? Exorcism demanded faith. Faith required relinquishing control, something Jake preferred not to do.

The sharply accented voice of the old Indian driver brought Jake out of his semi catatonic but self-reflective state. "We've arrived," he said.

Jake paid the driver a generous sixty Swiss francs. It didn't matter. Jake would expense it. He grabbed his valise and opened the door, almost smashing it into one of the large potted plants that sat in front of the building. The thick concrete casings actually acted as bollards and were meant to protect the building from a car or truck bomb, but they were currently a nuisance for Jake. He slid between two of the plants and moved toward the non-descript metal building.

The Claims Resolution Tribunal sat in the narrow entrance way on 141 Badenerstasse in a drab middle-class part of the city. Jake was surprised that CRT was not headquartered in the more picturesque portion of Zurich, closer to the major banks and financial institutions. On the other hand, he thought, it was probably wise to be as discreet as possible for security purposes.

Jake nodded at a couple of workers standing against the wall. He pressed the small intercom next to the door and announced his presence. "Jake Meyer here to see Henry Walsing."

A pleasant sounding female responded. "Of course Herr Meyer, please take the lift to the seventh floor, make a right and head down the hallway."

A loud buzz and sliding bolt allowed Jake inside. He entered the small elevator, barely large enough for three people, and lamented not asking if he could take the stairs. The thought of getting stuck in this miniature vertical moving box increased Jake's heart rate. He hated tight confines.

He breathed deeply through his nose as he exited the lift and headed down the hall. At the end sat a young woman behind a high desk. Her dark hair was pulled back into a bun. She stood and extended her hand. "The Special Master will be with you in a moment. Can I get you some coffee or tea?" It was the same voice Jake heard on the intercom.

"Coffee please, black, no sugar," Jake responded as the secretary led him into Henry Walsing's office.

Jake removed his overcoat and hung it on the rack next to the door and began studying photos sitting on a wood credenza and covering the left wall. They were pictures of smartly dressed men and women whom Jake did not recognize but guessed were important, wealthy or both. The common denominator in all of them was a large intimidating man, sometimes dressed in a black robe, with a red bulbous nose. Jake assumed it was Walsing. Apparently he was well connected, probably though financial status and a long career of judicial service.

"Admiring my wall of shame?" Henry Walsing asked as he strode into the office. "It's a little pretentious I know but the photos are a good way of documenting my professional journey."

Walsing looked similar to the man in the pictures, tall and overweight. But his once dark hair was now peppered with gray and his nose, though still big and round, had lost its crimson color, perhaps the result of a personal prohibition from alcohol.

"It looks like you've had a long and distinguished career," Jake said.

The head of the CRT gave a small grin as he shook Jake's hand. "I've been fortunate enough to have been in the right place at the right time. Everything in life is timing, wouldn't you agree?"

Jake squinted for a second, as if the question were a riddle. "Not always. The timing thing can be a crutch, a way to avoid personal responsibility."

Walsing smiled again. "You have a point Mr. Meyer. Please sit down. Thank you for coming."

Jake placed his 190 pound, five foot nine inch frame into one of the two chairs facing the desk and made himself comfortable.

Walsing continued the usual chit chat that preceded a business meeting. "How was your trip?"

"It was fine." Jake didn't feel the need to tell his new client the eight-hour flight had sapped his energy. More importantly it had triggered Jake's claustrophobia. The plane was full and he was stuck in coach, cramped between a fat man and a woman who had popped a couple of sleeping pills. The man's excess flesh rolled over the arm-rest and Jake had to hunch his shoulders and tuck his arms tight to his body. Even if he could have found some comfortable position to try and fall asleep, the woman had managed to knock herself out and snored incessantly. Jake imagined himself as live mummy stuffed in a sarcophagus. His nerves were shot long before the plane landed.

Having exhausted his already small amount of patience, Jake decided to get to the point, "What can I do for you Mr. Walsing?"

The bulky man dropped himself into the tall leather chair behind his desk and leaned back. "What exactly do you know about the CRT?

Jake shrugged. "Only what I told you over the phone. The Tribunal assists survivors of the Holocaust and their families to reclaim money from dormant Swiss bank accounts."

"Yes, but it is a little bit more complicated than that. In the mid-1990's a few wealthy and powerful people, leaders of the World Jewish Congress began an investigation into Swiss bank accounts opened by Jews who were attempting to keep their assets from the Nazis.

They found evidence that Swiss banks erected elaborate bureaucratic roadblocks for the survivor claimants. The banks even went so far as to use the concept of *bank secrecy* to deny information to claimants, while charging outlandish fees to conduct examinations of their own records.

The evidence proved embarrassing and the banks and the WJC agreed to set up an independent audit committee to determine which Swiss bank accounts were attributable to Holocaust victims. The committee was also tasked to investigate looted assets, Jewish gold and treasures confiscated by the Nazis and converted into currency by Swiss Banks. I was a part of this audit."

Walsing paused and shifted himself, but he never took his eyes off of Jake's face. "Shortly thereafter a few lawyers in the United States got wind of the investigation and filed a class action law suit against the banks on behalf of a group of victims and their families."

Jake was well aware that those outside the United States often viewed the dearth of American law suits as a form of legal bribery. It was one aspect of the U.S. judicial system that wasn't envied by foreigners. "I'll bet the Swiss saw this as a form of blackmail by Jews and their supporters."

"Exactly," Walsing stated. "The whole affair forced the Swiss to recognize that their behavior in World War II was not as innocent as they were taught to believe. They were not a party to the conflict, but some members of the Swiss community did commit despicable acts."

Jake nodded in agreement. The Swiss had long prided themselves on their neutrality and now they were forced to look hard at their national character.

The CRT head continued. "Eventually, the law suits were settled, the Swiss banks didn't want to incur any more bad publicity. The claimants wanted both money and justice since many of the Holocaust survivors were dying. The settlement allocated 1.25 billion dollars to the claimants of five different classes. The largest group, the Deposited Assets Class received eight hundred million dollars."

Jake raised an eyebrow. Even though he was painfully familiar with rewards doled out by the lottery known as the United States court system, 1.25 billion dollars was a mind- boggling number. "How did the Judge arrive at that amount?"

"The specific sum and the class distributions were the result of a three-year investigation by the Independent Committee of Eminent Persons, the auditing committee I mentioned earlier."

Walsing stopped when his assistant entered quietly with the coffee. She set it on the table next to Jake and left. "This is all very interesting, but I still don't see why you need my assistance," he said.

"Bear with me for a moment." Walsing explained that a notice was released to the media about both the settlement and the claim forms that were submitted by Holocaust victims or their heirs. The claims were reviewed to determine whether a victim did indeed own a dormant Swiss bank account and whether he or his heirs were entitled to compensation from Swiss banks. As a result the CRT was created to conduct investigations. Attorneys, accountants and other specialists were hired to examine the claims and match them with various bank records and other historical documentation.

Walsing paused and then continued, "Unfortunately, with such high stakes, there is an elevated risk of fraud. A few charlatans and others with questionable morals submitted suspect claim forms and supporting documentation. This renders the task of auditing and cross referencing even more difficult."

Jake took another sip of coffee and held the warm cup in his palms, trying to eliminate the remaining chill in his bones.

"While reviewing a number of bank records, one of our investigators, a bright and curious accountant by the name of Harold Burns, found some highly unusual entries from the mid 1930's. They were unrelated to any specific claims but he requested permission to look deeper into the accounts. I agreed as long as it did not interfere with the claims processing. He kept me updated on all of his work and filed timely reports. Burns became increasingly fascinated with the irregularities and requested extra time to complete his examination."

Meyer put down his cup and asked, "What did he find?"

Walsing pulled out a handkerchief and dabbed the small beads of perspiration that were forming on his upper lip. "I'm still not exactly sure about the significance of any of the information he gathered but I thought his initial findings warranted further examination. A number of the accounts belonged to some extremely wealthy and influential people of the time. My interest was peaked. As long as victims' claims were competently processed, I saw no harm in completing Burns' side work."

"So, a few old bank accounts caught your attention. That still doesn't tell me what you'd like from me." Jake was wondering whether coming to Zurich had been a good idea. He certainly had no intention of becoming a CRT claims investigator; not that Jake didn't believe in the work of the CRT, it just wasn't for him. Besides, his last experience with the Swiss banking industry had been disastrous.

Walsing rose from his chair and continued. "Mr. Burns was found dead a couple of days ago. The body was inside a trash bin near his apartment. His face had been badly beaten, his skull split open and his legs were broken."

Jake wasn't disturbed by Walsing's description, he'd seen much worse in a previous life, on his last stint in Europe. "It sounds like he ran into some thugs. This is a criminal case. I presume you called the police?"

"I have but there is a curious angle. The last meeting I had with Burns, he informed me that he'd be filing his final report soon. He seemed agitated, frightened and appeared disheveled, as if he hadn't slept in days. It was obvious something was bothering him. When I asked if anything was wrong, he merely said the report would explain *everything*."

"Do you have any idea what he was talking about?"

"Not the faintest."

Jake noticed a very slight twitch under Walsing's left eye. The Special Master wasn't being completely forthcoming but Jake wanted to see where Walsing was headed. "So you think he was killed because of the report?"

"Yes. Burns wasn't a stickler for protocol. He often carried papers in his briefcase instead of having them re-filed or placing them in the safe in his office. His briefcase was missing but thankfully, for once he followed procedure and the papers were actually in his office safe."

"How much of this did you share with the police?"

Walsing stared at Meyer "Some, but not everything."

"Why not? The Stadt Polizie have jurisdiction." Jake was becoming increasingly perplexed and hesitant about taking the job.

"Burn's was a U.S. citizen, a former special agent for the FBI. Given his manner and appearance just before his death, my instincts told me I should keep the papers as quiet as possible. Besides, given Swiss animosity toward the CRT, I have no doubt resolving the case wouldn't be a top priority."

"But withholding information will create further delays in their investigation."

Walsing titled his head. "Perhaps, but that is where you come in. I'd like you to assist the Stadt Polizie with their work and take a different angle." Walsing paused. "The police will look into Burn's death, but I want you to focus on his report, pick up where he left off. I want to know what Burns discovered."

Meyer was disturbed. He was being asked to deal with Swiss bank accounts and he didn't have much desire to do that again. A touch of anxiety crept through his soul. "I don't think I'm qualified for this sort of job. You may want to find someone else."

"Mr. Meyer, I need *your* help to find out the contents of Burn's report."

"Listen, I appreciate your concern for this man and his report but I've got petitions and briefs to file and trials to handle, and as you probably know the U.S. courts frown upon delays. I can't waste time with the murder of an accountant behind some strip joint. Moreover, this really is not my area of expertise."

Walsing reached forward and opened up a manila folder. "Don't be so modest Mr. Meyer; this is precisely your area of expertise. In fact, it says here in your file...."

"My file? Where did you get that? That information is confidential." Jake leaned forward, indignant that the Walsing had looked into his background.

"Mr. Meyer, this organization was sanctioned by the highest levels of government." Walsing nodded to the pictures on the credenza that Jake had admired earlier. "It really wasn't difficult to get your dossier. As an investigator for the United States Department of the Treasury, much of your work involved tracking the flow of money to and from terrorist organizations. In 1995, you were able to stop an attack in Seattle by chasing the funds that were wired from a Cayman Islands account to the terrorist so that he could purchase the necessary explosives. In 1997, you assisted in the apprehension of Mustafa Ibrahim for his attack in the Rome airport because you were able to gain access to some very secretive financial information. And of course there was the Yassin affair."

Well, there it was, Jake thought. His muscles tensed and his heart skipped a beat when Walsing mentioned the Yassin operation. The old wound began to bleed a little.

Walsing paused and then continued, "Your record demonstrates that you have found your way through the maze of banking and financial records. That knowledge is what is required here. Mr. Meyer, I wouldn't have requested your services if I didn't think that your skill - set are of utmost importance here. Please accept this assignment as a compliment to you and your experience."

Jake looked into Walsing's eyes and recognized a consummate diplomat. He displayed a confident demeanor and employed conciliatory words with the appropriate soothing tone. That's really why he'd been named Special Master to the CRT.

Jake pondered his misgivings about the job and the discomfort of working in Zurich again. Yet he realized he wouldn't refuse Walsing. He needed the money. More importantly, he might be able to put some demons to rest. "OK. Where do I begin?"

"By reviewing Burns' previous reports." Walsing pulled another large file from his desk. "I suspect you might want to then examine some of the accounts and transactions detailed in the reports. A list of the banks that Burns visited, along with addresses and contacts, are attached at the end of the file. If you have any questions you can reach me here at the office or at home. My assistant will provide you with the contact information."

Jake stood from his chair and was about to leave.

"One more thing Mr. Meyer, I'd like to be updated daily on your progress."

"That's not the way I operate. I provide a complete file when the assignment is completed and make contact only when I need clarification on an issue."

Walsing frowned. "Indulge me. I'll provide extra compensation for the change in your routine."

Jake stared at Walsing. The Special Master seemed desperate and desperate clients were the most difficult. They wanted to micro-manage the work, to be involved in every aspect of the investigation, to be a partner in the process. Yet Jake was becoming curious. Why was Walsing so anxious to learn about Burns' examination, especially when it appeared to be irrelevant to the work of the CRT? He was going to find out.

"Alright, you can have your frequent progress reports," Jake said retrieving his coat from the rack.

"Thank you." Walsing's tone was sincere.

"By the way Mr. Meyer, where will you be staying here in Zurich?"

"Hotel Schweizerhof. Why?"

Walsing raised his right brow, "Just in case we need to reach you."

Meyer nodded, turned and left the office.

CHAPTER 4

Alexandria, Virginia

The caramel sun slipped slowly behind a horizon of skeletal trees. A black Mercedes inched down King Street, stopping in front of the old brick building that was once a torpedo factory but later renovated for art studios. The passenger in the back seat opened the door slowly, pushed his cane out and hoisted himself up. He grunted and pressed forward through the steam of his breath toward the young man waiting on the corner.

As Lance Piedmont approached, Josh Dempsey's eyes widened with astonishment, and he failed to blink for a few of seconds.

Piedmont had seen the bewildered look before. He knew he was striking, if not mesmerizing - the bald head with thinning hair at the sides, the small straight nose, the penetrating eyes canopied by angled brows and, especially, the pointed goatee. Meetings with business and government officials, especially those versed in history, often began with quiet stares until someone worked up the nerve to swear he was looking at a ghost. Even people who had seen him before, including Josh Dempsey, found the likeness to V.I. Lenin stunning.

Piedmont did all he could to cultivate the resemblance, given the air of authority it created, and the similarities did not end with physical appearance. Like Lenin, Piedmont was warm and generous with family and friends, cold and ruthless where politics and business were concerned. Yet no one would accuse him of socialist sentiments. He was a capitalist in the purest sense of the term. Capitalism was the driving force of his life.

"Let's walk", Piedmont said, thrusting his cane before him.

"Wouldn't you prefer to sit somewhere? There's a coffee shop across the street," Dempsey offered, finally blinking.

"No, I need to move. It's stiff today." Piedmont's gait was robotic, his left leg snapping and locking. Doctors told him after the second hip replacement surgery that he'd never walk again. But they underestimated his extraordinary will and his absurd tolerance for pain. After two months of excruciating rehabilitation he was walking with an ornate onyx cane topped by a twenty-four karat knob, but walking nonetheless.

"Your message sounded urgent. What do you have for me, Joshua?" Piedmont's formality was purposeful; distance was useful in certain "business" relationships.

"We have a problem," Dempsey replied. They walked toward the marina and the docks hosting cruisers that ferried tourists up and down the Potomac in warmer weather. Dempsey pulled his coat collar over his knit scarf and thrust his hands into his pockets. "It's freezing out here."

"Not really," Piedmont responded, his overcoat unbuttoned and his hands ungloved. "The chill is invigorating."

Piedmont detested Dempsey's weakness. Not only was he physically weak, he lacked mental fortitude and discipline. Yet, he served a purpose.

Josh Dempsey was very bright. Had he spent as much time studying as he did drinking and frequenting illicit blackjack clubs at college, he might have graduated top of his class from Princeton. Somehow he managed to land a job with the State Department, and after tours in Nigeria, Morocco and Brazil, he was assigned to Switzerland. He worked back-to-back tours as a political officer where his natural charm forged solid connections with Swiss officials.

Thanks to the internet and modern telecommunications, Josh Dempsey also indulged his addiction to point-spreads, parlays and over-under numbers. He landed in the bad grace of a number of international sports bookies.

Dempsey's father learned of his son's problems and sought the assistance of a well connected high school classmate. "My son is a mess, and frankly I don't know what to do with him. He's thirty-two years old and pissing everything away. I'd be grateful if you could do something."

Lance Piedmont considered his need for a source and "errand boy" and decided Josh Dempsey's predilection for the *rush* associated with risk taking rendered him amenable to leveraged assistance. He enabled Dempsey to pay his debts and go on gambling and save his security clearance and job all at the same time. In return, Dempsey provided sensitive material and assistance when Piedmont demanded.

When Dempsey's tour ended, Piedmont pulled strings and had him assigned to the State Department's small but prestigious Bureau of Intelligence and Research where he spent his time researching various issues and assisting the cadre of experienced intelligence officers preparing *their* reports. And he had access to highly classified information, which Lance Piedmont found both valuable and lucrative.

"Tell me, what's the problem, Joshua?" Piedmont demanded as they reached the railing on the river's edge.

"Burns, the CRT investigator, is dead, too much sodium pentothal. He went into cardiac arrest before our Arab friend could ask him any questions."

Piedmont closed his eyes and rubbed the bridge of his nose. Decorum and etiquette had led him to acquiesce in a colleague's choice of who should handle the Burns matter. He should have insisted on *his* man. *His* agent had performed brilliantly in the past, efficiently eliminating Dissenters who threatened the Levant Group.

Burns had stumbled onto a secret whose veracity Piedmont doubted. Yet if the wrong people discovered it, the consequences for the Levant Group would be disastrous. From the little Piedmont gathered from a loyal group member Burns approached, the CRT accountant was looking into the distant past, investigating large withdrawals from Levant Group members' Swiss bank accounts. Some accounts were dormant, though most remained open, all family and corporate legacies. Piedmont knew that should the CRT investigator dig too deep, the Dissenters would be all too happy to use Burns to embarrass the Levant Group—and Lance Piedmont. He wanted to know everything Burns knew, including the Dissenters' account numbers so he could squelch the threat once and for all.

All that could have been accomplished easily, but the *other* agent, the Arab, bungled things. Badly. And Piedmont blamed himself. He should never have trusted anyone else's man to do the job.

"Did he at least obtain the contents of Burns' briefcase?" Piedmont asked.

"It was empty. Apparently Burns followed protocol this time and left the documents in his safe."

Now they had nothing. After years of running a hidden empire, he might get to watch it crumble because some imbecile couldn't fill a syringe and ask a few questions. Piedmont was tired of suffering fools.

"Has Walsing seen the papers?"

"Yes, though he doesn't seem to have any idea of their significance."

"Well, that's a relief," Piedmont snapped. "Find a way to get them. They'll tell us what Burns discovered and help us identify the remaining Dissenters so we can finish them once and for all."

Dempsey sneezed twice and responded. "But Walsing thinks the documents are related to Burns' death. He wants to continue the investigation."

"You learned all this from our contact in Zurich?"

Dempsey nodded. "Apparently, Walsing's worried about the Swiss authorities' disregard for the CRT's work and is bringing someone else in to look into Burns' death and finish his research. He wants objectivity."

Wind whipped across the river raised swells against the piers and the hulls of the boats. Piedmont enjoyed the sound of the waves and the breeze. They pacified him.

"Whom has he hired?"

"A lawyer and private investigator named Jake Meyer."

"What do we know about him?"

"That he worked with the Treasury Department." Dempsey paused.

"What else Joshua?"

Dempsey grinned.

"What are you smiling at?"

Dempsey told him what he knew about Jake Meyer, and while it wasn't obvious, Piedmont was delighted. The best news he'd heard in a while. "Well that is indeed fortuitous. Meyer may help insulate our associates."

"Exactly. Let him do all the leg work."

"Everything has been cleared through the appropriate channels?"

Dempsey nodded, still grinning.

The sun dipped below the horizon, and the street lamps switched on. Piedmont wondered whether his predecessors found managing the Levant Group so challenging. He was responsible for the well being of millions of people, quite a burden. But he wouldn't have it any other way. He could alter the course of world events, mold history as he saw fit. He found his lot in life intoxicating, and he had no intention of giving it up. He was committed to the survival and growth of the Levant Group. He decided that even with Meyer in, prudence dictated he take out an insurance policy.

"Joshua, why don't you place an order for some wine?"

The smile abandoned Dempsey's face. "I'm not sure The Merchant is still in business."

"I'm sure he is. I hear he's not ready to liquidate just yet." Piedmont chuckled at his own joke. The Merchant trafficked in liquidation, the mortal kind. "Apparently, he angered some of our English brothers. He'll need the work. Offer to buy a hundred cases of his best. Perhaps some Côte Rotie, 1999."

"Okay, but what if he wants to sell more? He's shrewd. He'll bring up our last order." Dempsey hunched his shoulders against the wind.

"Play the carrot and the stick. Remind him how much we appreciate his past work. Buy whatever he's selling, but make sure he understands the consequences of refusing to deal with us. I'm sure we'll be able to come to an arrangement."

"I'll get on that right away."

Piedmont turned from the river and watched Dempsey shiver. "You look awfully cold. Shall we go?"

"If you don't mind."

The pair turned and walked back along the boardwalk toward the torpedo factory. Dempsey opened the limousine door and Piedmont ducked inside. Before pulling in his cane, he leaned out and taunted the shivering informant. "I'm going to California this week. Weather should be in the seventies. You know how to reach me."

CHAPTER 5

Tel Aviv

In the communications room at the Institute for Intelligence and Special Tasks, the Mossad, the evening watch officer assigned to collect intelligence from sources in Europe typed the transcript. A conversation at the Claims Resolution Tribunal headquarters had come in a few hours earlier, and its mysterious nature caused Lt. Colonel Amir Eckstein some concern.

In the months since the order came down to monitor CRT communications, Eckstein had heard nothing out of the ordinary, mostly the names of claimants, the claim amounts and the CRT's ultimate disposition. On one level monitoring the information helped the Israelis make sure that people victimized by Swiss banks got justice.

On another level, a small number of intelligence officials viewed the CRT data to recruit *sayanim*, Jews in other countries who could be called upon to help Mossad field operatives in time of need. People figured that if Israel *helped* the claimants get their money back, they might be persuaded to return the favor.

Still, given the volume of raw intelligence from all over the world about more pressing matters, the CRT information was not a top priority. But something about the communication before him told Eckstein that Rafi Golan, head of Mossad operations, would be interested. And he preferred to risk Golan's legendary wrath with too much information rather than too little. He didn't want a blemish on his career.

Eckstein marched the transcript to the top floor of Mossad headquarters on King Solomon Street. In the outer office he approached Dalit, Golan's uniformed military intelligence assistant.

"Is he in? I need to talk to him."

"Yes, but he's pressed for time."

"That's okay. This won't take long."

Dalit pressed the intercom. "Amir is here to see you." She didn't use *sir* or any honorific. Things inside Mossad weren't formal.

A deep voice boomed from the loud speaker. "Send him in."

As Eckstein opened the door, smoke from Golan's Bolivar cigar violated his nostrils. Unlike most Israelis who smoked cigarettes as if they prolonged human life, Golan's taste ran to Cuban and Dominican tobacco. His humidors, in the office and at home, were always stocked.

"What is it? I have a briefing in half an hour." Golan hawked brown colored saliva into a spittoon.

Eckstein had witnessed the disgusting display before, but still winced. "I just received some information from CRT."

Golan turned around. He knew all about dormant Swiss bank accounts, looted assets and the Tribunal's work. His operation—a team disguised as a cleaning and maintenance crew—planted bugs and taps in CRT headquarters. But monitoring the CRT was no longer part of his workload. "I don't have time for this. Give it to Boaz. He handles the *sayanim*."

"This is different. Something strange happened in Zurich. An examiner was killed and Walsing is bringing in a person named Jake Meyer to investigate."

"What's this?"

Eckstein handed the transcript to Golan who exhaled smoke as he read through the conversation. He read it a second time. His face tightened.

"What else do we know about Burns' investigation?"

"Only what it says in there. We can go back through the tapes to see if there was anything other than the authorization for Burns to look into the large discrepancies."

"Do it." Golan took the top-secret stamp from his desk and slammed it onto the transcript. "Has anyone else seen this?"

"No."

"Good. I want to see everything else from CRT the minute it's transcribed. Clear?"

"Yes. What's going on?" Golan's reaction startled him.

"I don't know yet."

Eckstein studied his boss and then left the office. He knew the communication was strange but hadn't expected Golan to re-prioritize it. What made Golan's blood run cold? Eckstein was glad he had trusted his gut instinct to inform Golan.

Golan poked his head out the door. "Cancel my meeting, Dalit."

"What shall I say?"

"That I had to attend to something urgent. I need a file on Jake Meyer. He's American."

Back in his office, Golan picked up the transcript and stood by the tinted window. He read the conversation again and drew a deep breath into his barrel chest. *Some large strange withdrawals were made in 1936.* Was it possible? Could Burns have stumbled onto something? Would Meyer pick up the trail? The Pact, and hence the withdrawals, were the subject of conjecture among a small inner circle of the Israeli intelligence community. The mysterious deaths of a few elderly Swiss bank account holders a few years back raised some eyebrows—but not enough.

But what if the agreement, the Pact, had been reached? What happened to it? Where was the money? If proof of the deal surfaced, the consequences would be disastrous for the Middle East. That made even the hulking Golan shudder.

He had to find out what was going on. He needed to know if the rumors would turn into fact. He had an idea. Not perfect but it might work. Golan picked up the secure telephone line. "Get me Paris station. I need to pull someone in."

CHAPTER 6

Zurich

Jake paused in front of the Stadtpolizei headquarters on Banhofquai. The nineteenth century beaux arts structure looked like any other building housing a government bureaucracy, its stone face marked by rows of evenly spaced small windows and dormers jutting out like oversized blemishes.

A pair of policemen in blue jumpsuits with hand guns strapped around their thighs came through the large wooden doors, too engrossed in conversation to notice Jake standing on the bottom step. He sighed and entered the building with familiarity if not ease. He hoped he wouldn't be recognized; he didn't want to endure the stares or the glares, as the case might be. It had been a while. Maybe the turnover of staff and officers meant nobody knew about his past.

After receiving permission from the Chief Inspector's office, a guard let Jake through security. The thin man in a neatly pressed tunic handed him a visitor's badge. "Take the elevator to the fifth floor, make a right . . ."

"I know where it is, thanks."

As he walked to Chief Inspector Albert Kessler's office he wondered how his former colleague would receive him. They hadn't spoken since Jake left Zurich. Jake had wanted distance. Needed it.

He rapped lightly on the door and stepped into the outer office. Gertrude, Kessler's long time assistant, jumped smiling from behind her desk and hugged him.

"Herr Meyer! It's been so long. How are you?"

The warm welcome was a surprise, but Jake gently returned the squeeze. "I'm fine, Ms. Tinder, and you?"

"Well, thank you. My husband Heinrich is retired. The grandchildren come by once a week. The dogs are still barking, and work is busy."

Jake offered a faux smile. He remembered nothing about Gertrude's family and was glad she kept things simple. "You must be glad Albert brought you up with him."

"He didn't have much choice. I'm the reason he was promoted." She giggled just as Albert Kessler strode through the door.

"She's right. I'm too disorganized. My calendar is a mess, and there are papers everywhere."

Jake knew that was far from true. The Chief Inspector was orderly to a fault.

Kessler hugged Jake, another surprise. It made Jake slightly uncomfortable. He and Kessler had worked closely together, but as he did with most people, Jake shared few intimacies with the Chief Inspector. He figured a handshake would have sufficed.

Kessler led Jake into the inner office. "It's good to see you. Have a seat."

Jake sat in the chair across from Kessler's immaculate desk, centered by a single blue file.

"You look different. What is it?" Kessler asked after studying Jake a second.

Jake was thinner. He could tell by looking at old photos and then in the mirror. His cheek bones and jaw were more prominent, his torso less bulky. Frequent and vigorous exercise to release serotonin to the brain had that affect.

"I run on a treadmill six days, work out with lighter weights, watch my diet."

"Are you training for a marathon?"

"Not at fifty-five. I just decided I wanted to stay in shape." Jake didn't mention that his routine also fought the depression from his previous tour in Zurich.

Kessler patted his stomach lightly. "I'm afraid my shape is based on a steady diet of beer and bratwurst. I don't share your enthusiasm for exercise."

Jake just nodded. Kessler was lean, and the belly he referred to was nothing more than a coin purse on a thin torso. Was he trying to flatter Jake?

"Anyway, how have you been?" Kessler's tone turned serious.

Jake was unable to look Kessler square in the eye. He told Kessler about his practice and his quiet life. And then he returned the social volley. "Congrats on the promotion. Happened pretty fast, but you deserve it."

Kessler tilted his head in appreciation. "I put in my time as an investigator. Now I have to put in more with management responsibilities to boot. Though the increase in pay helps with the boys' tuition and Ilse's spending habits."

Jake wasn't so sure the promotion was *deserved,* but he said it anyway. Kessler was a good detective but not a great one. His skill was bureaucratic, a climber adept at the art of ass kissing, which came in handy when time and red tape got in the way. When they worked together tracking terrorist funds, Jake was the toiler, making the logical connections, putting pieces of evidence and intelligence together.

Still, Kessler was a diligent professional and Jake respected him. An apology was in order. "I'm sorry I never got in touch with you. It was difficult."

"Don't worry. I understand. It could have happened to any of us."

Jake was slow to respond. "But it didn't. It happened to me, and others suffered."

Kessler stared a Jake without judgment. "Nonetheless, at some point you must forgive yourself."

"That's what they tell me, though it's not that simple." He was glad when Kessler changed the subject.

"So, you've been to CRT, met Walsing and all?"

"Yes. He seems concerned but pleasant. Well-connected man. He knew a lot about me."

Kessler's face became serious. "Be very careful."

"Why?"

"Do you know the last straw that brought the CRT into existence?" Kessler asked, irritated. "That bank guard who filched documents from the shredding room at Union Bank of Switzerland and handed them over to a Jewish reporter."

"I remember. My contacts at the banks were not too pleased."

Walsing had mentioned the incident. The stolen papers showed that the Nazis had forced people to buy real estate they confiscated from Jews. They deposited the money in secret Reichsbank accounts in Switzerland. After the war, UBS took control of the real estate without informing or compensating the people the Nazis robbed. The evidence was damning.

"Union Bank was about to compound its mistakes by destroying evidence of a previous indiscretion," Jake said.

"But the guard violated the Bank Secrecy Act, which is a mortal sin here."

"Yes, I know. They ran him out of the country," Jake said with his own irritation. "He lives in California, I think." They disagreed on the matter, but it was no time to debate ethics, or morality or Swiss banking laws.

"Many Swiss believe the CRT is a Jewish bribery scheme. They resent it."

"As for Walsing," Kessler said, "he's a very wealthy man with the power to dole out CRT's funds. He's not held in high regard." Kessler paused. "And there have been rumors about his scruples."

"What sort of rumors?"

Kessler again was careful. "The unflattering kind, the kind that can lead to immense embarrassment."

Jake wasn't sure of Kessler's meaning. Did he mean sex scandals or bribery? Jake decided not to push the matter. He knew how to deal with problematic clients. "I'll take that under advisement. Tell me something. If you're not fond of Walsing, why did you agree to let him bring me in and run the Burns matter?"

Kessler pushed his glasses up the bridge of his nose. "Because I didn't want to deal with the headache, the public relations nightmare this was going to cause."

Well, at least he's consistent, Jake thought—playing the game, not wanting to antagonize the public or his superiors. *Probably has his eye on another promotion.*

"Beside, we're understaffed and spend all our time chasing terrorists. Jake, we're much busier than when you were here. The Yassin affair was *one* simple case compared to the dozens I have to manage."

Jake didn't recall the Yassin operation as *simple*; he found it devastating. But he held the thought.

"In any event, when Walsing asked for assistance and mentioned your name, it was fortuitous. I need the manpower—and distance from the matter. Who better than Jake Meyer? You know how things work here. You'll dispose of this quickly and quietly. The only caveat is that I need complete reports from you, as if you were one of my investigators. Would that be okay?"

"I'm being deputized?"

"Something like that."

He didn't have much choice. He'd have to give Kessler whatever he wanted. Walsing demanded frequent updates, so Jake would just pass the information along to his former colleague. "Sure, that's fine. What do you know about Harold Burns?"

Kessler sat down, flipped the lone blue folder on the desk open and turned it toward Jake.

"His body was found in a trash bin near the Barfusser with fractures to both femurs and multiple contusions on the face and skull."

"Could it be some kind of hate crime?" The Barfusser was a gay club. Maybe Walsing was wrong and Burns' death had nothing do with his extracurricular investigation.

"It's possible, though nobody there saw Burns in or near the bar."

"Okay," Jake said, "maybe it wasn't gay bashing, but you said a lot of people resent the CRT. Maybe some anti-Semitic group just happened to leave the body where another minority hangs out."

Kessler tapped his chin again. "Possible. From what I heard, Burns was a demon with claims. He may have antagonized the wrong people."

Jake had the sense that Kessler didn't want to deal with the Burns matter and not because he was busy. He took the file and flipped through a couple of pages. The damage to Burn's body was blunt object trauma, lead bludgeons, probably pipes, and the cause of death was subdural hematoma. But the toxicology report was curious. Burns had sodium pentothal in his blood.

"Do you have any theories about the sodium pentothal?" Jake asked.

Kessler shrugged. "No. It was minimal and unrelated to the brain hemorrhage."

Kessler was right. Had the sodium pentothal levels been higher Burns would have gone into cardiac arrest—and the report said nothing about a heart attack. Jake looked down at the report. The numbers next to the sodium pentothal levels were blurry. That was strange. He rubbed his eyes and flipped the page. The type was clear. It must be the jet lag, he thought.

There was little else in the report except a witness' statement that she saw Burns getting into a car with a dark-haired man on Banhofstrasse. But the old woman wore thick glasses and couldn't describe the man. Useless.

Finding nothing in the file about Burns' "side work," Jake decided to test the waters. Had Walsing really kept the information from Kessler? "Do you know specifically what Burns had been working on?"

Kessler didn't hesitate. "No. Just that he was investigating claims and bank records like the other CRT examiners. Why?"

"I thought it might give me a more precise place to start."

"You might get more detailed information from Walsing."

Jake already had what he needed from the head of the CRT, but he wasn't convinced Kessler didn't know Burns was moonlighting.

Kessler stood. "I'd like to thank you again for helping out. I'm really swamped. We should get together for dinner and catch up."

Jake took the cue and pushed his chair back. "Dinner would be good. And you should really thank Walsing. He's paying me."

Kessler grunted. Clearly, he did not trust the head of the man.

Before Jake stepped through the door, he wheeled. "Is our friend Pincay still in town?"

"Of course. I'm sure he'd be thrilled to see you." Kessler was sarcastic.

"I doubt that too."

"Shall I set up a meeting?"

"No, I'll call him myself."

CHAPTER 7

Paris

Maya Herzog crossed the Pont des Arts, the wooden footbridge spanning the Seine and linking the Louvre to the old mint. In a few months, it would be packed with couples walking arm and arm, picnickers on benches enjoying wine and cheese and artists sketching the Eiffel Tower or the Île de la Cité with Notre Dame's steeple in the background. That day however, the bridge was empty except for a few pedestrians scurrying across, bracing themselves against a cool wind.

Maya focused on a diminutive man in a dark overcoat and wool cap crunching through a thin layer of snow sixty yards ahead of her. She followed him off the Pont and up the narrow serpentine streets lined with shops specializing in old books and antique furniture. She lost sight of him for a moment when he rounded a corner and passed the art school, but she didn't panic. Thanks to Yoni, she knew exactly where he was heading.

Yoni Lippman was responsible for identification and surveillance on Maya's five member team. Slight and awkward with hunched shoulders and drab clothing, he looked more like a visiting academic at the Sorbonne than part of an elite intelligence operations unit. Only twenty-three, he was skilled and talented, especially with a camera. Every Thursday for six weeks, he watched and photographed the man take the same route from the Pompidou Center on the right bank to the Église Saint-Germain-des-Prés on the left bank. In the church he lit candles one of the six side chapels, sat in the nave along with a handful of old women stroking their rosaries. The entire exercise lasted fifteen minutes, no more, no less. Yoni briefed Maya with great precision.

"He's in," Yoni told Maya from an apartment above the Deux Magots, across the street from the church.

Maya—blue coat, gray shawl, plaid skirt, bag of charcuterie and bread over her arm—nodded and went into the café and took a seat at a window looking onto the church. She ordered mineral water and a croissant, her eyes on the entrance. She thought about the man in the church, her target. Abu Nassir was a member of Islamic Jihad, and for the past eighteen months, under the guise of attending confession, he'd been retrieving monetary contributions collected by Etienne Martel, a sympathetic priest. The naive Martel believed the money went to meet the Palestinians' social needs. In fact, Nassir used the alms to buy weapons to kill and maim Israelis.

Nassir was despicable, and Maya had no qualms about eliminating him. Nassir wasn't a freedom fighter. He was a murderer of women and children. Of that Maya was certain.

But for the first time in her career a shiver of remorse moved Maya's soul. Not for Nassir but for his family. According to his dossier, Nassir had a beautiful raven-haired wife and two sons, ten and eight. And in a matter of minutes Maya would change their lives. The woman would be a widow and the boys would be fatherless. They would have to learn how to cope with sorrow and anger. They'd learn to live without their father, but they would miss him, and they would be enraged by the way he left the world.

Maya's thoughts wandered back to a hill in Jerusalem on another chilly day. She watched her father's plain pine casket lowered into the ground. Her mother wept and the rabbi prayed, barely audible over the rustling trees. Maya permitted herself a moment of grief, and then like sliding bolts in a prison door, she went into emotional lockdown.

Her earpiece snapped her back to the present.

"Eight more minutes," Yoni said.

She didn't respond.

"Eight more minutes. Are you there?"

"Yes, I've got it."

Maya took a sip of water and lightly touched the pen in her pocket. She had practiced removing the cap many times when the pen was not full of poison. And now that it was, she wasn't concerned about pricking herself with the needle that replaced the ball point. What made her nervous were the ramifications of another failure.

Maya was part of Caesarea, an elite group of thirty Mossad agents who assassinated terrorists and their supporters abroad. Caesarea tracked and eliminated the people behind the murder of eleven Israeli athletes at the 1972 Munich Olympics. Maya was the first woman, accepted for language skills and ability to blend into various communities. The icing on the cake was she had been anointed the "hitter," reserved for only the best agents in a squad.

But ten years before, in Jordan, a couple of her colleagues had a poison pen hit on another terrorist with disastrous consequences. They were caught and to get them back to Israel, the government had to turn over an antidote and release several terrorists. This embarrassing incident caused the vaunted Israeli intelligence service to disband the Caesarea units.

But they were reactivated after a controversial politician visited a Muslim holy place and kicked off new violence. Maya didn't want to repeat the Jordan fiasco.

"Three minutes. Are you ready? Are you okay?" Yoni asked.

"I'm good," Maya mumbled into the microphone on her collar. She was about to prove a point.

Suddenly Nassir came through the church door.

"I've got him," Maya said. "I'm moving."

She left some Euros on the table, grabbed her bag and crossed the street to follow Nassir, about twenty yards back. Adrenaline rocketed through her as she closed the distance. Her focus sharpened, her senses eliminated useless information. The air stopped being cold, and the traffic fell silent. Everything in her sight was a blur save Nassim, the target. A couple of steps behind, she flipped the cap off the pen and held it at the edge of her pocket, the shopping bag hanging on her wrist.

At a natural gait, Maya took one more stride, swung her arm gently, touched Nassim's leg with the pen. To a casual observer, she bumped him with the shopping bag.

She dropped the pen into her bag as he caught her eye.

"Pardon, monsieur."

He smiled, nodded and kept walking. Heart failure would not occur for another few hours, after the poison seeped through his clothes and skin. Long after and far from the incident on the street, it would look like death from natural causes.

Maya rounded the corner and opened the door of a waiting car. She removed her hat and spoke into her scarf. "It's done. Let's go home."

"I will," Yoni said.

"What does that mean?" Maya asked, opening the window and tossing the pen.

"It means you are leaving Paris but not coming with us. Special orders."

"From whom?" Maya was surprised and a little irritated. She had just rejoined the team.

"Your uncle."

Maya paused, took a deep breath. "Shalom", she said as the car sped to Orly airport.

CHAPTER 8

Villefranche sur Mer, France

The Merchant reclined in a chair in the sun room of his villa, exhausted. The Mulberry assignment was unexpectedly taxing. Watching the Member of Parliament for four weeks brought difficult memories to the surface. As if he'd raised a sunken war ship on his own. He hoped that killing the MP would scuttle the ghost ship lurking in his soul.

It didn't.

He finished a glass of chardonnay, leaned back and stared out into the undulating cobalt Mediterranean. Whitecaps rose and fell, and within minutes The Merchant was asleep. His lean body twitched, and he muttered occasionally in German.

When he woke, his heart was pounding, and his shirt was damp with sweat. He took a moment to reorient himself. Everything in the dream seemed so real—the rank smell of alcohol on his father's breath, the sting on his slapped cheek, the desperate gulping for air when the leather boot slammed his stomach. He saw his mother turn away, afraid to helping her son. She was as much to blame as his father.

The Merchant took a deep breath and calmed himself. The thrashings ended long ago, when he was fifteen, when he turned his parents into the Stasi. He didn't complain about the abuse because the secret police officer would have laughed at him. Rather he concocted a story that his parents were CIA spies and drafted phony letters to support the charge. It didn't matter that the Stasi could have checked things out. In a police state, accusations *are* proof.

Once his pulse was normal, The Merchant got up, showered and dressed. His stomach grumbled, so he headed into town to grab a bite to eat.

Jumping on his moped, he descended the serpentine roads along the French Riviera. The chilly air was invigorating, and he breathed it in like an exhausted athlete. Through the narrow streets of Villefranche sur Mer he wound to the Crèperie du Soleil, a non-descript restaurant hidden away from the more touristy eating establishments.

He found the owner and sole occupant, Sophie Foucard, folding napkins and organizing silverware. Looking up, she smiled and came around the bar to hug him.

"Welcome back. How was your trip to London?"

The Merchant considered his response. "Relatively productive, I suppose."

"How many cases did you sell?"

"A hundred total. A mix of Syrah and Cabernet Sauvignon from Mas de Cadenet and St-Baillon."

"Not bad. Your client has good taste. Those varietals are the region's best." She went back behind the bar to retrieve a bundle of mail.

The Merchant knew Sophie doubted he was a middle man in the fine wine business, but she rarely questioned him about his travels. She accepted his lies and managed her curiosity. After twenty years, it was what he admired most about her.

He sat at an empty table, and Sophie brought the packet of letters and bills over.

"There's not as much as usual, but then again you weren't gone long," she said as she took a seat across from him.

"Thank you." He flipped through the envelopes.

Having his mail delivered to the crèperie was part of the cover he set up when the Stasi first sent him to Western Europe posing as a wine merchant from Provence. He learned all about wine and wine making, all about the best climates and soils for certain grapes. His palate could discern *fruity*, *smoky* and *flowery* wines. He was a quick study, and soon his knowledge rivaled that of a five-star restaurant sommelier. The self-proclaimed wine connaisseurs he catered to were often wealthy and politically powerful, often full of information important to East Germany and the Soviet Union.

He needed a cover for mail, though, someone stable who wouldn't ask questions about his absences, someone he could trust completely. So after casing Villefranche and getting to know some of his neighbors he decided to cultivate a relationship with Sophie Foucard.

Recruiting her was not difficult.

The Merchant had a natural charm and charisma that he perfected as a *Romeo* agent for Markus Wolfe, the East German spy master. He could approach any woman, strike up a conversation and within minutes raise a sparkle in her eyes. At that point he knew she'd do anything he wanted, including commit treason for him. He once recruited the wife of an American diplomat at a cocktail party in the Louvre while the husband stood by sipping champagne!

And The Merchant turned those skills on Sophie Foucard.

He stopped by the crêperie often to flirt and talk with her. He brought her bottles of wine and gifts from his travels, and they chatted over an espresso. After their third date, a sunset stroll through Antibes, they made long, passionate love. When he was certain she'd fallen for him, he asked her to hold his mail. Like scores of women before her, she accepted without question and never gave him reason to question her loyalty.

But unlike the other women, expendable when they no longer provided useful information, The Merchant developed a puzzling allegiance to Sophie. He knew better than to get too close to an asset, but he really *liked* Sophie. He enjoyed her company. She was a bright, strong woman. He trusted her. She was a friend, and for the first time in his life he felt safe with another human being. She became his sanctuary.

The Merchant felt her watching him, studying his face. "What is it Sophie?"

"Your face. There are more lines than before."

"I'm fifty years old. There should be lines."

"They're not from age. You're tired. Aren't you sick of all the traveling and work? Don't you just want to rest?"

The Merchant stared at her. She was still beautiful. Her green eyes remained captivating, and her dark black hair fell gently on her shoulders. Monthly salon visits took care of the gray. And her body was brown and taught from constant exercise underneath the Mediterranean sun. She still embraced some vanity, which The Merchant appreciated.

"Yes, I'm tired. And soon, very soon, I'll give up my business, and we'll go somewhere."

"I've heard that before," she said, raising a brow.

"I . . .we could use some more cash," he said quietly, reflecting on the sum he'd forfeited by killing Mulberry.

"I've heard that before too," she riposted. "I wonder if money is really the question."

Thumbing through the last of his mail, The Merchant came across an envelope without neither postage nor return address. It had been hand delivered.

"Where did this letter come from?" He raised the parchment colored envelope in the air. He often received such messages, but he wanted to know something about the messenger before he opened it. He had stockpiled his share of enemies, and one of them lacing the paper with something lethal was not so remote a possibility.

Sophie wiped her hands on a bar towel and came over for a closer look. "A gentleman dropped it off yesterday."

"What did he look like?"

"About average height and build, beady gray eyes, cropped white hair." She searched her brain for further details. "He had high cheek bones. He was actually handsome in an authoritarian sort of way."

The description was enough to trigger The Merchant's memory. It was okay to open the envelope. Still, considering who delivered the message, his jaw clenched.

He read the letter twice. It was only three lines.

We are in need of your assistance once again. Meet me in the spire of Grossmünster Cathedral at 11:00 P.M. Thursday night. By the way, we can clear things up regarding your indiscretion in London.

The Merchant's chest tightened. Of course the messenger was aware of the Mulberry incident. His organization had tentacles everywhere, and it was one of the few that could actually reach out and touch The Merchant. He knew the last line was more a threat than an offer of assistance. It might have read, *Do as we ask or we'll help some irate British politicians find and kill you.*

"What is it?" Sophie asked.

"Nothing." He tore the message up. "A client is thinking of making a large purchase from Presqu'île de St. Tropez."

A wave of guilt fell over him. "It's the last time, I promise."

"I know," her voice devoid of conviction.

The Merchant kissed her lips softly.

"Where is your business?"

"Zurich," he whispered.

CHAPTER 9

Zurich

The immigration official at Zurich's Klotten airport spent more time than usual examining Maya Herzog's South African passport. Mossad's forgers backstopped the document, so when the officer pulled up the name of Priscilla Vooten, a small business owner from Johannesburg who died six years earlier, the credentials cleared and Maya went through customs with ease.

After renting a car using cash and a Spanish passport with a different name, Maya drove to the Hotel Kindli where a reservation for Amanda Brighton, the name on Maya's United Kingdom passport and second MasterCard waited. She showered and lamented the fact she didn't have time for a nap; she had a meeting at a quarter to four that afternoon.

At the park near the Arboretum she sat on a bench near the water line. Had she been a couple of inches taller she could have paddled a toe in the Zürichsee. Wavelets lapped the rocks in front of her, and she pulled her coat collar up against the chilly breeze skimming the lake.

Covered sailboats bobbed up and down on the water, straining their anchor lines, and Maya's mind wandered. Why did they pull her out of Paris? What was going on in Zurich that agents already in the city couldn't handle? The soldier in her told her not to question orders, but the intelligence operative in her was curious. She was accustomed to emergencies, though she usually had some idea of what was going on. This time she was in the dark.

A familiar smell told Maya her contact was near. She couldn't see him; the hedges behind her were too tall, but the pungent scent was unmistakable. Her olfactory sense imprinted it on her brain years earlier, and it always triggered childhood memories, both pleasant and painful. Maya stood, walked to the park's path and fell into step with Rafi Golan.

In a dark overcoat, Golan moved elegantly for someone with short legs. A thick cigar jutted from his mouth like the plank on a pirate ship.

"It's good to see you," he said.

"You as well," she responded.

"I love coming to Zurich. I can get Davidoffs at such a magnificent price," he said, admiring the mocha colored tobacco stick between his fingers.

"That's really fantastic."

Golan raised a brow at the sarcasm. "How are you holding up?"

Maya knew Golan didn't approve of the way she mourned her father. She didn't speak at the funeral, and worse, she didn't sit *shiva*, the Jewish week of mourning. Rather she tended to her mother's needs, picked up groceries, cleaned the house. During her four week bereavement leave Maya shed not a single tear.

"I'm fine. And please don't lecture me on the benefits of traditional grieving."

"No, I wouldn't dream of it."

"He's the one who left when I was twelve, without warning or explanation."

"I know you're angry, but there wasn't any other way. We needed him to cut all ties. It was crucial for the mission and for everyone's protection."

"But I don't hear from him for twenty years, and then you call to tell me he's dead. You knew where he was and how he was doing all the time."

"Maya, you of all people should know it was an operational necessity. He was an illegal. What he did was vital for Israel's security."

Maya took a deep breath. "I'm aware of that." She knew the government put illegals in hard target countries to work undercover. And she knew better than to ask the details of her father's assignment, so secret that only three others knew about it: Golan, the head of Mossad, and the Prime Minister. But that didn't minimize her resentment, her confusion. Her father's work colored the rest of her life.

Taking her hand but looking straight ahead Golan said, "He loved you very much and asked about you frequently. He made quite a sacrifice."

Maya clenched her jaw. She knew Golan was right.

"I miss him," Rafi whispered. She felt warm and safe. Maya had known Rafi Golan since childhood. Her father and Golan met as orphans when they came to Israel after the Holocaust. The two boys forged a close friendship. So, while Maya had blood relatives on her mother's side, Rafi was the "uncle" from her father's side. She spent holidays and vacations with Uncle Rafi, and since he didn't have any children of his own, he treated Maya like a daughter. That was especially true after Rafi, newly appointed head of Mossad operations, dispatched Maya's father on his secret mission. Guilt and complicity drove him closer to her.

Maya turned her head back toward the park. "Does Shin Bet have any more information?" She referred to the investigation into her father's murder.

"Not yet, I'm afraid. Forensics has finished their work, but there wasn't anything definitive. They're leaning on informers, but nothing has turned up yet. It was a professional hit." Rafi frowned. Israel's version of the FBI usually had more by this point.

"Promise you'll keep me updated?"

"Absolutely. As I told you, you'll be the first to know."

They strolled a while in silence, stopped to examine a sign displaying the water fowl that lived around the Zürichsee. Finally, Maya asked, "Why are we here?"

Golan scratched his chin. "Are you familiar with the work of the Claims Resolution Tribunal?"

"Sure." Maya knew a small group of Israelis joined the Independent Committee of Eminent Persons to negotiate a final settlement with the Swiss banks and set up the CRT. She had no idea Golan was on that team.

"We've been monitoring things there for a while. The information from the CRT sometimes helps recruit *sayanim*. Yesterday a strange communication came in."

"What was it?"

Rafi ran over the conversation between Jake Meyer and Henry Walsing at CRT.

"What's worrying you about that?"

"I'm not concerned."

"Bullshit. You wouldn't have come here and pulled me away from Paris unless you thought this was serious."

"*Nachon.* You're right. But it's only a hunch, and I've kept it quiet.

"You didn't tell anyone about it?"

"I don't have to." Golan raised a brow, as if to remind Maya of his power within Mossad. "I want you to follow Jake Meyer and find out what he uncovers. Protect him if you have to."

"Protect him from what?"

"Anything or anyone he may come up against."

"Okay, that's simple enough." Maya didn't understand what had Golan so on edge, but she didn't want to push him. She knew better than that. "Any background on Meyer?"

"In the late 1990s he was a new Department of Justice investigator looking into terrorist funding. He promoted a secret counter-terrorist center between U.S. and European intelligence. After the 9/11 attacks CIA and their French counterpart, DSGE, set up Alliance Base to track transnational terrorist movement. Unfortunately, Meyer didn't get credit for his ideas, and he didn't get to work with them."

"Why?"

"He was in charge of the Ahmed Yassin affair."

"Oh." She remembered hearing about it. The young Yassin was a member of the Abu Nidal group that shot up the Rome and Vienna airports in 1985. Later he raised funds for Al Qaeda, Hamas and other Islamic fundamentalist groups. He was clever and shrewd and a target of U.S. counter-terror efforts.

"Meyer uncovered Yassin's network of banks, accounts and middle-men. He was on the verge of arresting Yassin and pressing him about the terrorist cells he funded. But Yassin escaped arrest, and Meyer took the fall. He left the Department of Justice soon after."

"How did Yassin get away?"

"I don't know. We never found out. Our contacts with U.S. intelligence in Europe went silent."

"And what became of Meyer?"

"He opened up his own law and P.I. practice in Philadelphia. Not doing too well. He barely makes ends meet. A bit of a recluse. He has few friends and spends his free time at a gym or some offbeat coffee house, reading and writing."

"Then the Yassin operation really messed Meyer up?"

"Yes," Golan assented, "but that's not your concern. Meyer is here because Walsing is scared of something. Find out what it is."

"Anything else?"

"Meyer is at the Hotel Schweizerhof, room 504."

Maya turned and kissed Rafi on the forehead.

CHAPTER 10

Zurich

Grossmünster Cathedral stands on the right bank of the Limmat River, the twin domed spires rising like giant helmeted sentries guarding the city. It is dedicated to the three patron saints of Turicum, the Roman name for Zurich, beheaded for trying to evangelize the city's inhabitants. The official city seal shows the martyrs carrying their heads underneath their arms. As The Merchant approached the portal of the romanesque/gothic church he wished he could remove his own head to stop the pounding inside his cranium that raged ever since he first read the message. He had little bargaining power. He was caught in a vise.

Under the portal he opened the large wooden door, normally locked at that hour. Inside he found the long nave softly illuminated by candles along the aisles. As least his contact had the courtesy to light the way.

The Merchant ascended the narrow, slippery steps in the south tower. Agile and flexible as he was, had there not been a rope banister he might have fallen. The stairs wound upward like the snake wrapped around the triangle of the Caduses, and just when The Merchant was getting winded, he reached a landing halfway up the tower and saw a light in an alcove to his left. A man sat in the recess, staring out an opening, an umbrella between his legs. He tapped the chair opposite him.

"Glad you could make it," he said.

"Based on your message I didn't have much choice." The Merchant's voice hid the irritation he felt.

"No, I suppose you didn't. But I'm sure you'll find working with us again more beneficial than the alternative." The man paused. "A few of our members in the House of Lords are furious."

"I didn't intend to kill Mulberry. I just snapped."

"Given your childhood, I'm not surprised. Mulberry's proclivities must have brought back some bad memories. Nonetheless, they want you dead. You went beyond your mandate."

The Merchant couldn't see the man's face in the faint light. But he knew the visage well. Hard and angular, with deep, cold eyes that could penetrate steel.

"But fortunately for you, we need your talents again."

"Is it the Dissenters?" The Merchant asked.

"Yes and no."

"There were a lot of bodies last time," The Merchant recalled. A few years earlier he took a job from the man's group which involved *wet work*. He didn't *like* killing for killing's sake; it lacked the subtleties of spy tradecraft and manipulation. But he was good at killing, and the skill was in high demand. Beside, it paid well.

"But you performed superbly," the man reminded him. "You left little evidence."

"And you took care of the residue."

The man pulled a folder from his coat and handed it over. "The photo inside is of an individual named Jake Meyer. He's looking into some things that may interest our organization. We want you to follow him and obtain any information he uncovers."

The Merchant lifted a candle to study the picture. The full head of white hair and matching beard was a stark contrast to his own shaved head and face. "That shouldn't be a problem. But where's the rub?"

"It's likely Meyer will come into contact with some Dissenters. If we knew which ones, we wouldn't need you. In any event, you are to eliminate any Dissenters Meyer meets but only once you have the information. Then terminate Meyer."

So, there would be more bloodletting.

Merchant stared at his contact. He didn't like the man. He'd dealt with him before, and the experience wasn't pleasant.

"For your efforts, you'll be compensated well," the contact said.

"How well?"

"Well enough for you and Ms. Foucard to move to that tropical locale you've discussed."

The Merchant's stomach dropped. How did he know about their plans? Surely Sophie hadn't told anyone else. Did the man's statement have a double meaning? Was he threatening Sophie as well? The Merchant wasn't afraid of death; it was an occupational hazard, especially as a freelancer. He was worried about Sophie.

"If you harm Sophie I'll . . . "

"You'll what? Why do you think you've survived all this time, despite the bounty on your head? You can't possibly believe it's because you're such a hot shot. You've had help from people who find you useful."

The man tapped The Merchant's shin with the umbrella. "But don't think for a moment you can act without consequence or hide from us."

The Merchant fought the urge to strangle him. He hated being cornered. But if he choked him to death, he'd never live in peace. The man's organization would hunt him down, probably kill Sophie while he watched, then slit his throat.

The Merchant crossed a catwalk to the north tower and stared at the lights on the Lindenhoff, the lime tree lined square in the center of the city, laid out atop the ruins of an ancient Roman customs post and stockade. During the day old men played chess with pieces the size of small children on squares painted onto the ground. At night, lovers strolled hand in hand and stopped along the walls underneath the swaying trees to embrace or gaze upon the old city. The Lindenhoff offered the tranquility and serenity The Merchant never thought he'd want until then—and might never have, because he had no options.

Or did he?

Options were like slabs of clay. They could be left as they are, dull and unappealing, never serving a purpose. Or they could be sculpted into something acceptable, pleasing, even useful. In the end clay is clay. The outcome is a matter of perspective and imagination. The Merchant learned that when he rid himself of his parents by informing on them. He made himself an orphan, but it was his choice.

Returning to the south tower, The Merchant asked, "How troubled is your organization about what this Meyer fellow might dig up?"

"We're concerned, and that's all you need to know."

The Merchant leaned forward. "I'll do this. But I want only half of the money."

Confusion and curiosity registered on the man's face. "Then what else do you want?"

Leaning forward, The Merchant told the man his wishes in detail.

The contact stared into his eyes without blinking. "Very well, we have an understanding."

"Good. Deposit the money in the same account as before."

The contact nodded.

"And stay away from Sophie."

"Meyer is at the Schweizerhof hotel, near the train station," the contact said, his head turned back toward the window.

The Merchant headed for the staircase.

"Careful on the steps," the contact called after him. "They can be slippery on the way down."

The Merchant grasped the banister and took the steps two at a time.

CHAPTER 11

Zurich

If patience were a virtue, The Merchant would go to heaven. He'd been nursing a beer in the Zum Hock bar on Linthescherstrasse for over an hour, watching the Hotel Schweizerhof employees' entrance across the street. The door was on the side of the building, sandwiched between the windows of the hotel bar and an upscale night club. It was inconspicuous.

The late evening pedestrian traffic was light. The Merchant saw a few people leave through the door, wrapped up, purses slung over arms or backs, laughing and chatting. But he had not spotted his mark.

Then he noticed a man round the corner onto Linthescherstrasse and head for the black door. Adrenaline warmed him . Finally, what he needed! A hotel employee about five feet, eleven, and lean. He timed his gait so he would meet the man right at the door.

"Hello," he exclaimed in the overly cheerful voice of one starting a new job.

The man looked up as he reached for the door. "Can I help you?"

The Merchant noticed the man's frown and blood shot eyes. His lips were slightly parted, and he barely blinked. The man was exhausted.

Good, The Merchant thought. Exploiting fatigue would be simple.

"Tonight is my first shift," The Merchant said. "They assigned me to room service and told me to come in here. I shouldn't be seen by the guests. But they didn't give me the code."

The employee studied The Merchant a second. Prudence dictated he go inside and check with the shift manager. But he was tired. He punched the numbers on a metal pad and held the door for The Merchant.

"Welcome aboard," the man said flatly. "You'll forgive my lack of enthusiasm. I had a crazy night, and I'm still hung-over." He unwound the scarf around his neck and extended his hand. "Heinrich Schneider. Nice to meet you."

Schneider's soft grip revealed a timid personality and a weak physique. More luck. The Merchant's job would be easier than he expected.

"Likewise. I'm Roger Thibault." The name rolled off his tongue. One of his many covers.

They rounded a corner in the bowels of the hotel, and the sound of industrial washers and dryers, great gusts of steam, roared from a room off to the right. Fluorescent lights glowed a lurid green. The innards of the posh hotel were as drab as a high school locker room.

The Merchant noticed that Schneider's bag was half open. He saw toiletries and a fresh shirt. *Perfect.*

"Listen, when I interviewed with Herr . . . Christ, I can't remember his name," The Merchant stammered.

"Gerard."

The Merchant snapped his fingers. "Yes, Gerard, that's it. Anyway, he said there was a changing room here, but he didn't have the time to show me. Do you know where it is?"

"Yes. Follow me." On their way, the employee said, "A bit of advice. Gerard's mousy appearance isn't deceiving. He's nosy and quite a taskmaster, so be careful not to mess up."

"I'll keep that in mind."

In the corridor, a waiter and his serving cart flew through swinging doors revealing a bustling kitchen, all but knocking The Merchant down in his haste.

Schneider smiled. "Welcome to Hotel Schweizerhof. Never keep a guest waiting."

The Merchant returned the smile and memorized the layout. The Room Service office was opposite the kitchen, he noted, and at the end of the hall was a bank of three gray service elevators.

"Where did you work before this job, Roger?" the guide asked.

"The Four Seasons, in Paris."

Heinrich whistled and raised a brow. "Really. I'll bet they paid! Why'd you leave?'

Schneider took a left just before they reached the elevators. "I just needed a change of scenery. I was tired of the same buildings, same bars, same parks. I like to move around a lot." His eyes scanned.

In the locker room red plastic benches lined up in front of the black metal lockers along the walls. Cheaply carpeted with soft lights, the room was about as cozy as an employee changing area could be.

"I know exactly what you're talking about. I think I might leave soon and get a job in Eastern Europe. I'd like to write, become the next Kafka."

"That's ambitious."

"You have to dream, you know."

"Absolutely." The Merchant knew exactly what Schneider was talking about. But his dreams involved sandy beaches, warm water, grilled fish, and solitude. All shared with Sophie Foucard.

Schneider opened his locker and pointed to the rear of the room. "Over there to your right is the men's wash room, and to the left is the ladies. I imagine Gerard has not assigned you a locker yet." He scanned the room and gestured to the far end where a smart looking brunette was changing from work shoes to heels.

"How about there, next to our little university student, Else."

The woman looked up. Full red lips flashed a sexy smile at The Merchant. He returned the flirt and walked toward her.

Else turned to Schneider. "This little student could teach *you* something."

"Excellent. I'm ready for a bit of tutoring."

"Not tonight," she giggled. "I have other lessons to attend to."

Schneider winked at The Merchant. "She's such a tease. But I do love women." Else paid no mind and sauntered out.

"So do I."

The Merchant opened the door to the men's room. Empty. He shut the door and locked it. He did the same at the women's room. He locked the hall door as well. Schneider, was half-way into his uniform, heard the sliding bolts and looked up from buttoning his shirt.

"What are you doing? Why did you lock the doors?"

The Merchant came toward Schneider.

"Seriously, what's going on?" He was scared.

The Merchant came on.

"Listen, if its money you want, I'll give you what I have."

"Nope. That's not what I need. Take off your clothes."

Confusion clouded Schneider's face. "I thought you liked women. That's what you just said." Schneider could not move, just stood before his locker as if Medusa had turned him to stone.

Schneider's fear pleased The Merchant. It simplified his task. He could avoid a bloody mess. He lunged forward and slammed his fist into Schneider's solar plexus, knocking the breath out of him. That would keep Schneider still.

The Merchant spun Schneider around and set him on his knees. His left hand on the hapless man's right cheek, right hand on his left arm, he jerked the man's head counterclockwise. Bone and ligaments snapped. The head fell limp.

The Merchant laid the body on the ground and undressed himself and the corpse. He put Schneider's uniform on, grabbed his name-tag, and stowed it in a pocket.

The Merchant pulled a laundry bin from the rear of the room, lifted Schneider by the waist and heaved him inside. He covered the lifeless lump with the dirty laundry and rolled the bin into the men's room. The Merchant checked himself in the mirror, smoothed the uniform and left.

He rounded the corner near the service elevators and peeked into Room Service. No one was inside so he went straight to the computer and punched in Jake Meyer. Room 504 had not ordered any room service. The Merchant decided to grab a cart of food and present it as a hotel courtesy.

He needed a key to Meyer's room. There had to be one there, but a search produced nothing. *The maids have keys,* he thought. The house keeping schedule showed that Room 508 was getting fixed up right then.

From the kitchen he filched a dining cart fated for Room 529 and barreled toward the service elevator. Inside he put Schneider's name tag on his vest and lifted the metal lids to check the bill of fare. After sampling the cheesy potatoes, he took his weapon, attached the silencer and stuffed it in his waist band underneath the vest.

On the fifth floor he found Room 508 where a short, chubby maid with dark blond hair pulled into a tight bun was making the bed. The Merchant stepped in and shut the door behind him. The maid looked up in surprise. "What are you doing? There is no one here to order room service."

He smiled and removed his weapon. The maid's eyes went wide at the dark black metal object and she tried to scream. What came out of her mouth was a high pitched yelp, like a wounded dog. The bullet slammed into her forehead.

The Merchant searched her body and found the master key lying in her cleavage. He ripped it from her neck and pulled the body into the closet. He covered her with bed linens, pulled her cart into the room and left.

A few steps down the hall he stood in front of Jake Meyer's room. He rapped on the door, but no one answered. He looked up and down and seeing no one in the hall, he laid his ear against the door and heard the shower.

The Merchant pulled the weapon from his belt and put it on the plate that once held potatoes. He opened the door with the master key, and there on the table before him was his bounty.

Pulsing hot water soothed Jake's aching neck and back. He leaned against the tiled wall, tried to ease his mind, push the exhaustion and stress of a long day away. But the relaxation he expected from a twenty minute shower was elusive. Instead, images danced through his mind: the meetings with Kessler and Walsing, dormant bank account numbers, Burns' broken body. Was the auditor's death really related to his side report? If so, why would bank accounts from over sixty years ago cause so much concern if they had nothing to do with the CRT's work? The mental collage abruptly morphed to the *affair* and the carnage his previous stint in Zurich caused. He shuddered and clenched his fists. *What the hell am I doing back here?*

He reached for the glass of Scotch on the sink and finished it off in one gulp. He shut off the water, pulled a terry cloth towel from the door and wrapped it around his waist.

A rattling in the bedroom startled him. Stepping from the bathroom without his contact lenses, he was surprised to make out someone leafing through the folder Walsing had given him containing Burns' findings.

The intruder looked up, equally surprised, and laid the folder back on the cocktail table.

"Who are you and what are you doing in here?" Jake retrieved his glasses from the nightstand.

"Room service, Herr Meyer. I knocked on the door and heard the shower running. When you didn't answer, I decided to use the master key." The waiter removed the cover from one of the plates. "We have a filet of salmon and . . . "

"I didn't order anything."

"Compliments of the hotel. I could bring something else if you'd like."

There was something wrong. Jake traveled a lot and knew there's no such thing as complimentary room service. Gift baskets with fruit and chocolate and coffee, yes, but never food and drink from the kitchen. Even worse, the waiter had let himself into the room, a violation of every hotel's policy.

Jake put on his glasses and got a better look. The burgundy vest, tight around the shoulders and waist, showed him slim and athletic. The name tag said he was Heinrich Schneider, but Meyer's instinct said that wasn't the waiter's real name.

The two men regarded each other carefully. The waiter made another attempt. "We have a bottle of Crystal in the bucket, and I could bring you a steak if you prefer."

"I don't want any food. I want to know who you are and why you were looking at the folder."

The waiter ignored him. "We also have a nice dish of potatoes au gratin." He uncovered another dish and produced a silenced Makharov pistol.

"I was hoping I wouldn't need this. You should have stayed in the shower." His conciliatory tone turned hard. He pointed the weapon at Jake and picked up the folder. "All I needed was this."

Jake's fear vanished, and his fight or flight adrenaline surged. As he leapt over the bed, he heard the silenced gun's soft *psst*. The bullet just missed his shoulder and smacked into the wall, spraying white plaster onto his wet head.

The towel flew off as he rolled off the bed and crawled behind the large armoire, his knees stinging with rug burn. He peeked around the cabinet and jerked his head back before the waiter fired another shot.

Jake knelt and put his shoulder into the heavy armoire just as he heard another pop and a shot sliced through the wood. At once came the loud double tap of an un-silenced weapon. Jake peered around again and saw someone else aiming a weapon.

Damn! Now there are two people gunning for me. He lay flat on his belly and crawled underneath the cabinet. The waiter screamed in pain as two more bullets tore through the wood. Then quiet.

Jake spied the room again and saw the waiter was gone and the file was on the floor. He slid into his chinos and pulled on a shirt. Down the hall he saw a long tail of hair whip around the corner. To his right feet pounded down the wide carpeted staircase to the lobby. Which one should he go after? Looking down he saw rivulets of deep crimson on the carpet leading to the stairs. At least he would have a trail.

Jake took the stairs to the lobby two at a time. There a well dressed man in a three piece suit sat on the lone white couch. He looked at Jake, then returned to his Martini and his newspaper. The clerk entering data into a computer at the front desk did not look up. Clearly neither had been startled by a waiter dashing through the place.

Jake walked into the hotel's dark wood paneled bar. A couple sat in a corner, holding hands and gazing at each other. Nothing had disturbed their world. The pretty bartender expertly finished off the head of a draft beer and set in front of a businessman sitting at the bar working on a Sudoku puzzle.

"Can I help you, sir?"

"Did you see a room service waiter run through here?"

"No."

"Thanks." Jake walked back into the lobby. He looked for more blood, but the trail had disappeared. No sign of the waiter.

Dumbfounded, Jake went to the front desk. "Is a room service waiter named Hienrich Schneider working today?" A manager stood by the clerk.

The desk manager's left eye twitched and his right brow arched as he examined the disheveled person before him. "Are you staying with us?" he asked softly.

Jake buttoned his shirt. "Yes, I'm in Room 504."

The manager nudged the clerk aside and struck a few keys on his computer. "You are Mr. Meyer?" he asked without looking up.

"Correct."

A moment later the mousy faced manager with beady eyes looked back at Jake. "Yes, Heinrich Schneider was scheduled to work the night shift. Is there a problem?"

Jake read the manager's name tag, "Yes, Mr. Gerard. What does Schneider look like?"

"I'm fairly certain he has blond hair and brown eyes. He's about five, ten, and slender."

As Jake suspected. The man in his room was bald with gray eyes. The real Schneider was either an accomplice or had suffered an ugly demise.

"I think you may need to find a new employee."

"What are you talking about?"

Jake recounted the intrusion into his room and the fight, but did not reveal that a woman was also involved. His gut told him to keep that to himself. She was the wildcard. Out of place. If she were backing the waiter up, why didn't she disguise herself as a maid? Something didn't make sense.

"I'll call the police and have security search the building immediately." Gerard picked up the phone and dialed.

Jake took the man's arm. Involving the authorities would complicate matters, creating bureaucratic delays and headaches.

"You don't have to call the police. I can handle this. I'm with Chief Inspector Kessler's office. You can check with him."

The clerk eyed Jake again, doubtful.

"I'll give you the Chief Inspector's phone number if you like," Jake offered.

Unconvinced, Gerard started dialing again.

"If you finish that call," Jake said, "the police will rope off the crime scene and make interviews. Lots of spectacle and problems for you and your guests. You don't want that, do you?"

The manager paused and replaced the receiver.

Figuring Gerard had the picture, Jake plunged ahead. "I'd like to view the security tapes of the hotel entrances and exits."

"Of course." Gerard came from behind the desk and escorted Jake to the elevators. "I'll have them sent up to you."

As they approached the lift doors opened, and an attractive woman emerged. Five feet, nine inches, three from high-heeled boots. She carried a large black leather bag and wore the wide grin of one ready for a shopping spree at the posh shops on Banhofstrasse.

"Hello," she chirped.

"Good afternoon, Fräulein," Gerard responded.

Jake nodded, embarrassed by his un-kept appearance. He stepped into the elevator and watched her saunter away as the doors shut. He had a fleeting thought she could be the other person who shot at him. But she didn't seem the type to handle a weapon. Too dainty. Besides, she had short dark hair, not a long auburn pony-tail.

Back in his room, Jake picked up the file and then slammed it back onto the cocktail table. What had he gotten himself into? He expected his return to Zurich to be emotionally taxing, maybe cathartic. He didn't expect mortal jeopardy. He should drop everything and tell Walsing to find someone else to investigate the withdrawals.

Jake pulled the bottle of Butler's Scotch from the wet bar and poured a glass. He'd update Walsing and Kessler later, after he studied the file.

He sat down and opened the folder. The first page was a copy of a 1936 deposit/withdraw sheet from Credit Suisse Bank, account 059481. A few more pages later he found copies of numbered accounts from 1936—dates and types of transactions, specific amounts withdrawn or deposited, remaining balances. Except for the font and the year, they looked like other accounts Jake investigated when he worked with the Treasury Department.

Jake found page twenty-one at random and skimmed account 126734. On January 4, 1936, a deposit of 15,000 British pounds. A deposit of 7,500 pounds on February 23. A withdrawal of 20,000 pounds April 14 leaving a balance of a million pounds. But what caught Jake's attention was the red asterisk, probably scribbled by the dead accountant Burns, next to a withdrawal on June 9: two million pounds. Jake turned the page to account 094387. He found an asterisk there as well. On June 7, 750,000 pounds withdrawn. Jake was dumbfounded.

He yanked another packet from the file, licked his fingertips and turned the pages. The accounts were from Banque Lyonnaise but contained the same information as those from Credit Suisse. And each account had an asterisk next to a large withdrawal made in June of 1936.

Clearly there was a link between the accounts and the timing and amounts of the withdrawals. More important, Burns' death and the shootout in Jake's room were somehow connected to the transactions. But why would withdrawals made half a century earlier create so much mayhem?

The legal and cultural complexities of Swiss banking would make connecting the dots hard. He understood the reasons behind numbered accounts, a policy established three centuries back, when French kings borrowed from Genevan money lenders, protestants of French origin chased out of France following the revocation of the Edict of Nantes by Louis XIV in 1685. They lent to French royalty because the monarchy paid the loans back and borrowed a lot. French royalty appreciated the discretion. God forbid their Catholic subjects learn they were borrowing from heretics.

But in the twenty-first century, terrorists and other criminals used the discrete Swiss banks to shield their money. Succumbing to international pressure to help fight crime, the Swiss agreed to provide limited information, including the names of account holders, to law enforcement agencies when evidence supported piercing the veil of secrecy. When evidence was lacking, agents like Jake kept tabs on terrorist and criminal monetary assets by following the funds from their source to the accounts of the criminals. Since bank checks are not issued to numbered accounts, such tracking involved normal surveillance, which was often time consuming even with state-of-the-art monitoring devices developed by the NSA and CIA.

How would he discover the identity of accounts from over sixty years ago? He was about to replace the packet but noticed a single page had dropped to the floor. On it Jake saw six hand-written names and a string of numbers next to each. The digits looked familiar, so he rifled through the logs and found the matches. Apparently, Burns managed to identify a few people. Jake's good luck. He might be able to bypass going to the banks directly.

He studied the names. How could he determine exactly who the people were, whether they were still alive, and if not, whether they had heirs who could explain the withdrawals? He could check census records and post office documents, but he didn't have a clue to the nationality of the names on the list. Where to start?

Jake rubbed his temples as the alcohol took affect. The tension in his muscles dissipated, his mind relaxed. Then an idea occurred. His experience as an investigator and attorney taught him that people in small communities know all about each other, especially the rich. Gossip, rumor and truth are social currency. He guessed some very rich people made the large withdrawals, and even though it was all long ago, possibly the account holders knew each other. If he could find just one person on the list, he might link them to the other names and find out exactly what Burns stumbled upon. It would be like spinning a spider's web of the wealthy. And Jake knew who had his finger on the pulse of Europe's rich. He closed the file and called Kessler and Walsing to tell them about the events at the hotel—and that the next day he'd call on an old acquaintance, Charles Pincay.

Damn, that was close, Maya thought as she shut the door behind her, ripped the brown pony-tail from her head and set her gun on the credenza. She threw the locks into a bag of hair extensions and wigs on the hotel bathroom floor, grabbed a towel and sat on the bed. She wiped the sweat from her brow and took off her clothes. Like any good operative she began personal debriefing as her mind replayed the events of the last fifteen minutes. Maya had been in her room when she heard a scream. She cracked the door and saw a room service cart and a housekeeping cart side by side. Suddenly a hand reached through the door and jerked the housekeeping wagon into the room. When the Room Service waiter emerged, Maya got her gun and followed him down the hall. She watched him knock at Room 504, then saw him open Jake Meyer's room with a master key. She knew room service waiters don't have master keys.

Through the doorway she saw Meyer emerge from the bathroom and recognized him from the photos she had. Maya strained to hear the conversation but could make out only something about Meyer not ordering food. Then the waiter lifted a cover and came up with a silenced weapon. Meyer jumped from her view, and the waiter fired a round. She took three steps into the hallway and fired twice at the waiter.

Her aim was off. One bullet grazed the waiter, and both hit the wooden armoire. The waiter screamed, dropped a brown folder to the floor and ran from the room. She could not decide whether to take the waiter out or to go after him. The indecision cost her. The next two rounds missed as well. She was about to run after the waiter when Meyer rushed out of the room. Maya ducked around the corner and reentered her room.

Now, as she straightened her skirt and pulled on her black boots she realized things were not as simple as she thought. She needed more information. She had to make contact much earlier than she planned.

She found her contacts. Her vision was perfect, but the lenses made her brown eyes a deep blue. She put on rouge, lip gloss and an orange wig from the bag on the floor. She coiffed herself and hid the pouch of fake hair in a suitcase. She grabbed a large black bag and her gun and headed for the elevator.

As the doors opened in the lobby Maya was face to face with Meyer and a man who looked like the hotel manager. Meyer was still wet and disheveled. For an instant she feared that he might recognize her but he just nodded. Either he did not see her face or her disguise worked.

She went outside and took a deep breath, then ambled to a quiet spot on Banhofstrasse where she would mark a street lamp, indicating she needed to meet her control.

CHAPTER 12

Zurich

Charles Pincay wasn't overweight: he just had a woman's pear shaped hips and fleshy jowls. That had as much to do with genetics as with his penchant for dishes heavy in carbohydrates and a strong aversion to exercise. Fortunately for Pincay, he had the means to compensate for the flaws in his appearance with suits tailored to hide his imperfections. So when Jake entered the Pizzeria Christophorus, he wasn't surprised to find Pincay in a navy pinstripe suit and yellow tie, enjoying a plate of *penne all'arrabiata* with prosciutto and a glass of red wine.

"Hello, Charles, it's good to see you again," Jake said at the table

Pincay's mouth was full, so he pointed his fork at the chair across from him.

Jake removed his jacket, sat down and scanned the dining room. The walls were covered with murals of seventeenth century merchant vessels sailing the oceans. Dark wood beams crossed the ceiling. Typical cheesy Italian.

"I would have thought you'd like to meet at Königstühl," Jake referred to the favorite eatery of Zurich's financial and banking elite.

Pincay scooped up a fork of pasta tubes. "I prefer not to be seen with you. It's not healthy for one's reputation."

"*Now* you're worried about reputations, Charles? Amazing how things change."

Pincay sipped his wine and glared at Jake. "I'm surprised to see you, Meyer. *I* would have thought you'd know you're *persona non grata* in Zurich. You left with your tail between your legs. How on earth did you convince your government to hire you again? Didn't you burn your bridges?" Pincay relished the payback.

"I'm not here on official business."

"Then what do you want? I hardly imagine this is a social call."

"You're right, I need some information."

"You want information from me? You've got balls to ask me for anything."

Jake understood the animosity. He had once threatened to destroy Pincay's life.

Charles was once the charming and affable managing partner of Pincay and Associates, one of Switzerland's oldest private banks. Its fund management specialty attracted the family trusts of Europe's elite, international institutions and charities as well as individuals.

Charles Pincay's intelligence, discretion and success at growing and safeguarding fortunes also attracted an unsavory set. Drug dealers, terrorists and other criminals sought the services of Pincay and Associates. They wanted their money laundered. And since Charles enjoyed accumulating wealth for himself, he took the business. He justified the higher fee by telling the less scrupulous it was "the price of the increased risk to the bank's business and my good name."

But Pincay took one too many dirty clients. Ahmed Yassin, a rich man who claimed to be a member of the Saudi royal family approached Pincay about opening an account "on behalf of a charity for the underprivileged and distressed in Palestine, Lebanon and Iraq." Most of the funds would come from the United States and Europe.

Pincay knew the charity was a front for some nefarious business. But he seized the opportunity, raised the bank's fee further and opened the account.

Unfortunately for Pincay, the Treasury Department was on to Yassin, and Jake Meyer was the lead investigator. He tracked contributions from Los Angeles, Detroit and Washington to the account at Pincay and Associates. After weeks of surveillance and gathering evidence, he put the screws to Pincay.

He showed the banker photos and played portions of tape recordings. Jake had then offered him a deal: help monitor and freeze Yassin's account and stay in business, or face criminal charges when it all went public. The latter would destroy both the bank and Charles Pincay.

Exhibiting a healthy preference for remaining out of prison and enjoying a privileged life, Pincay made the only choice and worked with Jake.

After weeks of gathering additional information, just as Jake was about to "roll up" everyone connected with the Yassin account, everyone and everything vanished. Someone tipped Yassin off. Jake was furious. He initially blamed Pincay and was about to turn everything over to the press, but as things turned out, he got blamed for the failed investigation and the human devastation it caused.

Now he needed Pincay's help. He was humiliated, embarrassed, and doubted Pincay would tell him anything without another stick and carrot routine. But Jake needed a starting point, and Pincay was as good as any.

"So, what do you want, Meyer?" Pincay asked, admiring something beyond Jake's shoulder.

"A history lesson." Jake turned to see a woman, stiletto heels accentuating her legs, leave the restaurant. He turned back and took Burns' list and pushed it across the table. "Any of those names familiar?"

The banker put down his fork and knife, pulled a pair of reading glasses from his breast pocket and unfolded the note. As he read the names, his hand quivered, and the smirk on his face disappeared. The color drained from his face.

"How did you come by these?" Pincay folded the paper and handed it back to Jake.

"Doesn't matter. Do you recognize any of the names?"

"Perhaps, but I need to check."

Jake knew Pincay had something. It was just a matter of fleshing things out.

"Don't do this Charles. Tell me what you know."

Pincay dabbed the corners of his mouth with his napkin and shifted uncomfortably in his chair. "A couple of them ring a bell, but I can't be sure."

"Which names ring bells?"

"Thyssen and Tilden."

"Who were they?"

Pincay shifted again and leaned forward. "Thyssen owned United Steelworks which controlled more than seventy-five per cent of Germany's ore reserves in the late twenties. At first Fritz Thyssen supported Hitler and the Nazis, gave large sums of money to the party. But as a Catholic he objected to the religious persecution and eventually fled to Switzerland. He then went to France, but the Vichy government returned him to Germany. They sent him to a concentration camp."

Jake rubbed his chin. If Thyssen were on the run from the Nazis, it was logical he'd make a big withdrawal. Maybe that's what all the entries in Burn's report were, getaway cash. But why did they happen at the same time in 1936? And why would that pique Burn's interest?

"Do you know anything else about Thyssen?"

"No."

Jake doubted Pincay was telling the truth. He'd push back later. "What about Tilden?"

The banker bit his lip. "William Tilden was an English chemist who developed a synthetic isoprene. The German conglomerate IG Farben used his work to create the buna-N and buna-S rubbers used in World War II."

IG Farben was the dominating element of a network of cartels spread all over the world in the twenties and thirties, but Tilden wasn't in Germany. He didn't need to flee the Nazis. How were Tilden, Thyssen and the other account holders connected? Nothing made sense.

"Did Tilden and Thyssen know each other?" Jake asked.

"I don't know."

"What happened to the bank accounts?"

"They were liquidated before the Nazis could get their hands on them."

"Really." Jake raised a brow. "Do you know what the families did with the assets?"

Pincay averted his eyes. "I have no idea."

Pincay wasn't just withholding the truth, he was afraid of it. As he stared past Jake, something clicked. Was it possible? Jake leaned forward. "Charles, did they have accounts in *your* bank?"

"I don't believe so."

"Are you aware of any unusual withdrawals Thysen, Tilden or others made in 1936?"

"I have a good memory Meyer, but it's not that good," Pincay quipped. Sweat beaded the banker's upper lip. Jake knew they had nothing to do with the crushed pepper in the pasta.

"Okay, but could you look into it? Do a little research?"

Pincay looked around. "That won't be possible. I'm extremely busy, and besides, Meyer, some stones are better left unturned."

Jake didn't want to do it again, but Pincay understood only sticks and carrots. "Charles, remember those pictures and tapes I had of you and Yassin?"

"You said they were destroyed?"

Jake shook his head. *He* was a good liar.

"You're bluffing," Pincay whispered.

"Willing to take that risk?"

Pincay's eye twitched. "It ends now. I want those tapes and pictures."

"You'll have them."

"Your word isn't worth much these days, Meyer."

Jake set his jaw for effect. "I said you'll get them."

"Fine. Come to my house tonight at nine. I'll have what you need."

Jake had kept his own copies of the Yassin surveillance file, though that was against the law. He had seen too many people lose promotions, jobs and court cases because they didn't have back-up documentation. He just didn't know how he'd produce evidence locked in his safe at home. But since it was early, he had a few hours to figure something out.

"Thank you," Jake said and tossed a couple of Swiss francs on the table. "See you later."

Pincay laid his napkin next to the plate, his hands still shaking. "I've lost my appetite. I'm leaving too."

They got their coats, and Jake followed Pincay to the door. Why was the banker afraid of names and accounts closed over fifty years before? And would he produce reliable information or feed Jake a story? How would Jake know?

As Jake left the restaurant, the waiter yelled *"Danke!"*

Jake looked back and waved. The waiter was leaning over a table talking to a woman with incredible legs. She was clearly teasing him, because she nudged his shin with her foot. Jake caught a glimpse of her profile, attractive, and noticed her hair. She seemed familiar. He decided to let it go and walked west, away from Pincay.

Maya took a seat across Pizzeria Christophorus with her back to Jake and the dressy man eating a hearty meal. She got her compact and put on lipstick while she studied the couple in the mirror. *Who's that with Jake and what are they talking about?*

A waiter walked by and gave her an appraising glance. She returned his smile.

When he came back she crossed her legs and brushed her foot against his shin as she ordered. "Oh, I'm sorry" she said coyly.

"Not at all," he responded, grinning.

She brushed his leg again, and he came closer.

"When I walked in, I noticed the fat man sitting in the back corner looking at you. I'll bet a lot of gay men come here just to ogle the handsome waiters."

The waiter looked over his right shoulder. "You mean, Mr. Pincay, the guy eating with the white-haired man? He's not gay. In fact, he's usually here with a young woman. I doubt it's his wife. Who would sleep with that pig?" His gaze returned to Maya.

"Not me. I need a fit, sexy man. Mr. Pincay is not attractive. I'm sure his appeal is in his wallet." She brushed his leg again.

"Oh, Charles Pincay is rich, all right. He owns one of the oldest private banks in Zurich."

"That explains it," Maya said.

The waiter smiled and licked his lips. "So, are you busy later tonight?"

This is too easy. "Sure. You're the type of man a woman could enjoy." Maya asked for his pen and wrote a fake name, number and time on a napkin.

The waiter folded the napkin and put it his pocket. He turned when he heard footsteps at the exit and saw Jake following Pincay out of the restaurant.

"*Danke*" he said. Jake waved back.

"For such a rich man, Pincay is a shitty tipper. I hope you're better." The cheesy line almost made her laugh out loud.

Instead, she grinned and winked.

Maya figured the waiter had been stood up before. He wouldn't be too upset. Beside, she needed to do some homework on Charles Pincay.

CHAPTER 13

Zurich

The night was not particularly dark. Thick clouds, glowing with reflected light, hovered over the city. And though Jake was extremely familiar with the streets of Old Zurich, he welcomed the illumination as he trudged through a light snowfall to Charles Pincay's house.

He walked up the Limmatquai, past small bars, cafes and shops. A handful of chic patrons smoking cigarettes and sipping coffee or cocktails late on the weeknight decorated the taverns. The store windows displayed Swiss souvenirs and trinkets, Swiss flags, chocolate, army knives, cheese and—most definitely—watches. All were established before 1830 and sold the only *real* and *best* timepieces in Switzerland.

Turning up a narrow alley, Jake stopped to admire one store's collection of pocket watches, gold and silver, some with thick chains, others with thin links, most with open faces though some closed. A silver watch in the center—without a design on the open cover, a simple clasp and large black roman numerals on the face—caught his attention. His father detective David Meyer had one just like it.

Silver haired and hunched, detective Meyer was a master manipulator, a skill that made him a good interrogator. His command of the language and ability to read human behavior often won the trust of perpetrators in custody. Detective Meyer probed for an emotional weakness, like guilt, or exploited a criminal's ego and obtained a confession. The problem was, detective Meyer couldn't turn himself off. He brought his interrogation methods home.

"Did you drink last night at the party? Did you finish your homework? Did you drive my car yesterday?" He'd ask Jake, pulling the watch from his pocket. He'd swing the chain; catch the watch and flip open the face in one fluid motion as if he were performing a magic trick.

No matter what answer Jake gave, his father listened carefully, then asked follow-up questions as the pocket watch sailed through the air.

"Dad, talking to you is like facing the Spanish Inquisition."

"So you think I'm persecuting you?" The watch swinging.

The memory of the pendulum pocket watch made Jake tense. He breathed deeply. He still preferred wrist watches.

Pincay was really frightened, Jake mused as he continued walking. Even during the Yassin affair, when his business was in jeopardy from international law enforcement and a sophisticated terrorist network threatened to kill him, he was scared yet remained composed. He went on with his life as if nothing was at risk.

But today, Pincay was terrified. What spooked him? How could accounts that no longer existed scare him? What secret was he hiding?

Jake made a right on Unt Zaune and walked toward Herschengraben. The house on the corner was Pincay's. Jake saw a the light in a second story window at the rear of the house. The banker was home.

Jake passed the sliding garage gate below the study. That Pincay had a place to park two cars in the old Zurich's tight confines was a testament to his wealth. Few could afford a garage in that part of the city.

As he rounded the corner toward the front of Pincay's house, someone blundered into Jake's shoulder, twisting him around.

"Excuse me," Jake said.

The person, bundled in a dark parka and a dark beret, did not stop to apologize, said nothing, just kept walking.

That was odd. The Swiss were usually polite to a fault. But that person was rude.

Jake noticed the gas lamps flanking the front door were not lit. *Something was wreong..* During the weeks Jake and his team watched Pincay's house during the Yassin affair, they burned constantly, even during the day. Jake once saw an irate Pincay berate his maid for letting them go out. Pincay wanted that alcove brightly illuminated.

Into the doorway he saw the lamps were smashed. Glass crunched under his feet. He wished he had his gun.

Jake knocked. No response.

He rapped harder and the door moved. It was open.

Jake went inside slowly. He opened the coat closet and checked the alarm. It was turned off. If someone other than Pincay was in the house, he didn't break in.

He looked at the light switch but decided against flipping it. He waited until his eyes adjusted to the darkness and eased toward the spiral staircase.

"Charles, are you here? Are you all right?"

Silence.

He climbed the stairs. At the top, he saw the light from the study down the hall and heard a harpsichord concerto by Bach. Pincay adored the composer's music. Then he smelled cigarette smoke. Pincay didn't smoke.

From the door Jake saw the bouncing red and green lights of Pincay's Bose stereo and the glow of the banker's lamp on his desk. The brown high backed chair was turned away, Pincay's brown hair visible above it.

"Charles? Hey, Charles?" The music was loud.

Jake tapped Pincay's shoulder.

Nothing.

When he pushed the chair around, Pincay's head dropped to his chest and his crumpled tie dropped into his lap. Someone used it as a gag. Pincay's arms and legs were tied to the chair, his shirt was ripped open. Tiny dark circles pocked his nipples, stomach, hands and forearms. Cigarette burns. On the floor he saw five butts. He lifted Pincay's head and he almost vomited. Burns all over his lips and nose. Pincay's left eye was little more than a blackened red pustule.

Jake saw at once he was into something far more complicated than Walsing led him to believe. He hated not being completely informed.

Maya waited outside the Hauptbahnhoff across the street from the Hotel Schweizerhof. When Jake came out of the hotel, she followed him. He headed east, across the river and made a right on Limmatquai. She stayed fifty yards behind.

Down the street the crowds thinned, and Maya pulled back another twenty yards. Jake was in no hurry. He admired the shops and restaurant he passed and showed no sign he knew he was being watched.

He stopped in front of a store, so Maya studied the menu outside a vegetarian restaurant. Jake lingered before the store. When he started moving again, he turned left on Brunngasstrasse, right on Froshstrasse. Maya realized he was running a classic "stair step" surveillance detection route. Either he knew she was behind him or he was just being careful. She fell back about a hundred yards, and when Jake took another right,, Maya made a left and headed back to the Limmatquai. She'd pick him up nearer Pincay's house.

Maya took a short cut to Speigelgasse and spotted Jake at the end of the street just as a man in a beret barreled around a corner and ploughed into Jake's shoulder but did not stop and apologize. Uncharacteristically rude by Zurich's standards.

Maya ducked back around the corner and counted to three. When she looked again, both Jake and the man were gone. She had no idea where the man went, but she knew exactly where Jake was.

Jake stared at Pincay's corpse. He was on the verge of calling Walsing to issue an ultimatum: *Either tell me everything or I'm out of here.* The last time he was in Zurich without all the facts, a lot of people died. He would not endure that again.

Yet two more men *were* dead, dead over some dormant bank accounts about which Jake was in the dark. All he had were a few records and names.

Names.

Jake thought about Pincay's reaction to the list of names. Apparently, he had good reason to be terrified. His battered body was evidence enough. But who were those people, and how have they reached into the present to wreak havoc? And who's doing the dirty work?

He pushed the body aside and rummaged through Pincay's desk. Jake recalled that Pincay considered the room his inner sanctum, off-limits to everyone—the maid, his children, even his wife. In the desk, Jake found monogrammed stationary, office stuff, pens, paperclips and Pincay's recent personal financial documents. He pressed a button he knew was beneath the desk, and a concealed drawer popped out. There he found letters written in a feminine hand, credit card statements and receipts unlike others he found. Pincay was having an affair. Pincay was weak: food, drink, clothes—and women. He was a hedonist, and hedonists succumb to the kind of pain Pincay endured. Jake knew Pincay had broken, but what he gave up he could not guess.

Nothing there. Jake turned his attention to the book cases and began pulling books, whose spines read like a liberal arts course in the classics, Chaucer, Dante, Shakespeare, Dickens. He was looking for the secret cabinet or storage unit, but apparently Pincay had it removed. Jake stopped and thought. He went to the bar and saw a bottle of Sambucca by the sink. Pincay liked to sip it while he read or worked. Jake pulled the lower cabinet open. A safe with its door ajar. *This is new. No safe here seven years ago.*

It was empty. Whoever was there took everything.

Jake turned to the computer and started opening the icons on the screen. An Excel spread sheet popped up, and Jake studied the data, but it was just Pincay keeping track of his own banking and expenses. The numbers were rather large. *What else?*

He opened the Trash, found nothing. He ran the e-mail. Ditto. And then he spied the internet icon at the bottom of the screen. A site was open. Jake double clicked and *voilà*. TheDissenters.com. Headings like Global Welfare, Corporate Responsibility, Important Links and Contact Us at the top. Jake clicked About The Dissenters and skimmed three paragraphs that described the organization's ideology, the usual "globalization is causing environmental and social disasters and injustice, and we need to heal the world" stuff.

But why was Pincay looking at The Dissenters? He was hardly the social conscience type and certainly would not have done business with a non-profit if there was nothing in it for him. What *was* he up to?

Jake opened Contact Us icon, and rather than a street address, phone number and e-mail address on the screen, he saw boxes requesting a Username and Password. In the Username box was CP1945. Charles Pincay was born in 1945. But the password?

He recognized a communications method terrorist groups used. To evade eavesdropping, terrorists kept their messages in draft files on websites that could only be accessed by those with appropriate usernames and passwords. The information in the files was difficult to trace because it was stationary. Evidently, Pincay was dealing with a group that protected its information and wasn't exactly what it portrayed itself to be. Whether it was a terrorist organization, Jake couldn't be sure. And whether it had anything to do with the dormant accounts, Jake had no clue.

But he did have a lead. He'd call in a favor to a friend at the National Security Agency, Paul Hollowel, a hacker he worked with in the past. He flipped open his cell phone, dialed the first four numbers before he heard noise in the hall. He reached for the second drawer, left side, of Pincay's desk. The banker used to keep a Sigsauer handgun in an old cigar box.

*   *   *

Maya hurried up the street and around the corner onto Herschengraben. Lights were on, broken glass littered the ground, the lamps were broken. Pincay's front door was open.

What's going on here?

Gun in hand, Maya went in. The coat closet door was open, but the alarm system was off. She recalled the light in a second story window. She reached the second floor and, like a moth to the flame, headed for the light.

Through the crack between the door and the jamb Maya saw Jake rummaging through Pincay's desk and the bookshelves.

He stopped poking around and turned to the computer. When he pushed the desk chair aside, Maya got a macabre glimpse of Pincay's battered body.

Did he do that?

Jake was dialing his cell phone, and Maya's thighs burned from crouching. She shifted her weight, and the floor complained.

Jake stopped what he was doing and looked to the door.

Maya sprinted down the hall. She thought about leaving through the front door but decided to take the stairs to the third level when she heard Jake yell, "Who are you, and what are you doing here?"

At the top of the step she bolted toward double doors to the right, likely a bedroom. Behind her, Jake pounded up the stairs.

In the bedroom, she saw an antique canopied bed on the left and an armoire on the right. She saw doors to a balcony but did want to risk breaking an ankle.

She had an idea.

She threw open the balcony doors and broke the glass. She ripped the drapes down on one side. She raced into a large closet to the right of the bed and hid behind the clothes. She looked down at her shoes, took them off and set them with the shoes lining the floor on the other side of the closet. Then she closed her eyes, tried to control her breathing and waited to see if Jake would buy the ruse.

Jake heard a crash and bolted for the open bedroom doors. He saw glass on the floor by the balcony doors where the sheared drapes flapped in the chilly breeze. He went to the balcony and scanned the courtyard and the garage but saw nothing.

The drapes. If someone had gone out via the balcony the drapes wouldn't have been shredded. And the glass. It wasn't scattered outward

The smashed window was a ploy, and the intruder, likely Pincay's murderer, was still in the house.

Jake stepped back into the bedroom, moving his weapon in a horizontal arc. His heart pounded like a bass drum as he checked under the bed. Nothing.

He checked the bathroom. A translucent shower door prevented anyone from hiding in the shower. The bathroom was empty.

In the closet, Jake scanned Pincay's suits and shirts neatly hung on the left side. On the right was an antique gilded dresser and straight ahead, a rack containing at least a hundred ties.

Then he saw the shoes. The problem wasn't the number of shoes. Pincay had a woman's penchant for footwear. But it was the undersized pair at the end of the row. As he bent to examine the casual flats, he felt searing pain in his back and thought he had burst a kidney. He fell forward and a foot pounded his solar plexus, pushing him out of the closet. The blow knocked the air out of him. Another kick and he almost vomited. He struggled for breath, swung his leg around and caught his assailant in the calf. He heard a thud as the assailant's head hit the floor.

Jake scrambled to his knees and looked for the gun. What his hands found was soft and silky and long. A pony tail.

He straddled Maya and clamped his hands on her collar bone. "What did you want with Pincay?"

"Nothing."

"Don't bullshit me. Why did you kill him?"

"I didn't. He was dead before you got here. I followed you."

"Why?"

"Orders."

Jake had no time for riddles. He was about to smack Maya's face when suddenly she pushed Jake's hands away and tilted her hips upwards. Jake flew forward, barely missing the bed post.

He stood and turned. Maya was facing him.

"Let's talk about this, Mr. Meyer. I don't want to hurt you."

"Are you kidding? Talk about what?" Jake snarled. He took a swing at Maya, but she easily knocked the punch aside.

"Please. Let me explain what I can. I'm actually on your side," Maya said as they circled each other.

Jake didn't answer. He wouldn't discuss anything until he had the upper hand. He threw another punch. Maya deflected it again and kicked Jake in the chest. The blow sent him tumbling backward through the doors and over the balcony.

He landed on garage's aluminum roof and thought his spine had been pushed through his chest. When the stars stopped swirling in his vision, he found himself staring back up at the window. The woman was on the balcony, watching him. Something about was familiar, her but he couldn't recall where he'd seen her before. His mind replayed the events of the last thirty six-hours and came up with the pony tail. *Who is this woman? What the hell is going on?*

Before he could ask himself any more questions, the woman on the balcony was in the air like a bat. She landed with bent knees, caught her breath and turned to kneel above him.

"Are you all right?" She asked.

Only someone with remarkable athletic ability or diminished mental capacity would have jumped from Pincay's balcony. "Yeah, I'm fine," he groaned.

"Good." Maya lifted him by the shoulders and saw that he was indeed fine. "Look, Mr. Meyer, I didn't kill the banker, and I'm not here to hurt you."

"You could've fooled me."

Maya turned the handle of her gun to Jake. "I was ordered to follow and protect you."

"By whom?"

Maya looked around. "My name is Maya, and this isn't the best place for that conversation. Let's get down from here, and I'll tell you what I know."

CHAPTER 14

Zurich

The snow had stopped and the wind had cleared the clouds. A silver moon gleamed above the Zürichsee. Jake and Maya walked along the water's edge toward Zürichhorn Park. Maya suggested they find a café or a bar so Jake could sit and she could get a brandy to warm her bones. But Jake said he did his best thinking outside, old habit.

"You shot the room service waiter in my room last night," Jake started.

"Yes." Maya gazed at the water.

"And you were at the restaurant today, putting on lipstick and flirting with the waiter."

"I needed to know who you were meeting."

"So you don't have a problem using feminine wiles to get what you want?"

"No. Where I come from you do whatever you can. It's a matter of survival."

"So where *are* you from?"

"Israel."

That explained the power and survival philosophy.

"I work for the government. They assigned me to follow and help you investigate the dormant accounts."

"Why is Israeli intelligence interested in this?" Jake had spent enough time in the U.S. federal bureaucracy to know that *government* was a euphemism for *intelligence*.

"I honestly don't know."

"Your superiors didn't tell you anything about the case?"

"Only that Burns, the CRT investigator, was murdered and that Henry Walsing asked you to look into his death and the dormant accounts."

"How did Mossad know that?"

"Again, Mr. Meyer, I don't know."

Jake doubted Maya was coming clean but pressed on. "Okay, tell me what you *do* know."

"Walsing is concerned about the dormant accounts for some reason, and you have experience following financial transactions. You were a logical hire."

Maya's use of *experience* probably referred to the Yassin affair. The counter-terrorism and intelligence communities were small, and events like the Yassin affair went straight to the rumor mill.

"Anything else?"

"Nothing beyond what you already know."

"Which isn't much, now that Pincay is dead."

"Who were you calling in Pincay's study?"

"The only lead I have right now." Jake produced his cell phone. "But first I should call Walsing. He'll want a report."

He dialed and, to his surprise, someone answered after two rings. "Hello."

"Mr. Walsing, this is Jake Meyer. We need to talk."

"Is everything all right?"

"No. Someone came after me at my hotel, and a contact of mine who knew some of the names on the bank accounts Burns discovered is dead."

"That's unfortunate. How will you proceed?"

Walsing's flat tone was striking. If the case was so important why didn't he seem more concerned about two people dead over those bank accounts? Walsing was keeping something from him.

"I'm not sure but I'll let you know when I figure out what my next step is."

"Very good, Mr. Meyer. Don't hesitate to phone again if you need anything else."

Jake closed the phone, and looked at Maya.

"What's wrong?" she asked.

"Something just doesn't feel right about him. I can't put my finger on it."

*   *   *

Back in his hotel room, Jake took four Advil to numb the aches and pains. He would be bruised and stiff the next morning. He propped himself up on the pillows and wondered about Maya. He wasn't sure what to make of her. She was attractive, gutsy, well trained. She could have killed him had she wanted. Instead she told him everything and offered to help. But how could he be certain she didn't kill Pincay and her offer wasn't a ruse to find out what the banker did not disclose even under torture? What did she want? Why did the Israelis assign an intelligence officer to "help" him?

Nothing made sense. Jake decided to call his techie friend, Paul Hollowel.

"Hey. buddy, how are you?" Jake chirped when Hollowel answered.

"Not so bad. It's almost quittin' time. Have tickets to the Wizards game tonight against the Lakers. Care to make a bet, Meyer?" Hollowel was a basketball fan and talked a lot of trash when Jake's home team came to D.C.

"You're on, fifty bucks."

"Hey, why don't you come down for the game? It doesn't start until eight. I can round up another ticket."

"I can't. I'm not in Philly. I'll take a rain check."

"Sure, you're not around. You just don't want to watch the ass kicking in person. Arenas is going to take Kobe down." Hollowel couldn't help dishing it out.

"No, really, Paul, I'm out of the country, and I need a big favor."

"Okay, what is it?" Hollowel knew Jake was serious.

"I need a password for a website."

"Are United States citizens involved?"

"I don't know."

"Jake, I can't keep putting my ass on the line. One of these days I'm going to get caught."

"I wouldn't ask if it wasn't really important."

"That's what you always say."

"I'm serious this time. Two people are dead already."

"You've gotten into some shit again, haven't you?"

Jake didn't answer.

Paul Hollowel worked at the National Security Agency for over fifteen years developing programs to crack computer hard drives and web sites. He assisted Jake on a number of terrorist funding cases by examining computer hardware confiscated during arrests and hacking into websites by uncovering usernames and passwords. He'd even helped with the Yassin affair.

"I promise. I won't ask again. I don't have any other leads." Jake hated pleading.

Hollowel sighed. "What's the site?"

"The Dissenters com."

"And the user name?"

"CP1945. It's Charles Pincay."

"Good old Charlie. " Hollowel remembered the banker. He tapped into a number of Pincay's professional and personal files a few years back. "How's he doing?"

"He's dead."

"All right then, let's see what I can do."

For three minutes Jake listened to Hollowel's fingers tapping the keys.

"I've got it."

"That was fast."

"Not really. We can usually break passwords in under two minutes."

"What do you have?"

"A message from Pincay to someone named Harrison Reiner."

"Is the organization legit?"

"As far as I can tell."

"What's the message?"

They may be getting close. Are you going to finish things this time? Will keep you apprised of developments.

"That's wonderfully cryptic," Jake said.

"Did you expect anything less?"

"I wonder who LG is. Another website user?"

Paul's fingers danced over the keyboard again. "No LG anywhere in the site's files. Sorry."

The message meant only that Pincay thought Harrison Reiner was in danger—and maybe it had something to do with the names on the bank accounts. "Look, Paul, can you get me any information on this Reiner fellow? It might be the only shot I have left."

"Okay, but I'm out of here in twenty minutes. I want to be at the game for tip-off."

"Thanks. I'll wait for your call.

When Paul called back, he had something.

"Harrison Reiner owns a company called Telon. His father was David Reiner who died from natural causes about fifteen years ago. At that point, Harrison, who was running the company, took over as board chairman."

"What else?"

"Reiner senior was born in 1902, founded Telon in 1926 and got government contracts to lay telephone and telegraph lines. Over the years it became a world leader in telecommunications. Operations in over 120 countries. Telon was among the first to take cellular phones and technology into underdeveloped countries."

"Do they have a stranglehold on the markets?"

"As tight as it can be without violating EU and U.S. anti-trust laws."

"Anything more?"

"Yep. Telon bought out its European competition a while ago and moved its corporate headquarters from New York to London. Telon was instrumental in merging US and European satellite systems like GPS and Galileo."

"What about Harrison?"

"He attended Harvard and Oxford and went into the family business. He managed the European operations for a while and then moved back to the States to oversee global operations. He's the one who moved Telon into the third world."

"Jeez, I wish I had stock."

"Me too. It even survived a federal investigation."

"Telon was audited?"

"Yeah. Corporate victim of the Enron scandal and the new accounting laws. Nothing really came of the investigation. Telon was clean."

Jake's experience was that when a federal investigation of corporate malfeasance punished nobody, somebody pulled strings way up. *Harrison Reiner must be connected.*

"Paul, one more question. Are the Reiners Jewish?"

"I don't know. What difference does that make?"

"A lot. None. Just curious. I'll be in touch."

Jake set the alarm for six and climbed into bed. He'd grab a few hours of sleep before preparing his report for Walsing and catch the ten o'clock flight to London. But his mind was racing around a puzzle track, and Maya was waving the checkered flag. What would he do about her? He could leave without telling her, but she'd probably track him down. The last thing he needed was another person looking over his shoulder. Maybe he'd take her with him. That way at lease he keep an eye on her. If she were a threat, she'd be easier to manage or eliminate. He decided to knock on her door at seven.

CHAPTER 15

Zurich

The Merchant sat in a red leather banquette at the rear of Café Odéon sipping an espresso and turning the pages of *The Brothers Karamazov*. Though the Odéon still catered to intellectuals, it was also a watering hole for the young and the hip who sought the panache of hanging out where Mussolini and Lenin once spent time.

A Swiss beauty of about twenty-five bumped The Merchant's wounded hand with her purse as she took the last seat at the curved wooden bar. He winced but then smiled, accepting her apology before she offered it. She returned the grin and ordered a drink.

The Merchant pulled his bandaged hand into his lap to avoid another accident. The question remained, who shot him? Jake Meyer didn't have a weapon. Did Meyer have an accomplice?

He looked at his watch. Nine o'clock. Fifteen minutes more.

The front door swung open and closed continuously as after dinner drinkers and revelers crowded in. The Merchant was lucky to get the booth he preferred, next to the window with a view of the entrance. He had two chances to spot his contact from Grossmünster Cathedral.

He revisited recent events. He escaped the hotel but without the file. Somehow, the Levant Group led him to Pincay but his visit produced nothing. He was failing. He was frustrated. Was he focused enough? Had he lost his edge?

The Merchant finished his espresso and looked at his watch again. Nine-fifteen. He looked out the window just as the contact strolled by, a newspaper under his left arm. That was the signal for The Merchant to leave the Odéon. Outside he saw the contact cross Limmatquai at the junction where the streetcars discharge their human cargo. The

Merchant picked up the contact's pace and within seconds he fell in beside him.

"It's a beautiful night," the man said.

"Yes, it is." The night sky was brilliant, with a radiant moon. Christmas lights twinkled on the masts of the boats docked at slips on the Zürichsee.

"Tell me what happened with Pincay?" The contact wasted no time. His voice hinted at accusation.

"Getting into his house was easy. The information you sent on his security system was accurate, and his wife and children were out."

"Of course the information we passed was solid," the contact sniffed. "Would you expect anything less?" The Merchant hated being talked down to, especially by someone he despised.

"So what did you learn from Pincay?"

The Merchant hated to admit another failure. "Not a word. May have been the first time he ever kept his mouth shut."

"And that with all the work you did on him. When the Stadtpolizei found him, some of them got sick at their stomachs. Did you learn that from your Stasi trainers?"

"Yes, but torture rarely yields reliable information."

"Or any information at all, as the case may be. And yet information is precisely what we are paying you for."

"It would help if you told me what Meyer is looking into. It would give me something to work with."

"The specifics are not your concern. All you need to know is that he is investigating some Swiss bank accounts from the 1930s."

Those accounts must be fairly important if the Levant Group hired him. But The Merchant knew he wouldn't get any more from the contact.

They navigated their way past a party yacht on the Zürichsee, dance music loud enough to be heard onshore.

"I bumped into Meyer as I left Pincay's house. I don't think he got a good look at me. He probably didn't connect me with the hotel."

"Don't be so sure. Meyer is sharp. He's got a photographic memory. He may recognize you one day."

The Merchant nodded. That was the first bit of useful information he'd received.

"There was somebody else at the Schweizerhof. Shot me in the hand. Does Meyer have an accomplice you didn't tell me about?"

"An accomplice? I was under the impression Meyer wounded you."

"I never said that. I only said a bullet grazed me."

"Where did the shot come from?"

"Behind me."

"And you didn't see anyone else?"

"No. That's why I'm asking you."

"I'm not aware of anyone working with Meyer." He wasn't lying. There was something he and his organization did not know.

They turned up Farberstrasse and headed toward Seefeldstrasse. The festive sounds faded, and the bright lights gave way to dim street lamps. Drab stone houses and apartment buildings lined the street.

"I'll look into this phantom shooter. In the meantime, you're going to London." Matter of fact. Arrogant.

"What's in London?"

"You couldn't get anything from Pincay, but Meyer did."

The contact hailed a cab on Seefeldstrasse. As he opened the door, he handed The Merchant a piece of paper. "Try not to mess this up. It's tiring doing your job for you."

The Merchant opened the note and read, "Telon Corporation: London, England. Harold Reiner, CEO."

CHAPTER 16

London

Jake stood in the executive lobby on the penthouse level of One Canada Square, the tallest building in Great Britain. He gazed through the large floor to ceiling window at Canary Wharf. In medieval times the area, known as the Isle of Dogs, housed the royal kennels. Later it hosted the West India docks, and in the 1920s the Royal Docks. Bombed in World War II, the docks closed in the 1970s, and businesses left. Gentrification later made it London's vibrant, ultra-modern business and financial center, home to transnational banks and companies—including the Telon Corporation.

Twenty-six thousand business people scurried daily along the streets among glassy skyscrapers, all in the requisite dark suits and light shirts. Watching them was a complicated system of security cameras, installed for their "protection," to fight crime and terrorism.

A woman in a perfectly tailored pinstripe suit tapped his shoulder. "Mr. Meyer, I'm Melody, Mr. Reiner's assistant. We spoke on the phone."

"Yes. Nice to meet you," Jake replied, stunned by the woman's beauty. She had straight blond hair, bangs falling seductively across her forehead, soft brown eyes and a silky complexion.

"A pleasure to make your acquaintance as well. Mr. Reiner will see you now. Please follow me."

At the end of the hallway decorated with photos of venerable twentieth century business machinery, they stopped before black double doors, and Melody knocked lightly.

"Come in."

With some effort Melody pushed heavy doors open and held out her arm for Jake to go ahead. Like the buildings in Canary Wharf, Reiner's office was a testament to modernity. Television monitors displaying news stations from all over the world lined one wall. Another offered contemporary art, bold colors splattered on canvas alongside black and white photos of buildings and people. There were a few odd sculptures on Lucite pedestals that Jake couldn't make sense of and, stylish furniture in black leather and chrome which hardly looked comfortable. And atop Reiner's desk of thick glass, sat only a sleek Apple computer, a date book and a telephone.

Reiner lifted his eyes from the monitor and looked past Jake. "Thank you, Melody. I'll call you when we're through." He stood and extended his hand. "Welcome, Mr. Meyer."

Though not tall, Harrison Reiner was stately. He brushed his thin, snow-white hair to the side. High cheekbones flanked a patrician nose. He wore a dark brown suit with a high vest that revealed only the knot of a patterned tie and a white collar. At seventy-three, he was still a handsome man.

Jake took his small hand. "Quite an impressive office you have here."

"Thank you. Though I must give credit to my daughter for the decorating. Her work is on all fifteen floors Telon occupies. Admittedly, it's not really my taste. I like things a bit more classical." Reiner smiled. "But I defer to her. That's what an adoring father does for his only daughter."

"Well, she's quite talented. She even uses televisions to decorate."

Reiner glanced at the monitors on the wall, then back at his guest. Jake noticed tension in his face, something he'd seen before on the faces of suspects. People with something to hide suffer from chronic paranoia.

"The monitors are as much for practical purposes as they are for décor. I'm a news junkie, obsessed with international business."

"Interesting choice of words."

"Why is that?"

"You said you were obsessed. Obsessions arise from paranoia."

Reiner flashed a fake smile. "What some call paranoia, others call healthy vigilance, Mr. Meyer. Telon has operations in every corner of the world. I need to know what's going on. Anything less would be a breach of my fiduciary duty to our investors." He motioned Jake to sit in an oddly shaped chair.

"Of course. I understand completely. I certainly didn't mean any disrespect. In any case, thank you for agreeing to see me. I'll try not to take much time."

"So, what can I do for you Mr. Meyer?" He leaned back and folded his hands across his stomach.

"I was hoping you could give me some information about your father."

Reiner's jaw tensed. "Mr. Meyer, we've complied with all the IRS audits and requests. There really isn't anything else to know. We were hoping to resolve the matter without the necessity of going to court."

Thanks to Paul Hollowel's research, Jake knew the U.S. government had challenged the distribution of assets from Frederick Reiner's estate. The authorities continued to pester Harrison Reiner, and he was at his wits' end.

"I'm not with the IRS or any U.S. government agency, for that matter. And I'm not interested in your father's estate as a whole, but rather just one detail."

"I thought you said you were an attorney. That's what you told my assistant on the phone."

"I am. But I'm also a private investigator."

"What does a P.I. want with my father?" Reiner's anger now included suspicion. "I think its time you leave." He moved to use the intercom.

"I'm here on behalf of the Claims Resolution Tribunal."

Reiner eyes narrowed. "Go on, indulge my curiosity."

"I'm looking into some discrepancies in a claim examiner's file."

"I'm familiar with the CRT's work, but neither Telon nor my family has made any claim with them. We didn't lose anything in WWII. What does the CRT want to know about my father?"

"No, it doesn't have anything to do with a claim. It's about some tangential work. I'm looking into some large withdrawals made in the mid 1930s."

"That's beyond the scope of the CRT's mission. Why would it be concerned with Swiss accounts the Germans didn't confiscate?"

"I'm not sure myself, but they're paying me well."

Reiner wasn't amused.

"Anyway, your father's name appeared a list of people who made significant withdrawals. I thought you might shed some light on what happened then, why your father all but cleaned the account out."

"I'm afraid I don't know." Reiner's eyes went to the television monitors, then back to his guest.

Jake figured Reiner was holding back. Jake read the signs, the body language, the hesitation before responding, eyes averted. He would have to lead Reiner if he wanted anything else.

"Well, do you know when your father first opened the account?

"I believe it was in the mid-twenties when he started Telon. And thank goodness for that. If it weren't for the Swiss accounts, he might have lost everything in the Depression."

Telon and the Reiners rode the Depression out. They would have needed cash for family, friends, employees. But then why wasn't the money pulled out earlier? And why were the withdrawals all within a few days of each other?

"And when did he close that specific account?" Jake asked.

"I'm not sure. Why?"

"Did he ever tell you what he did with the money?"

"I really don't think that's any of your business, Mr. Meyer."

"I apologize. Please understand, I don't mean to be insensitive or too intrusive."

Reiner's eyes checked the monitors. "I'll say this. I never examined the books from the period, but I suspect large withdrawals would not have been unusual for my father. He had a family and a business to support at a very difficult time."

"What specific problems did he face between 1936 and 1939?"

Reiner took a deep breath and licked his lips. "Look, I was a child then. I'm familiar with the history of the company, but my father was not the communicative type."

If Reiner didn't know anything about his father's account in 1936 why was he so uncomfortable?

Jake decided to take a different tack. "Mr. Reiner, are you familiar with the names Crowe, Kilgore, Davidson, Reisz, Brown, Gruenwald or Whitehead?"

Reiner smiled and held Jake's gaze. "Of course I'm familiar with those names. Actually, I'm surprised you don't know who they are."

"Why should I have heard of them?"

Reiner laughed. "Don't be coy, Mr. Meyer. Surely you know they are—or were—well known industrialists and financiers. They guided some of the world's largest companies."

"I honestly don't know anything about them except that they, like your father, made withdrawals from their Swiss bank accounts in 1936."

"Very well."

"Let me ask you something else. Do you know Charles Pincay?"

"Yes. For a while he was in charge of some of our accounts. Good man. Haven't heard from him in a while."

"Why did you stop using his services?"

"Telon was headed in a different direction, a more modern approach to our financial needs. We also needed to work with someone whose resources were larger than Pincay's. Like I said, he was a fine man and did a fine job for us."

The man was lying. Pincay and Associates, though small, was a Swiss banking institution and worked with the biggest companies. Reiner and Telon fired Pincay for something else. But then why was Pincay trying to communicate with Reiner?

"Is there anything else, Mr. Meyer? I do have another appointment." Reiner eyed the gold Rolex on his wrist ostentatiously.

"No actually. That's all for now. I hope I can call on you again."

"Perhaps, though I don't think I can be of any assistance to the CRT, and I'm not sure you can either. Though that is your decision."

An odd statement, Jake thought, and there was something ominous in Reiner's tone.

Reiner depressed a button. "Melody, Mr. Meyer is ready now."

Meyer started to leave but turned back to Reiner and said, "By the way, you should know that Charles Pincay is dead."

"I'm terribly sorry to hear that." Reiner was calm. Too calm.

Reiner stared at the TVs on his wall. He didn't need to listen to the audio; the images were sufficient. Demonstrators protesting fraudulent elections in the Ukraine, earthquake relief in Mexico, anti-Western riots in Pakistan and Indonesia, just enough chaos to allow Telon and the rest of the Levant Group to come to the rescue. The Levant Group was the world's caretaker, offering both carrots and sticks. Everything was moving according to their plans, had been for years. Yet Reiner watched the televisions with a combination of awe and anxiety. If the Dissenters were at it again, they could ruin everything.

Fifteen years ago, the Dissenters had obtained proof of the Levant Group's plans and projects. They were about to go public with the information, denouncing the mega multi-national as more powerful than any government, and claiming that the Levant Group's actions were the epitome of globalization run amuck.

Such a revelation would have cost the Levant Group trillions. Telon specifically. The communications giant was on the verge of a deal for control of African cell phone and cable television market. The Dissenters were on to the bribes, the kickbacks, the disruption of village life, despite the fact Telon, and the Levant Group more generally, was offering products and services for people who were otherwise cut off from the outside world. The Dissenters were so myopic, Reiner recalled thinking.

Lance Piedmont dealt with the threat. He asked for authority to take drastic measures. In two weeks, the crisis disappeared, and Piedmont earned the board's trust—and Harrison Reiner's.

Now, the Dissenters were stirring again.

At the last Levant board meeting they muttered about a CRT investigator, Harold Burns, snooping around, asking about members' Swiss bank accounts, specifically transactions in the 1930s. They believed Burns was working for the Dissenters.

But if the Dissenters were involved, why were they interested in those old transactions? Lance Piedmont said he'd handle it. But then Jake Meyer got involved. Did Piedmont know that? Reiner decided to bring up the issue at the next meeting.

Maya watched Jake go into One Canada Square, and when she was certain no one followed him, she headed back toward the Canary Wharf tube station. She and Jake agreed the night before that she watch his back when he went to Telon. Others were interested in the transactions, willing to kill for information.

In the underground, she rode the escalator down to the platform and caught the tube to London Bridge station. From there she walked east toward the *HMS Belfast*, the decommissioned war ship turned museum, moored between the London and Tower bridges. She was to meet Jake on board after his meeting at Telon.

Halfway up the gangplank her cell phone rang. "What have you got?" she asked, without the usual greeting. She pulled a pen and note pad from her purse and jotted down the information. "Excellent. Thanks for the help."

She passed the time touring the World War II ship. When she reached the control tower, she looked at her watch. Thirty-five minutes since she boarded the ship, time to meet Jake on the fifth deck, starboard. She found him standing against the railing.

"Enjoy your tour," he asked.

"Yes. How was the meeting with Reiner?"

"Not terribly productive. He says he knows nothing his father's account or the withdrawal in 1936. But he's worried."

"About what?"

"I don't know. He's hiding something. When I mentioned Pincay, he was hardly moved."

"So, no new leads?"

"Not one. What about you?"

He shared Burns' file with her in Zurich, including the bank account numbers and the list of names, not much to work with. But one name, Crowe, had the word "conductor" written by it. He asked her to see what she could find out.

She pulled a notebook from her purse and flipped the pages. "I had some friends at the Israeli embassy here trace the name and match it against employee lists from locomotive and transportation companies and unions."

"Like a conductor on a train?"

"Exactly. But no one named Crowe was a train conductor in Europe in 1936. Then I researched construction and engineering companies. Maybe someone like a foreman or designer. No match."

"Of course. What next?"

"Then it hit me, conductor might mean music, and sure enough, a man named Crowe conducted the Royal Philharmonic in the 1930s"

"Excellent!" he said with a grin.

"You knew that didn't you?"

"Yeah."

"You were testing me?"

"I needed to know if you were really on my side."

"I'm still here," Maya said. "What did you learn about Crowe?"

"There's a Crowe's Music Shop in the theater district."

"And its owned by Bethany Crowe, the conductor's daughter," Maya finished with a smirk.

"Precisely." Out of the corner of his eye Jake noticed a man in a navy blue coat and a dark knit cap. His nose was red from the cold, and he stood underneath one of the guns reading a guidebook. Occasionally he looked up, as if searching for different points of interest on the ship mentioned in the guide.

Then he headed aft and down the staircase to the lower decks.

"The ship has at least one other visitor today," Maya said.

"I'm not sure he's a tourist."

"What do you mean?"

"Most people find the big guns on a battleship fascinating. They walk around and around them. He took one glance and left. I just got the feeling he's interested in us."

"Do you think he heard anything we said?"

"Doubt it. But we should leave, maybe drop into Crowe's Music."

CHAPTER 17

London

The Merchant followed Meyer to Canary Wharf, but his Levant Group overseer told him not to go into One Canada Square. Harrison Reiner was not a Dissenter, and Meyer would learn nothing from him. But The Merchant did learn something: Jake Meyer had help.

Part experience, part intuition, The Merchant spied a woman keeping Meyer's back. She emerged from the Canary Wharf tube stop seventy-five meters behind him and kept pace. She kept her head straight, but The Merchant noticed the darting eyes. When Meyer went in, she stayed outside watching the entrance to One Canada Square. After a few moments, she headed back to the Tube. She was definitely with him.

The Merchant described her to his contact, who said he'd look into it. And he told The Merchant of Meyer's next stop. There wasn't much time. He needed to get on the road.

The drive south from London to Crawley was short. The town had grown beyond its 1940s designs when Gatwick expanded. Once light industry, everything was service, especially airport service. What was planned as a Brave New World was a pot pourri of immigrants and ethnicities, particularly Muslims. And it was a Muslim, Mahmoud Fawaz, a former "classmate" of The Merchant at a Stasi training facility, who brought him to town.

The Merchant turned onto Birkdale Drive, went two blocks past the address he'd been given and parked the rented blue Ford Escort. He checked the scene, then turned the car around and stopped across the street from the plain two bedroom house. At first glance, the house looked normal. A narrow walk snaked through a poorly manicured lawn to a white front door. When he knocked, The Merchant saw someone close the drapes at a second story window.

A few moments later a young man in his early twenties opened the door. He had short black hair and wore dark gabardine pants and a light blue Oxford shirt. He looked like a student, not a jihadist. The Merchant eyed him and stepped inside. Once the door was closed, the young man shoved him against the wall and another, bigger man pushed his forearm hard against The Merchant's throat while the first one frisked him.

"Sorry about that," Mahmoud Fawaz bellowed as he pounded down the stairs. "Under the circumstances, you can't be too careful."

The two men stepped back, and Fawaz grabbed The Merchant's shoulders and kissed both his cheeks.

"Come, let's talk. Can I offer you some tea or Turkish coffee?" Fawaz asked.

"Coffee would be fine, thanks,"

The Merchant followed his host down the hallway and into the kitchen. Fawaz was fatter than the last time The Merchant saw him. But that was almost twenty years earlier, when Fawaz was in his late teens, slim and agile. Now, The Merchant guessed he was way over two hundred pounds and waddled under the weight.

Fawaz poured two miniature cups of thick coffee and set them on the kitchen table. He grunted as he sat and waved The Merchant to a seat. "What can I help you with, my old friend?"

The Merchant sat straight, held the tiny cup with his thumb and index finger, and took a sip of the heavy liquid. "I need some materials I suspect you have."

"Such as?" Fawaz tapped a cigarette from a carton on the table and lit it.

"Manure, remote control devices, switches, all the toys we learned to play with at camp."

"Those were good times." Fawaz laughed.

The two met and became friendly competitors in 1988 at a Stasi terrorist training base in the North Schwein region of East Germany. The Palestinian Liberation Organization sent Fawaz, and The Merchant earned a seat in the class thanks to superior work and good contacts. They both excelled at the training, and when The Merchant graduated first in the class, Fawaz' feelings were hurt. Since then, they had spoken rarely, usually a quid pro quo basis rather than from friendship or loyalty.

"We had fun. Things seemed simpler then. There were only two sides, the enemy was clear," The Merchant said.

"There are still only two sides, Western imperialism and Islam."

Either Fawaz was religious or the fanatics were paying really well, probably the latter. Fawaz was as much a mercenary as The Merchant.

Fawaz downed the bitter coffee in one gulp and set the cup down. "What do you need the materials for?"

"A job, obviously."

"But if I sell them to you, I may be jeopardizing our own operations."

The Merchant knew Fawaz wanted to know more.

"You know I can't tell you anything else, client confidentiality. But let's just say that what I have in store will benefit your cause. You can even take credit for it."

"Your operation will bring the world closer to *sharia*?" Fawaz played the game well.

"Absolutely, my good friend," The Merchant smiled.

"Very well, let's go shopping."

Fawaz led The Merchant to a small yard behind the house bounded by an eight foot brick wall. Near the far perimeter was a green tool shed. Fawaz opened the aluminum door and put the lights on. The Merchant saw a work bench with an electric saw. Paint cans and brushes were stacked against one wall. Hammers, drills, gardening tools, including a bag of fertilizer, neatly arranged in a corner. "There must be more", he said.

"Of course."

Fawaz pushed the work bench aside and took a hammer with a red grip from the wall. Then the floor opened up. Fawaz started down a ladder in the hole.

At the bottom was a workspace two times the size of the shed above. The room held three tables topped with desk lamps, swinging magnifying glasses, pliers of different sizes and soldering irons. Underneath each was a stockpile of electrical wire, clocks, used cell phones, remote controls, ball bearings, nails, backpacks, and switches. Along the walls were jars of chemicals, aluminum powder and bags of fertilizers. The Merchant was in a bomb factory.

"Find what you want, and I'll give you a price," Fawaz said.

The Merchant picked up electrical tape, the joystick box from a remote controlled air plane, wires and some other stuff and put them on a table. "I'll also need to two cans of aluminum and three bags of fertilizer."

"Very well." Fawaz nodded and calculated on his fingers. "Ten thousand pounds."

"That's rather pricey, don't you think?"

"No haggling. This isn't the *shouk*," Fawaz snapped. "You could get it cheaper at home improvement shops and toy stores, if you like."

The Merchant reached into his pocket and unfolded a wad of bills. He handed them to Fawaz who licked his fingers to count them. "It's good doing business with you, my old friend. Can I help you assemble your device?"

The Merchant looked at his watch. He was in a time bind. "That would be great, thank you."

It only took an hour. Occasionally The Merchant asked Fawaz to remind him where and how to attach the wires. "Don't you remember?" Fawaz relished the opportunity to prove he should have been first in the Stasi class.

"Why don't you have your buddies come down here and haul the fertilizer up?"

"Certainly," Fawaz replied with a smile. *He* wasn't about to carry a bag of manure up that ladder.

The Merchant grabbed a bag and went up the ladder. Outside he lay the bag down, ran to his car, backed up the driveway, and opened the glove compartment. When he had the muzzle screwed to the barrel, he headed back to the shed.

The two men came out carrying bags of fertilizer on their shoulders.

The Merchant raised the weapon without losing step and fired a silenced round into each man's head. He walked past the bodies into the shed. Fawaz was halfway through the opening in the floor, device in one hand, joystick detonator in the other. He looked up as The Merchant aimed.

"Please, no. You can have everything for free."

"No haggling here." He put two rounds in Fawaz's chest and one in his head.

The fat terrorist slumped forward, stuck in the opening. The Merchant pried the explosive components from his hands and pushed Fawaz backward. The ladder snapped, and the obese corpse thudded to the floor.

"May Allah be with you," The Merchant intoned.

CHAPTER 18

Palm Springs

The winter sun was warm and soothing, the air quiet and still. Even the Santa Ana winds were quiet. The weather was only one reason Lance Piedmont kept a house in Palm Springs. The other was his deceased wife.

Ellen Piedmont loved Palm Springs. She enjoyed hiking in the mountains above the Coachella Valley and playing the emerald green golf courses dotting the brown desert floor. It was her escape from New York or Washington or wherever Piedmont did business.

Palm Springs was also where Ellen Piedmont spent her last days, dying of lung cancer. On her death bed, she made him promise not to sell the house, and while he did not share her love of the desert, Piedmont was too grief stricken to refuse.

He lay in a chaise longue on the patio, considering what he'd just heard from Josh Dempsey about events in Switzerland. The Merchant had neither gotten the Burns file nor eliminated Jake Meyer. Worse, Meyer knew about Harrison Reiner even though The Merchant had liquidated Pincay. Still worse, Piedmont was no closer to finding out whether it was all just another threat from the Dissenters to expose the Levant Group or something deeper.

In fifteen minutes he would have to update the Levant Group board, but what would he tell them? They did not tolerate failure.

Piedmont wanted to speak privately with one member before dialing into the conference call. He wanted to make sure he controlled the flow of information to the Levant Group. He didn't need some dimwit spilling the Burns matter to the board.

He grabbed his cane, hoisted himself up, and hobbled through the living room, which remained decorated in the bright red, yellow and green colors his wife preferred, into his office. He punched a few a numbers a pad and a moment later the man's face appeared.

"*Salaam Alechem*, Mr. Piedmont," the man said.

"Thanks for calling a bit early," Piedmont replied. "I won't waste time since the other members will be dialing in soon."

"As you wish. I imagine you would like to discuss Hamid."

"Yes. You assured me he would take care of Burns and get the information on his examination. Simple. I understand he used too much sodium pentothal. The CRT investigator went into cardiac arrest. Now I have to explain that Levant Group is still in jeopardy because your man failed, because you failed."

"I apologize for Hamid's mistake." The man wanted to distance himself. "He was trained by our security services and came highly recommended. He has been dealt with."

Piedmont nodded. Hamid probably died a painful death. "Nonetheless, we still have a problem. The CRT has contracted someone else to pick up Burns' work, and we still don't know where that will lead. The only thing clear at this point is that it involves our members' bank accounts when they formed the Levant Group."

"That was a long time ago. Shouldn't cause problems. The Dissenters didn't exist back then."

"True, but you are aware of what happened in 1936? If the Dissenters knew, they wouldn't hesitate to use it against us."

"But they wouldn't have any proof. The Pact was lost. It doesn't exist."

"They don't need proof. Rumors and lies are worse than the truth. Hamid's failure could be much more than a mistake."

The man slid his thumb and index finger over his moustache. He was beginning to understand the gravity of the situation.

"Don't worry," Piedmont said. "I'm taking care of the situation, and I won't mention specifics to the board. Let's keep this conversation to ourselves for the time being. We'll talk soon. I'll be going to Davos shortly to prepare for the World Economic Forum. Perhaps you should make arrangements to meet me."

"Yes, I will do that, Mr. Piedmont. Thank you."

"Not at all. I believe it's time for the others to dial in. See you in a minute."

Piedmont closed the line. He was pleased. When the agenda turned to the question of Burns, the old bank accounts and the Dissenters, he wouldn't have to worry about anyone complicating things.

Piedmont punched numbers on the pad again, and the screen crackled to life, split into twelve sections, a face in each box. The last face to pop was Harrison Reiner's. Telon Corporation was part of the Levant Group.

"Good afternoon, gentlemen. Or good evening as the case may be" Piedmont said.

A chorus of greetings in various tongues followed, the faces staring back at Piedmont serious and taut.

"You all should have received the minutes from the last conference call and today's agenda from Mr. Kim." All twelve heads nodded. They represented multinational companies dealing in everything from oil and renewable energy to pharmaceuticals to electronics and communications to aeronautics to finance, powerful men whose companies shaped the global economy.

Lee Byung Kim was the secretary of the Levant Group, CEO of Hyundsam, the vast South Korean conglomerate.

"Mr. Kim, are there any additions to the agenda?" Piedmont asked.

"No. We are ready to proceed." Kim answered.

"Good. Let's start with litigation and government action. Mr. Kilgore, what is the status of the case against GlascoMartin?" GlascoMartin was a troublesome member of the Levant Group that spent an inordinate amount of time in courtrooms. They always won.

"The class action suit was filed in U.S. District court in New York, last week," Kilgore said. "Rathmussen and Bird will work with our in-house counsel."

"A wise choice. Their lawyers know exactly how to deal with such pests," Piedmont had worked with Rathmussen before.

"Yes, Rathmussen assured me they'll challenge the plaintiffs' standing, and his junior associates are already pounding the environmentalists with discovery requests that should run their legal fees into the millions," Kilgore said.

"There's a good chance they'll go bankrupt," Piedmont said. "The case could die before it really starts. Keep us updated. We need this to go away."

All twelve heads nodded in agreement.

"Now, Mr. Thierry," Piedmont resumed, "what about the EU anti-trust investigation?"

"I've taken care of the problem," Thierry answered.

"Pray tell, Jacques, how have you done that?" another member asked.

"I persuaded a university classmate of mine, a member of the EU Parliament anti-trust committee, that the investigation should be dropped, or at least determined in our favor."

"What makes you so sure he'll follow through?" Piedmont asked.

"Because he'll lose his title, position and a whole lot more if he doesn't. We have some compromising information, including photos."

Piedmont warned Thierry about the risks associated with bribery and pushed the meeting ahead through several other dicey questions. But when a particular item came up on the agenda, he fell silent. He left the board members to stew in the interval. Finally Harrison Reiner spoke.

"Mr. Piedmont, I had a visit from a fellow named Jake Meyer the other day. He got an appointment by claiming he was an attorney with questions about my father's estate. He asked about the Swiss bank account my father he opened when Telon was formed in 1916."

"What did he want to know?"

"He asked if I knew anything about a large withdrawal made in 1936. Of course, I had no idea about it and told him so." Reiner paused. "But since other board members have had similar inquiries from that Burns fellow from the Claims Resolution Tribunal, I wonder if there is a connection."

"Indeed, there is," Piedmont said. "Harold Burns died before we could find out what he's after. Apparently, Jake Meyer was hired to finish the job. I'm on it."

"Well, do you think this is the Dissenters looking for something damaging?" Kim asked.

"Too early to tell."

"Meyer also said Pincay was dead."

"So the Dissenters *are* involved."

"I'd bet on it," another said. "But they're focused on the 1930s. What could have been happened so long ago that would cause us problems now?"

"I'm not sure," Piedmont lied. The 1936 transaction was the subject of rumor. No written record existed. And should the Dissenters learn of the terms, they would have to provide evidence. And there was no proof.

"Regardless of what happened seventy years ago, we have too much at stake to let the Dissenters get hold of something. The malcontents should be eliminated," Kilgore said. "I assume that's where you're heading. Right, Piedmont?"

"Uh, yes. I've engaged someone to deal with the threat."

"Well, he better take care of the Dissenters in a hurry. Your World Economic Forum is less than two weeks away, and we don't need any unnecessary distractions."

"Correct," Piedmont responded half heartedly.

Kim finished things out. "Well, the last item is in fact the WEF. Mr. Piedmont, are there any issues?"

"No. We'll gather at my chalet as usual. I'm leaving soon."

"Excellent. I believe we can adjourn the meeting then," Kim said.

Piedmont hung up, found his cane and went back to the patio, turning things over. *What if?* repeated in his head like a broken record. *What if* the Pact existed? *What if* he could get his hands on it?

He lowered himself onto the chaise longue and looked out across the valley. He closed his eyes and let his mind tumble further. Like anyone with immense power, he wanted more. The thought of the Pact intoxicated him. Finding it would be akin to finding the Holy Grail. The Pact would be a bargaining chip and keep the Levant Group on top for years. Piedmont would be a king - the absolute master of global destiny.

But first he had to determine if the Pact existed, and for that he'd have to rely on The Merchant and hope his recent failures were anomalies.

CHAPTER 19

London

Even with a map Jake and Maya had difficulty locating the store. The winding streets between Leicester Square and Covent Garden are maddening even for people with a solid sense of direction, but bumbling through the maze in a cold rain was not appealing.

Eventually they found it, tucked away on a street near the Garrick Theater. Jake was surprised Crowe's Music was still in business, given its remoteness, and inside Maya felt like she'd stepped into a time machine.

The bells on the door chimed, and they sniffed rotting wood. There wasn't much light, and it was colder inside than outside. In one aisle, wooden cases displayed sheet music, from classical to jazz, from musical theater to opera. In another were instruments—violins, flutes, even a small harpsichord. In the third aisle were books, toy figurines of composers and musicians like Mozart and Beethoven and an array of concert posters.

A woman bounded down stairs in the back. The grace and ease of her movement, her back straight and toes light, gave her away as a dancer. She was petite and thin with white hair pulled into a bun. Her eyes, dark like chestnuts, were big and brilliant and alive. Despite the lines around her mouth, Bethany Crowe was a stunning woman.

"Can I help you?" she asked

"We'd like to talk to you about your father, Ms. Crowe," Jake said.

The twinkle in her eyes disappeared. "May I ask what about?"

"An old Swiss Bank account in the name of Daniel Crowe," Maya said.

Bethany Crowe slid behind the counter and slid a Sati CD into the stereo. "I have already spoken with a young gentleman about that. Do you work for the CRT as well?"

"Sort of," Jake answered. "Was the man named Burns?"

"I believe so. Why?"

"He's dead, Ms. Crowe."

The old woman tensed. "When did that happen?"

"A couple of weeks ago."

Silence. Then, "I spoke with Mr. Burns about a month ago."

"What did he want to know about your father's account?"

Bethany Crowe seemed to be lost in her head, her eyes going from Jake to Maya and back to Jake. Then quick as a cobra, she pulled a 9 millimeter Beretta from under the counter and pointed it at her visitors. "Burns warned me about you. Said you might come calling and that I should protect myself." She tilted the weapon to one side. "So I invested in this gun. I won't hesitate to use it. I won't end up like father."

Jake and Maya saw she had no idea how to use the weapon. The safety was still on and the magazine was not fully clicked into the grip. "We're not here to hurt you, Ms. Crowe," Maya crooned.

"How do I know that?"

"Because if we wanted to kill you we would have already," Jake said.

Bethany Crowe didn't put the gun down.

"What did Burns tell you?" Jake repeated the question.

"That you or they killed my father."

"Who killed your father, Ms. Crowe?" Maya asked.

"The Levant Group."

Jake looked at Maya, then back at Bethany Crowe. "We're not from the Levant Group. We want to find out what happened to Harold Burns. Apparently the information he was gathering got him killed."

"Who are you then?"

Jake knew when to tell the truth and when to conceal it. With a frightened woman in front of him and a trail of bodies behind him, he opted for partial honesty. "I'm an investigator hired by the CRT, and this is my colleague."

Bethany Crowe relaxed a bit, but she kept the Beretta up. "What do you want to know?"

"Why don't you tell us what you told Burns," Maya suggested. "Like why your father opened the account in 1933."

"My father loved music, theater and dance. He was first violinist with the Royal Symphony and earned a nice living. He opened this shop when I was two years old. We weren't wealthy, just very comfortable and certainly did not need a Swiss bank account. He opened the account as a favor."

"For whom?"

"Edmund Rothschild."

"*The* Rothschilds?"

"Yes. My father's career as a musician put him in contact with high society. Edmund often attended concerts and admired my father. Eventually they became friends. They dined together and spent hours discussing history and politics."

"Could you elaborate on their relationship, Ms. Crowe?" Jake asked.

"Before World War I, none of the Rothschilds were in favor of the projects for a Jewish settlement in Palestine. But Edmund's theories on colonization and investment were compatible with the Zionist movement, and my father shared most of his views."

"Was your father Jewish?"

"No, but he was a realist. Imperialism was a drain on Britain, and he realized a prosperous future for the country required disengaging from the colonies and creating investments and business relationships all over the globe. He and Edmund believed it was in Britain's best economic and political interest that a Jewish homeland be created in Palestine. They agreed it was one of the best chances for Britain to maintain its influence in the Middle East.

"The conclusion of the Great War and the Depression only enhanced Edmund's belief in the need for investment. He learned of a group of industrialists and financiers that shared his beliefs that capitalism and business are better suited than governments to meet people's needs. He wanted to join them but decided to keep his distance. Instead, he asked my father if he would join and attend the meetings and let Edmund back him. My father agreed, and in 1933, Edmund opened a Swiss bank account in Father's name. When the group wanted money, Edmund deposited it in the account."

"Why did Rothschild want to keep his distance? Certainly they would have welcomed him."

"Because he didn't want to alienate the rest of the family with his liberal beliefs. He ran the risk of losing his title and fortune."

"And your father told you all this?" Jake asked.

"Yes, shortly before he died."

"What else can you remember?"

"I vaguely recall attending a few meetings with my father when I was a child."

Jake's mind jumped. Crowe had just given them another possible connection to explore.

"Who else was at the meetings?" Maya asked.

Bethany Crowe grinned. "I really don't know who was there. I just remember the estate. It was *so* beautiful. I felt like a princess when I walked inside. There were magnificent lawns and gardens behind the house. While the men were inside, the children played outside. The women sat and watched us from benches and tables under umbrellas. Servants brought food and sweets and games to keep us occupied. I had never been around such wealth." Crowe paused, closed her eyes. "I spent hours dancing around the fountain, pretending I was a prima ballerina performing for the royal family. It was like a dream."

"Where was the estate?" Jake asked.

"It was in Salisbury. I remember because we passed by the marvelous cathedral when we went to the meetings."

"And who owned it?"

"Oh, it was such a long time ago." Crowe put her fingers to her lips and bent her head. "Reisz. The family name was Reisz." She lifted her head. "Elizabeth Reisz was the daughter's name. She was a teenager at the time."

Jake had a name. "Why did your father make a large withdrawal from the bank account in 1936?"

"My father told Edmund the group was making a major investment. Edmund put a significant amount of money in the account and told my father to forward it to the group. My father wasn't as excited about the venture, but Edmund ignored him. By the late 1970's, my father began to see the suffering the Levant Group's policies caused. He was ashamed to be a member even in name. He decided he had made a grave mistake."

"What kind of mistake?"

"He didn't say, only that he had to make amends and expose the Levant Group."

"And you believe the Group had him murdered for his dissent?"

"My father was in excellent health. He exercised regularly and drank rarely. A sudden heart attack seemed very strange, especially just before he was going to take damning information on the Levant Group to the press. I'm certain the Levant Group murdered him."

Bethany Crowe stopped, considered something and then continued. "Its interesting you should use the word dissent."

"Why is that?" Jake asked.

"Father said he had become a Dissenter, a member of the Levant Group who became opposed to its activities and policies."

"Did he mention any other dissenters or anything about the Levant Group's initial investment that caused his crisis of conscience?"

"He never mentioned any of the others by name and said it would be better if I didn't know anything about the investment, that it might put my life at risk."

"And why did your father tell you all this?"

"Probably because he wanted me to know everything before he went to the press. Some sort of absolution from his only remaining family. Or I suppose that since keeping secrets can be a solitary endeavor, he didn't want to be alone." Crow shrugged. The reasons seemed immaterial.

A church bell somewhere tolled twice. Jake and Maya looked at each other, both thinking the same thing. They'd hit a dead end.

"Thank you for your time, Ms. Crowe. You've been very helpful," Maya said with a smile.

"Not at all."

As Jake nodded his thanks something in the mirror behind the counter caught his eye. A car pulled up and parked in front of the store. A man got out and began walking away from the store. *That's odd*, he thought. Parking wasn't permitted.

The Merchant got back from Crawley with time to spare and had no problem picking up Jake and Maya as they left their hotel. Initially, he followed them without much difficulty, but when they left Piccadilly Circus and marched through Leicester Square, he lost them. He knew where they were headed so he got a map and found the street.

After a few turns through the theater district, The Merchant caught sight of Jake and Maya entering Crowe's Music. He drove a block past the street and pulled over to the curb. He grabbed the package he constructed at Fawaz's and made some adjustments. He'd never actually used a homemade bomb before. He was more familiar with fists, knives and guns.

He attached the device to the fertilizer in the trunk of the car. Back down the street he was dismayed to see *No Parking* signs. He hadn't done his homework. Parking would be conspicuous. But as he pulled in front of Crowe's, he saw Jake and Maya at the counter, talking to Ms. Crowe. No choice.

He got out of the car and walked away, the remote control underneath his overcoat. He didn't look back. He headed across the street and north, counting silently. When The Merchant got to ten he pushed the button. He felt the shockwave before he heard the blast.

Jake's gut sent him a warning. He knew he should trust it, and then he knew why. Jake recognized the driver as the intruder at the Schweizerhof. He interrupted Ms. Crowe. "Is there a way out the back?"

"Yes, behind me."

"Let's go!"

"What's going on?" Maya asked.

"Ms. Crowe, follow me. We have to get out of here now." Jake pushed Maya around the counter and grabbed Ms. Crowe's wrist.

She struggled. She figured they were trying to kidnap her. Maya bolted for the back door and Jake followed, pulling a flailing Bethany Crowe. Just as they burst through the door, a bright light and a shock wave threw them forward. Debris rained down on them.

When things settled, Jake lifted himself, then turned to help Maya. "Are you okay?"

"Yeah, I think." Maya dusted herself off.

They turned to find Bethany Crowe lying in a pool of blood. The blast had flung her against the brick wall and smashed her skull.

"She didn't deserve that," Maya gasped.

As they hurried south, Jake tried to clear his head. What next?

It came to him in a couple of seconds. "We have to get in touch with the Salisbury county recorder's office."

"What for?"

"To see who owns the Reisz estate now."

"In the distance, sirens keened.

CHAPTER 20

Jerusalem,

Professor Steiner trudged toward his office on the third floor of the Social Sciences Building at the Hebrew University of Jerusalem on Mount Scopus. He shunned the shirt-sleeves and slacks many of his colleagues wore on campus in favor of a suit and tie. He thought such attire commanded deference from students and lent an air of authority.

The professor of modern history and international relations was returning from lunch in the Lamport Botanical Gardens across the street and opened the door to his spartan office. Though he had tenure and was entitled to plusher surroundings, Professor Steiner was on campus only two days a week and figured extravagant furniture and décor were unnecessary and a waste of university funds. He preferred to work, read and write at home, where there were fewer telephone calls—and no students.

He sat at his desk and gazed a moment at the Jerusalem skyline. Jerusalem was particularly important to Professor Steiner. It had been his home most of his life.

A knock on the door. *Damn.*

"Yes," Steiner grumped.

A plump woman in her mid-forties with bright red hair and freckles marched in. "Here are your messages and mail from the past week, sir." Steiner's secretary laid the notes in his inbox.

"Thank you, Leah."

"Is there anything else you need?"

"No, I'm fine."

"May I leave a little early today, Mark has a soccer game."

"Of course, nothing is more important than your children," Steiner smiled.

Leah left and Steiner rummaged through the envelopes. He eventually came upon one with a return address at the Prime Minister's office. He opened it, read the note and took a deep breath.

Professor Steiner had informed his government contacts he no longer was available to consult on Foreign Policy and Arab Affairs. He was tired. He had done his share. Beside, there were others, in and out of government, even some of his students, younger and better able to handle the stress. Yet, the government stayed after him.

He picked up the phone and dialed the number from memory. "Avram Sills please, Joseph Steiner calling."

A moment later the jovial voice of the Prime Minister's chief of staff assaulted Professor Steiner's ears. "Good morning, Professor. I hope everything is well."

"It is, Avram, thank you."

"I take it you got my note?"

"I did, and my answer is the same as it has been the past six months. I'm finished with consulting. It's amazing. I think that after I'm dead you'll have the chutzpah to call me in the grave, even if *my* last request was for eternal peace."

"Professor Steiner, please. We're at a crossroads with the Arabs."

"We're always at a cross roads with the Arabs. It's been that way for years. Madrid, Oslo, Camp David, Gaza. One step forward, two steps back. Beside, you don't really want my advice: you want me to tell you what you want to hear. And no matter what I say, the Prime Minister, and not just this one, does what he or she wants. There are others who can give you advice to ignore."

"Listen, Washington is pressuring us to move forward with the Palestinians."

"What's new, Avram?"

"They're serious this time. Threatening to cut aid."

"Should have done that a long time ago. Maybe we'd have peace."

"Is that what you really think?" The Chief of Staff probed for an opinion.

"After all these years, I've come to the conclusion that my thoughts are relevant only when they echo the government's."

"Its not just the Americans," Avram went on. "Despite our military deals with the Turks, Ankara has some religious parties in power that want to side with the Islamic fundamentalists."

"Don't worry. The secular military won't let that happen."

"The Syrians are offering to talk, and as usual they'll want the Golan Heights on the table. But we still don't know if and how to deal with the different Palestinian factions. We need your wisdom, your connections. We'll triple your fee and keep your identity a secret." The Chief of Staff sounded desperate.

"Avram, don't insult me. It has never been about the money, and you know that. If I wanted a government career, I would have accepted any number of offers for cabinet positions. I prefer the academic world, especially at this point in my life. Thanks but no thanks."

"The Prime Minister will not be happy. What shall I tell him?"

"The truth. I'm too old and no longer have the energy."

"He won't accept that."

"Maybe not. But I have no doubt you'll find somebody else."

"Perhaps you would agree to just one more meeting?"

Steiner thought about it. He loved his country, even if he disagreed with its policies at times. And peace with Israel's neighbors . . . How could he stop now? Besides, they'd hassle him until he gave in. The Israeli way. "Fine. But you promise it's the last time?"

"Of course."

"Yes, of course." Steiner hung the phone up, wiped his brow and looked at his watch. Thirty minutes before meeting with a student to discuss his thesis. He deployed his feet on the widow sill and took a raft of newspaper from his bag.

He scanned the front page of *The International Herald Tribune* and then turned to the European section. He read an article reporting the deaths of two men whose only connection to each other seemed to be their wealth and influence. But Professor Steiner's gut told him there was something more.

His read the article a second time and his heart skipped a beat. He knew the deceased. Not personally, just by their family names, seared into his memory years earlier.

He read the article a third time. *Could it be happening again?*

From the safe in his credenza, his trembling fingers took a folder of clippings. Five years ago Martin Lindt and Peter Childress died of unknown causes. A year later Daniel Ostroff was found dead in his apartment, and a year after that, Margaret Davies disappeared. Her decaying body was eventually found on the banks of the Seine, outside of Paris. The striking thing about all of them was that while they were old, nothing indicated they were sick. All could have died by coincidence, but Professor Steiner doubted it.

There was no coincidence. They had said the wrong thing, spoken to the wrong people, done something to irritate the Levant Group. All were Dissenters.

Steiner knew when to keep quiet, had said nothing to anyone. But the Levant Group had tentacles everywhere, even in academia. Could the Levant Group know his secret? As far as he was aware, none of the Dissenter's knew him. But what if someone did? He could not let the Levant Group uncover the secret. He put the papers away, took his briefcase and left his office. In the hall, he met the student.

"Professor Steiner, where are you going? We have an appointment to review my thesis."

"We'll have to reschedule. I need to take care of a personal matter."

CHAPTER 21

Davos

The helicopter's whirling blades kicked a cloud of snow up from the landing pad. Lance Piedmont watched from behind the windows of his mountain chalet as the Sikorsky's hatch opened, the stairs dropped to the ground and his guest emerged. Piedmont didn't go outside to greet him.

Piedmont's visitor, bent to avoid the rotors and headed toward the chalet, his body guard after him. He crossed his arms over his chest, unaccustomed to the chill; he spent most of his time in warmer climates.

When Mustafa Ibn Azziz, confident and advisor to one of the many Saudi Arabian crown princes reached the door, Piedmont groaned. It wasn't the hypocrisy. Azziz publicly espoused strict adherence to Islam, but privately drank alcohol, ate pork and engaged in sexual perversion. And truth be told, Piedmont shared some of his guest's proclivities, even enabling them on occasion.

Rather, Piedmont thought he was dumb. To some, Azziz looked intelligent and successful, but not Piedmont. He figured Azziz got where he was by favor, not merit. What else could explain the rise of such an incompetent man?

Azziz, for example, insisted that *his* man deal with Harold Burns, but when the CRT accountant was killed, the Levant Group was left in a bind. *Christ, the fool really bungled that one,* Piedmont thought. *But if the Pact exists and I can get my hands on it, some good may come of this.*

"Welcome to Davos. Nice to see you again."

"And you as well, Mr. Piedmont," Azziz beamed. "Allah has given you quite a home."

"Thank you. The chalet serves its purpose."

Azziz was about to take off his coat when Piedmont said, "Come, let's walk. It's too glorious a day to be inside." Piedmont knew the cold air didn't agree with Azziz, but pride would keep him from rejecting a stroll in the mountains behind the chalet.

The Saudi tilted his head in assent and the two men headed down a paved footpath. Azziz' bodyguard and one of Piedmont's protectors followed thirty feet behind

"Its splendid here," Azziz said, his teeth chattering. "Why did you choose Davos?"

"It's a third home actually. I love the mountains, and I grew up skiing and hiking. Before my hip problems, Davos was the perfect playground. Now it's become sort of a sanctuary." Piedmont chuckled. "Speaking of sanctuary, did you know Davos used to have a number of sanitariums for treating tuberculosis?"

"I didn't know."

"Yes. People believed the altitude, the fresh air, the long hours of sunshine soothed the lungs and alleviated some of the disease's symptoms."

"The air certainly does have an effect on the lungs, though I would rather call it a burn", Azziz grimaced.

Piedmont smiled. "You probably don't know this either, but Davos has a literary history as well. Robert Louis Stevenson finished *Treasure Island* recuperating here, and Davos inspired Thomas Mann's *Magic Mountain*. His wife was treated for tuberculosis here."

"That's very interesting. I've never read Mann, but I rather enjoyed *Treasure Island*."

That figures. "In any event, I like Davos because it is more secluded than Zermatt or St. Moritz." He didn't mention the other reason for the chalet, its proximity to the World Economic Forum—and Piedmont was among its major, all be it silent, sponsors.

Unlike the governments and businesses that openly supported the Forum, Piedmont's support was anonymous, handled through front companies. The rumor mill churned endlessly about the identity of the Forum's major benefactor, but it was all gossip. Piedmont's agents gathered information about companies, governments, and the global business environment at the bars, coffee houses and lecture halls in

Davos during the WEF. And it was this intelligence that Piedmont used to chart the course of the Levant Group.

"I too prefer privacy, Mr. Piedmont. It provides freedom, companionship, release and relaxation," Azziz said with a sparkle in his good eye.

Piedmont recognized the veiled request for female company. "Well, in order to maximize your private time, let's discuss the Meyer situation." He'd take care of his guest's urges later, somewhere in town.

"Indeed. The crown prince is very concerned."

"Yes, I imagine he is. The royal house could find itself in a precarious position." Piedmont briefed his guest on what Jake Meyer and The Merchant were up to.

"You are confident this man, this Merchant, will succeed?" Azziz asked.

Piedmont ignored the impulse to remind him they wouldn't be having this discussion if Azziz's man had appropriately dealt with Burns.

"Yes, his skills are a bit more refined than Mr. Hamid's." The statement was calculated to burn. "We've used The Merchant in the past."

"I did not know that," Azziz muttered.

"You didn't need to know the specifics. The Merchant wanted his part kept quiet."

"What did he do?"

"He eliminated a few Dissenters."

"Ah, yes, I remember. A few years ago. The Dissenters were threatening to expose us."

"Yes. The Merchant performed well. He earned his keep. And if Burns was about to uncover the Pact and Meyer follows his tracks, The Merchant will finish the job."

"Good, because if it does exist and people find out, there will be a revolution which would make Iran in 1979 look like a Ramadan dinner. The desert would turn a bright crimson."

Piedmont let the man articulate his hesitant thoughts.

"The chaos would be disastrous for the Royal Family. And the Levant Group. The princes, the clerics and the mullahs would stop cooperating with the Group."

The threat was tiresome. Any time a Persian Gulf ruler took issue with the Levant Group, they hinted at withdrawing, tinkering with the oil spigots, generally causing trouble. They were like spoiled children who want to take their toys and go home if they don't get their way.

But if Piedmont got hold of the Pact, things would change. He'd have the biggest and best toy. "It seems Meyer has help."

"What do you mean?"

"Apparently the Israelis got wind of Burn's investigation and his death and were curious about Walsing's decision to hire Meyer. They pulled in a Mossad agent to 'protect' Meyer and to spy on *his* investigation."

"Do you think they have any idea of the Levant Group's connection to the Pact?"

"They only know what Meyer knows."

"And this Mossad agent, what's his name?"

"*Her* name is Maya Herzog"

"They assigned a woman?"

"Their female agents are quite capable," Piedmont replied. "Better than most Arab male operatives."

The path u-turned around a large fir tree and led the pair back toward the chalet. "Where are Meyer and Herzog heading next?" Azziz asked.

"I'm not entirely sure," Piedmont lied.

"But you are positive The Merchant is on top of them and will get the Pact if they find it?"

"Absolutely."

"And destroy it?" The question was partly rhetorical.

"Of course. Don't you trust me, Azziz?"

The Saudi studied Piedmont carefully. "I don't have any reason to doubt you. You are aware of the consequences if the Pact is exposed."

"Most definitely. Tell the crown prince not to worry. Everything is under control."

Azziz waved, and his bodyguard rushed to open the helicopter door. The blades started spinning slowly, and Azziz stepped up into his seat.

"I thought you wanted some company?" Piedmont asked.

"No, I'm no longer in the mood. I need to return and inform the Prince of these developments. Some other time?"

The rotors picked up speed and snow began lifting from the ground.

"It would be my pleasure." He lied again.

As the Sikorsky vanished in the distance, Josh Dempsey came out of the chalet wearing a black parka and a knit ski cap, and stood next to Piedmont.

"That man is a fool," Piedmont declared as his eyes followed the helicopter over the horizon.

"How much did you tell him?"

"Not enough for Azziz or the Prince to cause trouble." Piedmont changed the subject. "When are Meyer and Herzog going to see Elizabeth Reisz?"

"Tomorrow."

Piedmont nodded. "The Merchant has her address and everything he needs?"

"All has been taken care of by my contact in Zurich," Dempsey answered.

"And what did you learn from your colleagues at INR about the relation between Maya and Chaim Herzog?"

"She is Herzog's daughter."

"That's what I figured." When Piedmont first learned Maya Herzog was monitoring Jake Meyer, he had Dempsey find out about her background. During the search, the name Chaim Herzog, a highly decorated but recently murdered Mossad agent, surfaced. Dempsey uncovered nothing about the death, but what he did learn made Piedmont chuckle with irony.

"Can we go inside? I'm freezing," Dempsey chattered.

"Stop whining, Joshua. Did you find out anything about how Herzog died?"

"No. Are you going to say anything to The Merchant?"

"No. He'll figure it out on his own, if he hasn't already. Beside, I don't want to do anything to disrupt his focus." Piedmont stuck his cane to the left and turned on his heel around the stick.

Inside, Piedmont eased himself into a leather chair. "Pour us a Bourbon, Josh."

Dempsey went to the bar, filled two tumblers with Maker's Mark. "Do you think the Pact really exists?"

Piedmont took a sip of the warm liquor. "I certainly hope so. And we'd better get our hands on it first, or we'll miss a golden opportunity to rewrite history."

CHAPTER 22

London

Jake lay in Maya's bed, arms behind his head looking at the ceiling. He knew she was staring at him, but he said nothing.

A car with its brights on sped by the hotel and briefly lit the room. Jake turned and caught a glimpse of her silky brown hair and full lips. She looked sad.

"What happened with the Yassin *affair*?" she asked.

The question did not surprise him. He knew the Israelis kept information on the operations of friendly governments. "I can think of better subjects for pillow talk."

"I can't." She propped herself on an elbow.

"What do you know?"

"Only that you left the Treasury Department right after Yassin got away."

Jake wondered whether he was about to purge his soul or take a leap of faith. Maya had saved his life a couple of times. That bought her a certain amount of trust didn't it? "I was stationed in Zurich as part of the U.S. counter-terrorism and drug interdiction efforts. My job was to investigate, follow and cut off Al Qaeda's, Hezbollah's and the FARC's money trails."

"Not easy."

"There are a lot of obstacles. You understand how it is," Jake said. "But I was in with the Swiss authorities and the banks, and they were very helpful, especially after 9/11. We closed a lot of accounts and stopped a number of operations."

"Including Yassin?"

"Yes. He was smuggling poppy seeds from Afghanistan into the Baltic states and some of the former Soviet Republics with big Muslim populations. They processed it into heroin and took it to Europe and the U.S. The money went into banks in Zurich and the Cayman Islands. Yassin gave some of the terrorist cells access to the accounts to fund their work."

"How did you put the pieces together?"

Jake told her about Yassin's accounts with Pincay and the banker's predicament. Pincay told Jake and his team when withdrawals were made so Jake could watch certain cells and seize the accounts. Interrogations of cell members led to phone numbers and computer hard drives which led back to Yassin's direct associates. "We shut a lot of it down, but"—Jake paused—"Yassin got away."

"Do you know how?"

Jake got up, took an Evian from the fridge in the kitchenette, and sat on the edge of the bed. "Yassin was less than thrilled about losing his stream of income and his status as terror broker. He was good. He set me up." Jake seemed to leave the present. "Her name was Anna Constantine. She was fantastic. Intelligent, playful, sexy."

"Where did you meet her?"

"At an art gallery. She told me she was in Zurich buying art for her home in St. Petersburg. I was careless. I lost control. I was obsessed or possessed."

Maya said nothing.

"I was in love with her for six weeks. Then I got word that Yassin was gone. Two days later five of my team and two diplomatic security agents working with us were murdered. The same day, Anna disappeared."

Still silent, Maya nodded.

"I guess she copied the keys to my apartment and stopped by when I wasn't there. Apparently she was good with computers."

Maya finished the tale. "She hacked her way into your hard drive, found your notes, reports and information about your team members and relayed it to Yassin."

"That's my best hunch. At some point Yassin got wind we were watching him and put Anna, or whatever her name was, into play."

"There was no way you could have known."

"I should have checked her out. I was stupid to keep personnel information and case notes at home. Those men and women deserved more from me. They were my responsibility."

Jake took a sip of water. "Anyway, they didn't ask me to leave. I quit."

Maya touched his back.

"It's funny. I became an investigator and took the job with Treasury because I wanted to be somebody, do something important. I was never satisfied just being an ordinary Joe, no real purpose in life. Maybe it was ego, I don't know. But after the *affair*, I was happy being nobody." His voice trailed off. "No glory, but no pain."

Maya shifted in the bed, and Jake pulled a sheet over his naked lap. "So what's your story?" he asked.

"I don't have one."

"Everyone has a story."

Maya didn't respond.

"Quid pro quo," Jake said. "I gave you something. You owe me."

Maya seemed hard. "My father was murdered a few months ago."

"I'm sorry."

"I know you are," Maya said. "Maybe I'll tell you some other time."

"Sure."

"Come back to bed."

After they made love, his heart was pounding. "I can hear you," she said.

"I'm sure you can." Jake didn't know what else to say.

"We've got an early morning. We should get some sleep," Jake said, but Maya was already out. He closed his eyes and fell into the first deep sleep he'd had in years.

CHAPTER 23

Riyadh

Azziz sat on a plush lawn chair by a fountain that fired a stream of water fifty feet into the air and rained down into a pool of colored tiles. The fountain was part of an immense courtyard of green grass, tall palm trees, an Olympic swimming pool, pillows and tables for guests to recline and dine, and an area for lawn bowling. It centered a rectangle surrounded by bright white marble columned walkways.

Azziz was waiting for an audience with crown prince Faisal. He did not have to gather inside with the others awaiting His Royal Highness. His unique relationship with the Prince let him bask alone in the hot desert sun. He needed thawing after the trip to that ice box, Davos. *Only mad people could live like that,* he thought.

Speaking of madness, a vision of Piedmont waving the Pact in the air flashed into his mind, and he shuddered. If the Pact really existed and if Piedmont got his hands on it, the consequences would be disastrous. Not just for the Saudis but for the entire world. What was he going to tell the Prince?

The crown prince emerged from the great hall. Tall and lean, a soft rope belt cinched his flowing white robes at the waist. He wore the red and white checkered keffiyeh, signifying that he lived in a monarchy and had made the Hajj, the pilgrimage to Mecca demanded of Muslims. The prince moved with elegance and grace, his shoulders back, his steps slow and fluid. Azziz admired him.

"*Salaam, Alechem.* Hello, Azziz. Welcome home. Would you like some tea?"

Azziz stood and bowed his head,

"*Alechem, Salaam.* Tea would be nice, thank you."

The Prince snapped his fingers and an attendant disappeared inside.

The two men embraced and kissed each other's cheeks. "Sit down, *habibi*. Surely you are exhausted from your journey."

"The cold does sap one's energy." Azziz dropped slowly back into the chair. Another attendant brought a seat for the prince.

The first servant appeared with magnificently decorated porcelain cups and saucers and set them on the circular table between the two men. He heaped sugar into each cup and poured the black tea. Prince Faisal and Azziz sipped the warm sweet liquid and engaged in the customary chit chat, inquiries about their families, the Saudi national soccer team's prospects, current events. After thirty minutes, Faisal got to the point. "So, Azziz, what did you learn from Piedmont?"

The royal advisor set his cup down and leaned forward, formed a pyramid with his hands and rested his chin on his finger tips. "He's brought in someone called The Merchant to finish what our man, Hamid, failed to accomplish. He's a mercenary and has worked for the Levant Group before. Apparently, he's very good."

"Tell me more."

Azziz relayed the information about Jake Meyer and Maya Herzog.

The crown prince raised a brow.. "So Mossad is involved?"

"It would seem that way, Your Highness, but I doubt they know any more about the Pact than we do."

Faisal closed his eyes. "This is terribly important. The position, if not the lives, of the royal family may be at stake. Our fanatical co-religionists will use even a rumor about the Pact as propaganda against us. The entire region will turn upside down and suck the rest of the world in. Perhaps we should be more involved, put some of our own people on Meyer, Herzog and The Merchant. Where are they now?"

Azziz calculated his response. "If we involve our own people, Highness, we expose ourselves, and we don't need to do that yet. We have the luxury of using our agents as a last resort. Beside, Piedmont said he didn't know where Meyer, Herzog and The Merchant were. Of course, I don't believe him."

"You don't like Piedmont, do you Azziz?"

"I don't trust him. He's an arrogant man. I am certain he doesn't like us and resents our membership in the Levant Group."

"Likely he's not alone," the crown prince smirked. He meant the conservative clerics and some of the royal family. They could tolerate a relationship with the West to hold onto power, but membership in a secret organization like the Levant Group, a cabal of multinational corporations, was heresy. Oil rich Saudi Arabia didn't need to be so tight with infidels, it could survive quite well on its own. Membership in such a group just opened the doors to empty, evil Western values.

So, when King Faisal, the crown prince's father, joined the Levant Group, he kept it quiet. The Prince, educated in the West, agreed with the group's basic tenets about global business and trade; and when the oil dried up, and eventually it would, a seat at the Levant Group's table would assure access to other resources, trade and wealth. Membership was an insurance policy.

"I fear," Azziz said, "that if the Pact does exist and Piedmont gets it, he'll use it against us."

"What makes you say that?"

"Gut instinct. The look in his eyes as we walked and talked. They burned with fantasy and unbridled ambition."

"So you think that if Piedmont finds the Pact, he will bribe and blackmail us? We shall no longer be partners but servants to the Levant Group?"

"That is what I fear, Your Highness."

The Prince stood, dipped his hand into the fountain and cooled the back of his neck. "You know I have always valued your wisdom Azziz, ever since we were boys. What do you advise we do?"

He was about to present the only option he could think of, one Prince Faisal might question. Faisal was his friend and protector from school days when the young nobleman befriended the pockmarked kid everybody else picked on and thereby won his undying loyalty. Azziz nevertheless chose his words carefully. "The other princes remain unaware of our membership in the Levant Group?" He asked.

"Yes, only the king knows."

"Someone else hopes the Pact does not exist as much we do."

"I know. The Israelis."

Good, Azziz thought. *He's opened the door himself.* "Exactly. They know what's at stake. Mossad is already involved. Perhaps if we made an overture to the right person we could use our membership in the

Levant Group to get inside information and help the Israelis handle the matter."

The prince folded his arms across his chest. "I don't know about that, Azziz."

"We would keep our exposure to a minimum, Your Highness."

"Yes, but talking with the Israelis is always delicate. The West praises us, but we risk riots and violence at home. Our own people call us traitors."

"I understand your concerns. But it's not as if we've never dealt with them before. We've had secret talks about the Syrians, the Iranians - even the Palestinians."

"With little result," the Prince rejoined.

"But the stakes are greater now, Your Highness. And the enemy of our enemy is our friend." Azziz used the old cliché.

"That is true." The prince looked up brightly. "Ironic, isn't it, Azziz? Poetic justice. Dealing with the Jews is how we got ourselves into this mess in the first place."

Azziz didn't want to address the past. "I'll keep everything unofficial, very secret."

"I trust your discretion. Do you have a point of contact?"

"I might. But speaking with him won't be easy. He'll doubt our motives and may even refuse a meeting."

"But do you think he can really help?"

"He's the only one."

"Then you must speak with him. Use the charm and intellect that has served you so well in the past, because our future truly depends on it."

"Of course, Your Highness."

CHAPTER 24

Salisbury

The Merchant sat at a picnic table enjoying the Stilton cheese and thick bread of a traditional ploughman's lunch. The weather was crisp and chilly, but he preferred fresh air to the stifling smoke inside the Old Mill pub. Beside, the view was spectacular.

He sipped ale and watched the clouds above the cathedral's spire. The scene was peaceful, but The Merchant wasn't at ease. Something gnawed at his gut, and after another moment staring at the cathedral he realized what it was: faith.

Though he thought beliefs, faith, trust, were vulgarities, recipes for disappointment and disaster, faith kept him working. People who demanded action in the name of the one true god paid well. Faith was a delusion, a luxury The Merchant did not need.

He looked at his watch. Noon. His contact should be waiting inside the restaurant.

When The Merchant opened the door he noticed the patrons were glued to a television above the flagstone bar. An attractive brunette BBC reporter stood at Ten Downing street, talking about the bombing in London's theater district. The Merchant wasn't surprised to learn the authorities blamed Islamic militants. It's what he banked on when he took the explosives from Fawaz. He and the Levant Group would be nowhere on Scotland Yard's radar.

Not spotting his contact, The Merchant walked past the crowd and into the large but cozy dining room. Built in 1135, the building was Salisbury's first paper mill by 1550. Water from three millraces cascaded through the restaurant.

He scanned the room and spotted his man at a table near one of the millraces, nursing a beer and stuffing his face with bangers and mash. The Merchant walked up and pulled out a chair.

"Have you been here long?" The Merchant didn't want to waste much time with pleasantries.

"About fifteen minutes."

The contact sipped his beer and stared at The Merchant. "Are you German? I wouldn't have guessed by your accent over the phone. You almost sounded English. But you look German. You have the cheekbones, the nose, and even with the glasses your eyes are arrogant. I never much cared for Germans."

The Merchant smiled. "You are entitled to your opinions, though I hope they don't interfere with your work. The people I work for don't tolerate failure."

"Don't you worry about me. Do you have the money?"

The Merchant slid an envelope across the table. The contact looked inside, flipped the bills, then slid it back. "That's not enough."

"It's a lot. You should be set for life. Beside, it's what we agreed on." The Merchant stayed calm.

"That was before I knew you were a Kraut."

The Merchant studied the man. He couldn't blame him for wanting more. And the man had him at a disadvantage.

After the explosion at Crowe's Music, The Merchant learned that Jake and Maya had survived and were headed to Salisbury. How the Levant Group knew that was a mystery, but they gave him the number of someone who could and would help. In fact, the man sitting across the table was perfect for the job.

"Consider that a two-thirds down payment," he said. "My benefactors will wire the rest to you when you finish."

"That's more like it," the contact grinned. "Now, what exactly do you need?"

The Merchant took another envelope from his jacket, explained its contents, and gave the man detailed instructions. Then he said, "Let me repeat the last part. You do nothing until I call you. Is that clear?"

The man nodded.

"Failure to follow the instructions I just gave you means you forfeit the rest of the fee. And more than likely you'll get an unpleasant visit from some unpleasant people."

The man's face went red. It was The Merchant's turn to smile. "We Germans make good businessmen, wouldn't you say?"

CHAPTER 25

Salisbury

The drive from London to Salisbury was quiet. Jake and Maya didn't speak much; the memory of the night before was like soap residue on a shower wall. Jake listened to music while Maya watched the lush green countryside through a steady drizzle.

"I found my father's body," she said a propos of nothing.

"You don't really owe me anything."

"I want to tell you. Last night you were vulnerable. Quid pro quo, remember?"

"Okay." He wasn't in the mood to argue.

"He'd been working abroad. Obviously, I have no idea where, but he came home suddenly. Things must have gotten hot wherever he was, and they pulled him out."

"He was in your line of work?"

"Deep in it. Remember Yayee Ayash, the Engineer?

"Sure. The Hamas bomb maker. Responsible for a number of suicide attacks. Killed by a booby trapped cell phone."

"The government denied involvement to avoid retaliation by the Palestinians. It was father's operation."

"That one was well done." He remembered that the U.S. intelligence community was impressed, even jealous, though they couldn't say so publicly.

"Anyway, Abba had been back for two weeks and I was about to leave on an assignment. We had breakfast at his house overlooking the Mediterranean in Netanya. He didn't answer the door. I used my key and found him in the living room in his lounge chair, two bullets in the chest, one in the head."

"Professional hit."

"The killer knew what he was doing. He didn't leave many clues. Shin Bet has had a hard time. I wanted to be part of the investigation but they wouldn't let me."

"Makes sense."

"I know. I took some leave, but I spent most of the time fighting with my mother."

"Then I had to fight with my boss to come back to work," Maya went on. "I was at the new post just three weeks when they assigned me to you. My boss promised he'd update me if they found anything out about my father's death."

"Have you heard anything?"

"Not yet."

Jake turned off the highway, and Maya brightened as the cathedral spire rose into the sky like Excalibur. "Stunning!"

"Yep. Tallest in all of England." Jake turned onto New Bridge Road. "Cathedrals fascinate me. Maybe I associate them with romance and chivalry.

"Are you religious?"

"Not particularly. Why?"

"Your obsession with cathedrals."

"They are as much art as religion."

"You're right."

"Would it matter if I were?"

"Not at all."

At the end of Lower Road, they found themselves at the drive of a grand estate. They had reached the residence of Liz Boyles, maiden name Reisz. Jake eased up the pebbled drive between great guardian trees that gave way to a large courtyard flanked by a hedge maze left and immaculately manicured gardens right.

The manor itself was a face of chiseled marble and stone, exact lines and symmetrically placed windows, three stories high and the length of an aircraft hanger.

Jake parked and the pair walked up three steps to a large and intricately carved entry door. Maya swung the heavy bronze knocker three times. Moments later, a man in a navy lamb's wool turtleneck and khakis opened the door. Broad shoulders, neatly cropped gray hair, veiny muscular forearms.

"May I help you?"

"Yes, we're here to see Liz Boyles." Jake figured he was more than a butler.

"And who might you be?" The accent was refined cockney, sounding as though the man were taking diction lessons from Professor Higgins.

"I am Jake Meyer, and this is Maya Herzog."

The bodyguard asked for identification. They presented their passports.

"And what is your business with Mrs. Boyles?"

"We'd like to speak to her about her father. We phoned earlier," Maya said.

"Ah, yes, you're the couple from London."

"That's right," Jake said.

"Come in. I'll let Mrs. Boyles know you are here. I'm Reginald, by the way," he offered without extending his hand.

Reggie disappeared down a long hallway, leaving Jake and Maya in the foyer.

"He appears to know what he's doing," Maya said.

"Yep. I'd guess he was probably in the Royal Marines. The personal protection business attracts people with special-forces training."

"Give me your weapon," Jake said, taking his own gun from the small of his back.

"Why?"

"Because Reggie's going to frisk us, and if he finds anything there's no way we'll get to talk with Boyles."

Maya handed her weapon to Jake, and he slipped the guns behind an ornate grandfather clock. "On the way out you tell him you have to use the toilet, and I'll get the guns."

Reggie was back. "She'll see you. But let's have a check."

After he frisked them, Reggie led them down the chandelier lit corridor. Renaissance art hung on the paneled walls between evenly spaced doorways. At the end of the hall, Reggie opened double doors that led into a large salon. Upholstered couches and wing chairs flanked a tea table. A silver tea cart sat by the marble fireplace.

They followed Reggie through the room to more double doors. He knocked, then opened the doors into a cozy library. A frail woman, with white hair and reading glasses slung around her neck, sat in a leather chair that seemed to devour her. Her stockinged and slippered feet rested on an ottoman. A knit afghan fell over her legs and a copy of *The Times* lay open in her lap.

"Mr. Meyer. Ms. Herzog. Welcome. I trust you found me easily enough."

"Your home is hard to miss," Maya said. "And so beautiful."

"Thank you, my dear," Liz Boyles smiled. "The estate has been in the family for a long time. Sort of a vacation home. I'm fortunate to spend my last years in such comfortable surroundings."

The woman appreciated her lot in life, Jake thought. Reggie took up a position behind her chair.

"Please, have a seat. May I offer you some tea?" Boyles asked.

"No, thank you." Maya said as she and Jake sunk into the couch facing Ms. Boyles.

"Well, then, what would you like to know about father?"

"We'll try not to take up too much of your time. What was your father's involvement with the Levant Group?" Jake asked bluntly.

Liz Boyle's face tightened. "Reggie, leave us alone. I'll be all right."

"Yes, ma'am. I'll be just outside if you need me."

CHAPTER 26

Salisbury

The Merchant drove the Land Rover down Lower Road but turned off the pavement and headed into the woods before he got to Liz Boyles' estate. When he was certain the vehicle could not be seen from the street, he parked and took a black duffle bag from the back seat.

He slung the bag over his shoulder and walked into the trees. In the distance to the left he could make out the buildings of the estate. After ten minutes of hiking in a semi-circle, The Merchant was three hundred meters from the main house. He found a clearing with a view of the rear of the estate. He lowered the duffle to the ground and found a pair of high powered binoculars that took him right into the library. He looked at his watch. He still had time.

As he waited, he took something that resembled a gun from the bag and plugged it into a laptop. He attached earphones, and soon the screen showed a graph and a dialogue box asking if the user wanted to listen, record or both. Both.

The Merchant raised the binoculars and saw Jake Meyer and Maya Herzog on the couch, talking to someone in a tall chair. Reginald Summers came behind the chair and leaned against the window. He brushed his arm along the glass and drapes, fumbling to attach the silicon piece The Merchant gave him at the Old Mill.

The Merchant pointed the gun at the window and pulled the trigger. An invisible laser beam locked on the target. The glass window vibrated with the sounds in the study. The laser responded, and the computer translated the movement into words.

"Reggie is suspicious of everyone. Please, don't take it personally."

"We understand. He takes his job seriously," Jake said.

"He does indeed. He served under my husband Charles during the Falklands crisis. They were very close. Reggie saw Charles as the father he never had."

"What did they do in the Falklands?" Jake tested the waters.

"I'm afraid I can't tell you. I don't know. State Secrets Act and all."

"Of course." Her response confirmed his suspicion of Reggie's military background.

"And though he's not the brightest fellow, Reggie has been very loyal, honoring Charles' last wishes and looking after me."

"We can appreciate that," Maya said.

"Mr. Meyer, as to your original question, my father was secretary of the Levant Group, but he became a Dissenter."

"A Dissenter? What do you mean?"

"Dissenters are the people who eventually came to disagree with the Levant Group's policies and plans. They tried to stop it. But the Group was too strong." Boyles noticed the expectant look on their faces. "What do you know about the Levant Group, Mr. Meyer?

"Not enough. But as far as I can tell it's a group of very rich people and multi national corporations who were interested in buying land in British Mandated Palestine years ago."

"And how did you find that out?"

Jake told Boyles that Burns uncovered some strange withdrawals from Swiss bank accounts and that he was hired to look into them further. He said he was trying to find the names associated with the bank accounts, had met account holders or their families. He described the suspicious circumstances surrounding the deaths of some account holders, including her father.

"They were Dissenters. That's why they killed them."

"I'm sorry, Mrs. Boyles, I don't follow."

"Let me explain, Mr. Meyer. My family had a long and profitable history in the textile business in Manchester. The city was the prime source of the world's textiles from the end of the nineteenth century until the 1950s when cheap foreign imports flooded the market. In 1920 my father inherited the family business, and he built it up even further. He was well known in the financial and industrial communities. He was on the board of Avro."

"Avro. Didn't they build the Lancaster bomber in World War II?" Jake asked.

"Yes. I'm impressed, Mr. Meyer." She resumed. "When the Depression hit, my father and some others had enough cash to insulate them from disaster, but in true Manchester economic tradition, they knew they would have to take steps to avoid future financial crises."

"What economic tradition do you mean to?" Maya asked.

"My dear, the industrial revolution that transformed the city also generated thought. Academics and economists created the Manchester School to promote free trade and laissez-faire economics as a means to benefit everyone in society, not just business owners. In theory, anyway."

"So Daniel Reisz formed the Levant Group to promulgate a philosophy?" Jake asked.

"Not exactly. The group already existed. Initially, it didn't have a name. It was just an organization of like-minded financiers and industrialists. My father agreed that businesses and corporations serve society's needs better than governments. They meant to invest, not dominate, to create jobs and build up economies. People would have better living standards, and the companies would earn profits which could be reinvested. They were the forerunners of globalization, Mr. Meyer."

"Economic imperialism," Jake rejoined.

"Perhaps. The Dissenters certainly came to believe that. They saw no world-wide social benefits, only greater disparity between the rich and the poor. They broke with the Levant Group, and for a while they were a threat. Anyway, the group was formed in the 1920s and initially consisted of large companies and wealthy individuals from the United States, Britain, Germany and France. My father joined in the early 1930s."

"And your father hosted meetings of the group at this estate?"

"Why, yes. How did you know?"

"Bethany Crowe," Maya said. "She recalled spending weekends here with her father."

"I don't recall a Bethany Crowe." She closed her eyes then opened them wide. "Wait, I *do* remember her. She was a dancer, right? Ten or twelve years younger than I. While all the other children played in the hedge maze, she pranced around in the back yard. The little prima ballerina, we called her."

"That's the one," Maya said.

"How is she these days?"

"She died," Maya answered.

Jake didn't want to lose momentum. "What do you recall about the meetings, Ms. Boyles?"

Boyles looked at the photos on the book case. "I was eighteen or nineteen then. The members brought their families, and they stayed here for the weekend." A smile began to creep back. "The men, anywhere from twenty to forty, met in the dining room. The women socialized, and the children played. I spent my time peeking around corners or pretending to read, just waiting for the meetings to end."

"Why?" Maya asked

Boyles blushed.

"I was in love with one of the participants." She looked at Maya. "You were looking at the pictures behind me, Ms. Herzog were you not?"

"Yes. I'm sorry for being nosy."

"Not at all. The photos are my window to the past. Here, bring me the one with the couple picnicking by the river."

Maya stood and found the silver framed photo. She noticed something familiar about the man, sporting a navy blazer and white pants. She handed the picture to Boyles, whose eyes grew wide with fond memories.

"What company was he with?" Jake asked.

"Oh, he wasn't a businessman. His name was Michael Freeman, special assistant to Chaim Weizmann."

"What did Weizmann have to do with the group?" Jake asked.

"He was soliciting money for an investment," Boyles said. "It was the group's first project. They were going to be the first to develop and invest in a new democratic, capitalist country. They would have a strong financial and industrial foothold in the Middle East without the strain of traditional colonial issues. That's how it came to be known as the Levant Group."

Jake's mind spun. The large withdrawals from the Swiss accounts were beginning to make sense. If Freeman were still alive, he could explain why the Levant Group's initial investment was causing trouble seventy years later.

"What happened to Mr. Freeman?" Jake asked.

Boyles frowned. "Time doesn't heal all wounds," she said softly. "The Levant Group eventually agreed to Weizmann's proposal, and Michael accompanied him to Palestine to complete some deal. He didn't return. I heard that a mob attacked Weizmann's entourage in Jaffa during one of the Arab riots. Michael was killed."

So much for Freeman filling in the blanks.

"You must understand that I loved my husband. Charles Boyles was a brave, good man, but Michael was my soul mate. He was kind and supportive with a brilliant mind and great vision for someone his age. He understood the problems associated with Weizmann's grandiose plan, and he had reservations."

"Ms. Boyles, what was the plan? What were the investment terms?" Jake asked.

"Michael never told me. He said only that it involved an immense land purchase, that it would change history. But he worried about it."

"Why?" Maya asked.

"Social issues, mass migration, potential for future conflict. I don't remember exactly, and I didn't ask. But even so, he believed the purchase was necessary, the lesser of evils." Boyles smiled. "Michael was so adamant and passionate about things. He had a charming gesture, circling his hand from his abdomen up to his chest, outward and then back down again when he explained. I teased him about it."

Maya looked up from the photo. "Could you show me the gesture?"

"Oh? It was nothing. Just like this."

Maya's face froze. She had a feeling that she knew Michael Freeman. But that didn't make sense. He died long before she was born. She never met him.

"What ever happened with the deal?" Jake asked.

"It was a pact. Michael called it *the* Pact."

"What happened with the Pact?"

"It fell apart. For a while there were contentious meetings about the investment. They lost a great deal of money, and some threatened legal action. But nobody did anything. Then Nazi Germany and the war took center stage. It generated a lot of business, and the Levant Group turned its attention to opportunities that would follow the end of the war."

Jake leaned back into the couch. Another dead end . If the Pact fell through, why was it so important now? The Levant Group could never recoup money it lost over seven decades ago. They'd need proof, and large withdrawals were not enough.

CHAPTER 27

Salisbury

The Merchant listened as Meyer told Boyles what he knew about the Dissenters and he nodded at the mention of Daniel Reisz, Liz Boyles' father. He was one of the original targets when the Levant Group hired The Merchant years ago. Reisz was about to go to the press with some embarrassing information, and despite his age and ailing health, the Levant Group had The Merchant liquidate him. Killing an old man was distasteful, but they paid very well.

The conversation in the distance turned to the Levant Group's history, then to Michael Freeman and Liz Boyles' ill-fated romance. The Merchant learned of a Pact, as Boyles called it, that fell apart. But soon it was clear that Boyles knew nothing else and that Meyer and Herzog were at a dead end. He was ready to go, but first he needed to clean up. He dialed Reggie Summer's number.

"I have what I need. You can finish up."

The kettle on the stove whistled and Reginald Summers poured steaming hot water into a cup. Three bags of Earl Grey floated to the top. Reggie took his tea strong and the caffeine would keep him alert. He sat down and pulled the sleeves of his sweater over his thick forearms. His cell phone lay on the kitchen table. *The call should come shortly.*

Reggie had been with the Boyles household a long time, ever since Captain Charles Boyles hired him straight out of the Royal Marines. They were a lot alike, he and the captain, both from rough stock, not over bright but robust and rowdy. The main difference was that the Captain was handsome and married well.

Reggie was treated well and adored his boss; but he loathed the boss' wife. Elizabeth Boyles was arrogant. She talked down to Reggie, and she treated the captain as badly. Once Reggie saw her humiliate him in front of guests. So when he placed the bug that let the German listen to the conversation in the study, he felt no guilt. He'd stayed on after the captain died. He needed the money. But that was no longer the case. The German was paying an unbelievable sum of money.

The cell phone vibrated. He flipped it open and listened, then stood, screwed the silencer onto the gun and walked calmly toward the study.

The doors burst open. Jake heard a pop and saw Boyles' head snap back against the chair. A small red hole centered her forehead. Maya dove for the floor and reached for her weapon—which wasn't there. Reggie came into the study, sweeping the gun from left to right. Jake leapt behind an oak desk as Reggie fired again. His gun, like Maya's, was in the foyer.

Maya, on the floor and out of Reggie's sight, caught his arm with a spiked boot heel. She scramble to her feet and aimed a kick at Reggie's gut, but he caught her leg with one arm and slammed an elbow into Maya's thigh.

Jake tackled the bodyguard, and all three went down hard. Reggie's gun slid across the floor.

"Maya! Get the gun!"

She didn't move. Out cold.

The men grappled and fumbled for the gun as furniture buckled and bibelots flew. At length, Reggie got Jake's head in a lock and all but choked the life out of him, when Maya came to and spotted the gun. She swept it up, aimed it and shot Reggie in the foot. The bodyguard's grip loosened like a blood pressure cuff, and Jake slid to the floor. Two more shots and Reggie hit the carpet, a gaping mess of blood and flesh where his eyes had been.

"So much for loyalty," Maya snorted. She stepped over the corpse and took the picture of Boyles and Michael Freeman off the bookcase.

Jake stood up, rubbing his neck. He stared at Maya. She had too much energy. Her presence of mind after a fight was too good. But what about Reggie? How did the Levant Group find him? How did they know Jake and Maya were going to Salisbury? How did they know about Bethany Crowe? Or Reiner? Was Maya part of it?

"Let's get out of here." Maya headed for the door. Jake lingered, a little dazed, not quite ready to go. He walked over to the window behind Liz Boyle's corpse to see what was moving outside, and his eye picked up something on the window, something small, circular and clear. He peeled the bug off, stuck it in his pocket and followed Maya out.

In the foyer, Jake snatched their guns, and they ran for the car. Suddenly, pebbles and rocks from the driveway burst up around them. There was another shooter!

They made it to the vehicle unscathed. Jake hit the gas and sped down the driveway.

The Merchant was about to turn off the laser listening device and pack it in the duffle bag when something told him to stop. He aimed the device at the window again and raised the binoculars in time to see Reggie slam into the study and shoot Liz Boyles, scuffle with Meyer, and die at the hand of that woman. *Damn.* The Merchant knew Reggie would screw things up. That's why he had back up. He made another call and threw the equipment into the bag for the sprint through the forest to his car. But as he ran for cover, he saw two people leave the main house, Meyer and Herzog. He rushed toward the pebbled driveway, shooting as he ran. He knew he had little chance of hitting either of them.

Sure enough, their car sped off in a cloud of dust. The Merchant stopped, turned and jogged back toward his vehicle. Perhaps he slowed them down enough for the back up team to get into place.

CHAPTER 28

Salisbury

"**L**ooks like we're clear," Maya said as Jake slammed the car down the lane—which was true until he rounded a curve and saw a car parked across Lower Road. Two figures got out and starting shooting.

"Where did they come from?"

Maya looked up just in time to see the passenger side mirror fly off.

Jake pushed the hammer to the floor and aimed the BMW's right front bumper at the car to spin it off the road. It worked. He whipped right onto Downtown Road and checked the rear view mirror. Nothing behind them. Jake let himself breathe.

"You all right, Maya?"

"I'll be okay," she said. "And I'd be a lot better if you got back on the right side of the road."

He made the correction and checked the rear view mirror. A Land Rover was coming up fast. "We've got company."

He sped to New Bridge Road and on into Salisbury's narrow streets, the Land Rover gaining on him and peppering the BMW's rear end with bullets. Pedestrians screamed and scurried out of the way.

The heavy Salisbury traffic ground to a stop. "We've got to get back to a major road," Jake said. He wasn't sure which way to go, so he navigated off the cathedral spire.

Maya snapped a magazine into her weapon and fired through the window at the car after them.

"How far back is he?" Jake yelled.

"About twenty meters and gaining."

Jake made a left on to bumpy cobblestone streets. "Hold on! We're in for a ride!"

They bumped and bounced past the cathedral, back onto pavement and straight toward the London road. He checked the mirror. The other car was so close he recognized the driver instantly.

"It's he," Jake said.

"Who?"

"The driver. It's the room service waiter from the Schweizerhof."

The Land Rover jammed the BMW's back bumper, and the cars did a high-speed, slow-motion *pas de deux*. Jake and the room service guy went through a classical poste/riposte maneuver from which Jake finally pulled out. He managed to get a little distance between the cars and raced ahead. "You can slow him down now, Maya."

She fired three shots, two into the other vehicle's windshield, the other into the grill. The chase car dropped back.

"Maya," Jake screamed, "I am going to pull a drift block!" He brought the BMW back across the road. "You get out and hit the driver, and I'll take out the wheels. Got it?"

He rolled down his window. "One, two, three!"

Jake pulled up on the emergency brake and the car spun sideways and stopped. Maya jumped out, aimed over the roof and fired twice, straight at the driver. Jake stuck his gun through the window and took aim at the wheels, but the car veered off the road before he could get shot off.

Maya stared at the driver, his head fallen to the right.

"Get in! Let's get out of here."

She climbed back into the car. Jake straightened out and pushed the speed limit to London.

"That was some driving! Where'd you learn to do that?" Maya asked.

"A friend in the diplomatic security service showed me a few pointers."

"He did a good job."

"*She.* Vicky was as good as anybody in the Secret Service. I still practice in an empty parking lot. Never really thought I'd need it."

"Well, thank goodness for parking lots." Maya found the photo she had took from the estate and studied it.

"What is it about that photo, Maya?"

"It's crazy, but I'm fairly certain I know Michael Freeman."

The Nag's Head pub was just off the Mall, well away from the bustle at St. James' Palace and not a tourist destination. Jake and Maya found a corner in the dimly lit pub and arranged themselves on stools and tables so small that Maya thought they would do better for a child's tea party rather than adults gathering to drink.

Jake went to the bar and returned with two glasses of London Pride. "You said you knew Michael Freeman. What did you mean?"

"He was my professor at Hebrew University."

"That can't be. Boyles said he died long before you were born."

"I don't think he's dead. At least he didn't die in the Thirties."

"The picture was old. He probably just resembled your professor."

"It wasn't just his face, Jake. It was the gesture Boyles mentioned. Professor Steiner did the same thing."

"That's quite a stretch, Maya. Why did you call him Steiner"?

"Because that was his name."

"*Was* his name? You're not making sense."

"I absolutely am, Jake. What if Michael Freeman didn't want to return to England? He could have faked his death, changed his name to Steiner and started a new life in Palestine."

"Even if that were true, it begs the question: why? And what's it got to do with what's happening now?"

Maya shrugged. "I can't answer that. I didn't get that far. But we might as well look into it. Boyles didn't give us anything else. We're at a dead end."

Jake grunted. *Dead* was the operative word. "There may be another way."

"What's on your mind?"

"Are you sure nobody followed us to Boyles?"

"Yes."

"Then they knew exactly where we were going. Which means the Levant Group is either omniscient or they've got help. Remember that phone call I took last night? It was a friend of mine who's good with computers and research. He did a little digging for me and based on what he said, I have a pretty good idea about the leak."

"Who is it?"

"Walsing"

Jake saw the shock on Maya's face. "Grab your things. Go to Israel and check out your old professor."

"Where are you going?"

"Zurich. I need to brief a client and close the account."

CHAPTER 29

Paris

It was as much the source as the content of the message that brought Rafi Golan to a flat in the eighteenth arrondissement. A request to meet with an emissary of a country technically still at war with Israel piqued his curiosity.

The note did not come through official channels. When Golan was certain it was authentic and not an elaborate trap, he arranged for a meeting in a rarely used Mossad safe house. A French painter, a *sayan*, owned the place, though he lived in Avignon and kept it for only for Israeli intelligence. Hidden in the narrow streets of Montmarte, the eclectic shops and eccentric artists drew attention away from it.

Golan took precautions. He had the house swept for bugs. The guest and one bodyguard were to fly to Amsterdam and meet two of Golan's men who blindfolded them and drove them around for hours in a van to disorient them. They'd have no idea they were in Paris.

In the utilitarian apartment, two black leather couches faced each other across a glass cocktail table. Track lights hung overhead. A Lucite armoire held a flat screen Sony and a Bose stereo. The place looked more Scandinavian than French.

Puffing on a cigar, Golan peeled a thick blackout drape back and peeked over the roofs at people climbing the top steps at Sacré Coeur. Ironic. A Jew was about to meet a Muslim in the shadow of the Basilica of the Sacred Heart. A white van drove through the archway below into the courtyard. Golan couldn't see but he knew one of his men got out to shut the gate.

"He's here," Golan told his own guard. He shut the drape and waited while his assistant answered a knock. Two Mossad escorts nudged the blindfolded men forward.

The tall one — close cropped beard, navy suit, no tie — was of no interest and Golan sent him into the kitchen. He recognized the other man immediately from photos Mossad profilers kept. The thick jowls and a mustache ending exactly at the corners of the mouth were unmistakable. Golan had the blindfold removed. Mustafa Azziz let his eyes to the light.

"Shalom," Azziz said as Golan stepped up without extending his hand.

Golan led his guest to a couch and sent the other bodyguards out. "Do you want some tea or something to eat?" he asked coldly.

Azziz indicated the tobacco between his host's fingers. "Do you have another one of those? And some vodka, perhaps."

From the couch opposite Azziz, Golan shouted something in Hebrew back towards the kitchen. "Tell me, what's so important that we had to meet?"

Azziz unbuttoned his blazer and crossed his legs. "There is a serious matter of common interest to both our countries. Do you know what I am referring to?"

Golan knew but shook his head.

One of the guards returned with a glass and a cigar and set them before Azziz. He took a small sip of vodka, rolled the cigar between his fingers and returned his attention to Golan. "You have an agent, Maya Herzog, working with an American lawyer, Jake Meyer. They are looking into some very old bank accounts, correct?"

Golan was surprised but didn't flinch.

Azziz played the game. "That's all right. I understand. Let me put it this way. Meyer and Herzog are discovering things some very powerful people would prefer they not know. Their snooping could lead to disaster and not just for them."

"Even if that were so, why would you or your superiors care?"

Azziz sat forward. "Look, you know those two are leaving a trail of bodies and have only narrowly escaped with their own lives. The Levant Group will do anything to protect its interests."

"Which are?"

"Everything. They're into industrial machinery, pharmaceuticals, telecommunications, computers, construction companies, investment houses. They own a lot of land. They exert a lot of influence."

"So why is Saudi Arabia so concerned?" Golan asked.

"Some members of the royal house have a tight, albeit secret, relationship with the Levant Group. There are common interests."

Golan nodded. "Oil."

"Among others. In the 1920s and 30s, when Arabia first tapped the oil resource we needed steel, we needed engineers and scientists. So British and American companies competed for the right to develop that oil. Standard Oil of California won."

"Tell me something I don't already know."

Azziz bit his tongue. "Certain companies in the Levant Group provided other assistance. Communications, construction, infrastructure. But it was the petrochemicals that cinched our connection to the Levant Group. You see, petrochemicals go into everything, and the Levant Group has irons in all the fires."

"So the Levant Group needs Arabia, and Arabia makes money on them?'

"The Levant Group doesn't need *us*, they need our *oil*."

"Meaning that as long as they stay tight with whomever controls the oil, they get what they need"

"Precisely. We are actually subject to the oil blackmail." Azziz paused and changed his tone of voice. "Quite frankly, I need your help."

Golan stood and walked to a window. "You can't be serious. Last week we intercepted a suicide bomber at the door of a coffee shop in Jerusalem." He pointed the glowing tip of the cigar at Azziz. "Do you know what we learned from him?"

The room went quiet for a moment.

"Your boss gave him money to take care of his family after he died."

"Not mine specifically," Azziz rejoined softly.

"Well, your government. And he's not the first, is he?" Golan's voice rose. "A lot of terrorists and Islamic radicals come from your country, and you're asking the country they hate, the country they attack, for help? Have you lost your mind?"

"Perhaps. But the Crown Prince is not like the rest of his family. He knows Israel is a reality. And the radicals are a threat to our government as well. They call the House of Saud infidels. They want to overthrow the government. Why do you think we're pressuring our clerics to reeducate them? We can't tolerate the situation either."

Golan knew Azziz was telling the truth, but he wanted to get back to the matter at hand. "Is the Levant Group blackmailing the Crown Prince?"

Azziz took a long sip of vodka and swallowed hard. "Not yet. I'm sure you are know why the group was founded."

"I thought the Pact was only a rumor. Apparently it wasn't. Thank God, it's disappeared."

"But what if it showed up? What if that is exactly what Mr. Meyer and Ms. Herzog are after?"

It was Golan's turn not to answer.

"What if the Levant Group gets to the Pact first? We'll be blackmailed. We'll have to give in. And do you know what will happen if we dont?"

Golan wasn't a fool. The Middle East's legions of poor, unemployed, disenfranchised, would see the revelation of the Pact as proof that the West and Israel meant to subjugate the Muslim world. Radicalization would escalate; moderates would be silenced. Chaos would metastasize throughout the region.

"The royal family will fall. Other regimes will fall, and Israel will face a greater threat of destruction from new theocratic regimes. The West will intervene."

"That's exactly the scenario I've come to," Azziz agreed. It's a path to Armageddon, from which only the Levant Group will benefit. They must be stopped."

Golan knew his guest had a point. And though helping Azziz bothered him, he had no choice. "We'll deal with the Levant Group the way we deal with terrorists. We'll cut the hydra's head off. Do you know the group's leader?"

"I do."

"I assume he has connections with the United States."

"Deep ones."

"Then neither of our countries can afford to be involved." *Jew, Muslim, Christian, none of that matters at this point*, Golan thought. "I have an idea."

CHAPTER 30

Paris

Tense and deep in thought, Rafi Golan strode through the Israeli embassy basement on Rue Rabelais. Those who recognized him were either too stunned to see him in the bowels of Paris station or too frightened of his obvious contemplative mood to say anything to him.

He was on his way to the communications room. He just got word that the information he asked headquarters for had arrived. He punched a code on the panel and opened the door. A young woman led Golan to a cubicle and handed him a file.

"Is it all here?"

"Yes, including the enhanced photos you asked for."

"Good. Has anyone else seen this?"

"No sir. Well, I have, but I didn't read it. I just skimmed the pages."

After she left, Golan opened the thin file and scanned the pages. The first page was a summary of the man, his recent activities, his personality. The rest was background information, such as date of birth, childhood history, years of service, and significant operations.

The last two pages of the profile were an overall character assessment. And there Golan found what he was looking for.

Subject frequents high class adult entertainment establishments and has a propensity for dropping significant amounts of cash for personal dances and other services in private rooms. This behavior may suggest subject has issues with intimacy or sexual addiction both of which are dissociative conditions.

Golan leaned back in his chair to mull over the options. *Where was Maya when she last made contact?* London. On her way to meet another name from Burn's list. Perfect.

Golan turned to the computer next to him and entered his password. He scribbled notes on a piece of paper and put them and a photograph in a new envelope. Then he called the communications officer in.

"Have the station chief follow the instructions in this envelope and contact the appropriate people immediately." He paused. "And don't skim it this time."

"Yes, sir. Anything else?"

"Not now."

The plan had risks but it was solid. Well, not exactly. Maya wouldn't like it. In fact she'd probably be furious. What would he tell her? That her father would have done the same thing? She'd feel betrayed but she'd understand, right? It was for Israel. Golan grasped at justification.

For the first time in his long career he felt dirty. He had no choice. He'd have to deal with the devil.

CHAPTER 31

London

The Merchant sat in a corner of the tea room at Brown's Hotel. Most of the hotel had undergone renovation to bring the decor into the twenty-first century, but the tea room remained characteristically Victorian with dark wood paneling, tall chairs, shelves lined with classic books and a deep crimson carpet. The waiters, in black vests and bow ties, spoke softly so they would not disturb the patrons - though there were precious few on that evening.

The Merchant enjoyed the room's charm, especially the crackling embers in the fireplace. They took his attention off his pounding head and his throbbing shoulder.

A waiter brought a glass of Châteauneuf du pape, and set it on the table next to him. As He sipped the smooth wine, his thoughts turned to Meyer and Herzog. They escaped him in Salisbury. Worse, their conversation with Liz Boyles taught him little. The next step eluded him, and he was embarrassed, personally and professionally, to have to tell his Levant Group contact he'd failed again.

He could not handle failure. When he ratted out his parents — a drunken father who beat him, and a passive mother who failed to intervene — he felt nothing, and the Stasi officer who came for them assured him he'd done the right thing.

"You are free now. Your parents failed you, but you have not failed the state. You are a good citizen, Dieter Fuchs. The state will look after you, educate you, train you. And you will pay the state back with loyalty and service. There is no greater honor."

The state indeed educated him and more. After *Gymnasium*, the Ministry for State Security put him through intense training where he learned how to manipulate, seduce and charm people to get information. He learned how to kill. He already knew how to disassociate, to turn his humanity off. His father's beatings taught him that. Distancing himself to kill was no stretch.

And the state taught him fear, especially fear of failure. Failure meant, among other things, that he would never disentangle himself, never be independent, never find his way out of the morass to a better life. A life with Sophie Foucard, say.

His recent failures, however, put all that in jeopardy. The Levant Group was ruthless. If The Merchant didn't produce, the Levant Group could and would take everything. He decided on a visit to his favorite club, to get some distance. He finished the wine in one gulp, shouldered his leather coat, left the hotel and made a right out the door.

On Great Windmill Street he came to Windmill International, ducked inside, paid a cover and found a booth. He wanted to be alone, to drink, to watch the women, to numb his mind. But not five minutes later, an attractive brunette slid in beside him.

"Buy me a drink?" She wrapped an arm over his injured shoulder.

He winced. "Please remove your arm. I hurt my shoulder."

The woman asked for a glass of champagne, and he squeezed her thigh, a signal that he wanted to leave the booth.

"There are private rooms upstairs," she said.

She toweled the red lipstick off. Wrong color. She chose a clear gloss and eased the tiny brush over her lips in soft, smooth strokes. She touched up her mascara and leaned toward the mirror to study her work. Claire Roberts, née Glassman was one of about two thousand active *sayanim* in London, Jews in many countries who help Mossad operatives in many ways. Claire did two things: she ran a car rental agency in West London and obtained vehicles for agents without a paper trail. She supplemented her income dancing at a bar, and her Mossad handler found that useful too.

She agreed to get Mossad targets drunk and pump them for information. She'd worked on at least ten cases when her handler asked her to do something slightly out of the ordinary, something risky. A blind commitment to her ancestral homeland ingrained in her since childhood led Claire to agree. The *katsa*—handler—explained what she had to do and handed her a packet. He told her to study it, especially the photograph, and burn it when she finished.

Claire adjusted her garters, squeezed into a red and black bustier, and slipped into a fitted black skirt slit all the way up the side. The place was hopping, so before going into the main room, she imagined the face. Hard and angular, high cheekbones, and deep oval eye sockets. Not lovely but attractive. She sauntered into the room, and six hundred eyes checked her out. She scanned the crowd for the face.

Fighting off a couple of amorous drunks, Claire took a lap around the club but did not see what she was looking for. Her boss caught her eye and sent her to a table of hard drinking, hard smoking clients where she hustled drinks and flirted until one of them, a blond fellow with a snout for a nose — asked her for a lap dance. Reflexively she slid her long legs over his beefy thighs and went through the motions. That was when she saw it. The face came into the Windmill International cautiously, but she had her mark.

She finished off the pig, swiped the money off the table without taking her eyes off the mark and ignored the others pleading for their turn.

"Buy me a drink?" She slid into the booth and laid her arm over his shoulder.

"Please remove your arm. I hut my shoulder."

"Sorry. I didn't know."

"I know you didn't." He looked her up and down and turned away.

"I'll have a glass of champagne." Claire licked the corner of her mouth. He didn't respond. He just squeezed her thigh.

"There are private rooms upstairs."

"There always are."

"We could retreat to one for a special show?"

"I don't like being filmed."

Claire rubbed her thigh against his. "Maybe I can do some persuading and have the cameras turned off."

The VIP room on the second floor was cozy and warm. Velvet couches, soft music. Peaceful compared to the frenetic activity downstairs. And they were alone.

He poured Champagne from a bottle waiting on the table. He took off his coat and sat on the couch. Claire took a sip and squeezed in next to him. Her hand found his crotch.

"Please, don't do that. Just sit across from me."

What does he want? Claire eased into the chair across the cocktail table. The man stared at her.

"Tell me about yourself," He picked up the flute and took a sip of champagne.

"What do you want to know?"

"Anything."

"My name is Anne." She gave him a cock and bull story about a rough childhood, needing money for school and plans to become a barrister.

When she was done, he said, "That's an interesting story. Next time you should spice it up a little. Your customers will appreciate it. If you're going to lie, at least be creative"

"You don't believe me?"

He raised a brow.

"All right then, what's your story? It better be good."

"I don't have a story." Self-pity oozed from him.

"What would you like then?"

"Peace of mind."

They drained their flutes, and she refilled them.

"Dance for me now," he said.

She stood and started swaying to the music, her hips as smooth and regular as a slow metronome. She flipped her hair and ran her hands over her breasts.

He watched her intently, but did not react.

Claire put a leg on the table and slid her fingers from her ankle to the back of her thigh. She felt the bulge in the back elastic of her stockings. *Good. It's still there.*

Still no response.

Finally she eased herself onto his lap and slid up his torso so her chest was at his mouth. She grabbed his hands and put them on her rump as she pressed into him.

He took his hands off her and laid them on the couch.

She ground on him, rubbed his chest, kissed his ears—yet nothing.

She reached behind herself and loosened her bustier, and suddenly he grabbed her arms. He was very strong, and his hands dug into her biceps.

"You're hurting me! What are you doing?"

Just as quickly he turned her loose and stood. "Sorry. I'm sorry."

"So, you're the rough type?"

"No. Not really." He went to the window to look down on the second floor. Now was her chance.

She slipped the pill from her stocking and plopped it into his glass. "Not to worry, honey. Come back and have some more champagne. We'll just tell each other some more stories."

He returned to the couch and took a long gulp from the flute. Claire sat across from him and crossed her legs. She started talking again, and again he looked through her. Soon his eyes grew heavy and his head tilted to the side. She stood up just as he fell to the couch. She put a run in her stockings with a fingernail and dabbed champagne on her lashes to let the makeup run. She went to the phone and dialed the number she memorized. She waited five minutes and called the bouncers on the house phone. Moments later, two goons burst through the door.

"Are you all right, Claire?" one asked.

She tussled her hair and feigned exhaustion. "Sure. He was just a bit playful. Too much to drink, I guess."

"All right, let's get him out of here." The bouncers grabbed him and took him out the back where a taxi waited. Claire whispered something in the driver's ear. He nodded and sped off with The Merchant in the back seat.

CHAPTER 32

Zurich

Jake was irritated with himself. He hadn't learned from his past mistakes. He should have checked out Henry Walsing before he accepted the assignment. Kessler had warned him about Walsing, but Jake didn't listen. Thank goodness for Paul Hollowel. Better late than never.

The techie ran a background search and found that the details of Henry G. Walsing's life were unremarkable for a man born into modest means who bootstrapped himself up to wealth and privilege. Hailing from upstate New York, he earned an MBA from Columbia and went to work on Wall Street—where he quickly moved up the corporate ladder. But his social status solidified when he married in 1968.

"Paul, are you sure that was her maiden name?" Jake asked.

"Yes."

"Do me another solid, and run her name."

"Sure, it'll only take a couple of minutes. Stand by."

Walsing had not told him everything. What the hell was he up to?

Hollowel clicked back in and told Jake about Walsing's wife. What he said brought Jake to the front steps of the opera house.

Jake leaned against a lamp post until Walsing emerged from the Neo-baroque auditorium alone, taking the stairs slowly and adjusting his gloves.

"How was the show, Mr. Walsing?"

"Splendid, Mr. Meyer, just splendid. Pity you couldn't join me."

"I'm afraid *Carmina Burana* is not my cup of tea."

"To each his own," Walsing responded. "My car is just over this way."

155

Walsing's car was second in a line of limousines, and his burly, baldpated driver waited by the door. "Rolfe, this is Mr. Meyer. He will be riding with me."

When Rolfe drove off, Walsing started in. "So, Mr. Meyer, what's new with the Burns matter? It must be important since you wanted to meet in person."

Jake motioned for Walsing to close the partition. "Elizabeth Reisz is dead, just like Ms. Crowe and Reiner."

"I'm sorry to hear that. Do you have any idea what's happening?"

"I have a hunch." Jake pushed the barrel of a Beretta 9000 Maya gave him into Walsing's left kidney.

"What are you doing Mr. Meyer?"

"I'm fixing a problem with my client. There seems to be an issue of confidentiality. Whoever is behind the killings knows every move I make."

"Do you think I would do that?

Jake twisted the barrel. "As the client and at your request I have kept you up to speed on all the details. You're the only one who could have known."

Walsing rolled down the partition. "Rolfe, Mr. Meyer and I would like to walk."

Rolfe fixed his gaze on Jake. The message was clear. *If anything happens to Walsing, you're dead.* He made a left on Quaibrucke, a right on Fraumünsterstrasse, pulled up before Fraumünster Cathedral, and let the men out. Jake had a notion about the bodyguard, but he couldn't put his finger on it.

"The windows inside are by Chagall," Walsing said.

Jake was in no mood for an art history lesson. "Let's walk, Mr. Walsing."

Walsing turned his coat collar up and folded his arms. "Why would I deceive you, Mr. Meyer? I'm paying you handsomely."

"I don't know. Maybe it's your connection with a name on Burns' list. Warburg. As in Emily Warburg."

"I got lucky. Who would have thought the son of a factory worker would find himself part of a family that banked royalty. The Warburgs had connections I could only dream of. Marrying Emily was a sound decision."

"So your marriage was a business deal?"

"To an extent, I must admit. I love Emily, but I don't think I was ever in love with her. I just saw there was more there than a relationship. "I hired you because when Burn's hinted at what he had found, I suspected my wife's maiden name would show up."

"And you wanted me to confirm your suspicion?"

"Yes. And to determine the status of others on the list. You are now aware of the Levant Group."

It wasn't a question, so Jake didn't answer.

"No doubt they have infiltrated the Treasury Department, but you are in private practice. I figured that since you don't have to report to any superiors, the risk would be greatly reduced. Obviously, I was wrong.

"Burns was on to something big. A number of names on the list disagreed with the Levant Group's direction. The people you've discovered, including my wife, are the remaining Dissenters."

"What exactly is your wife's connection?"

"Her father was a founding member."

"So he was not a Dissenter?"

"Heavens, no, quite the contrary. He believed business meets people's needs better than governments."

"And industry does such a great job of distributing the wealth?"

"Well, Emily disagreed, though she did not tell her father. She was the apple of his eye, the brightest of his children. He told her his secrets, including the Levant Group. She was horrified. When he died, he left her in control of his estate. After that she disavowed the Levant Group. She became a Dissenter."

"Earlier you said 'remaining Dissenters.' What does that mean?"

"A few years ago, some of the Dissenters, like Mr. Crowe and Professor Steiner threatened to reveal the existence of the Levant Group, and they conveniently expired."

"Did you say Steiner?"

"Yes. Why? What else have you found?"

Jake decided not to tell Walsing about Maya's hunch. "Nothing."

"In any event, their bodies were found in a few days. Death by natural causes was the explanation."

"Where is Emily?"

"In New York. She's very active in politics and charities. She visits frequently, but with the Burns incident, I told her to stay home."

Jake wasn't sure he believed Walsing. The Dissenters were not the primary issue. A piece was missing.

Jake had two options. He could cut with Walsing, forego the fees and walk away. But by then he and Maya clearly knew too much. They would be Levant Group targets in perpetuity. He had to take the other option. "Who heads the Levant Group?"

"I suppose that's the crux of the matter now," Walsing said. He shook a finger at Jake. "You won't stand a chance, Meyer. The man is an emperor. He's untouchable."

"Well, he's sure out of reach if I don't know who he is."

Walsing took a deep breath. "His name is. . ."

Jake saw the red dot circle for a second and steady. He'd been on enough raids with Treasury to know what a laser sight finding its mark looked like. He knew what was about to happen, but there was no time to react.

The first shot, through the heart, killed Walsing. The second was assassin's insurance.

Jake dove into the alcove of an apartment building as another bullet slammed into the wall above his head.

The tip of the beam searched for him. He tried the door, but it was locked. The beam was still moving. The assailant didn't have sight of him yet.

Sight. That was the solution. A single bulb lit the alcove, and if Jake jumped out, he'd be dead. But the shooter was looking into the light. He shot it out, vaulted into the street and broke into a run.

The laser followed him. He heard footsteps behind him but didn't look back.

Jake took a set of stairs two at a time and found himself in the Lindenhoff, the park at the top of Zurich's old city. Another bullet whizzed by his ear. He bolted across the Lindenhoff, past the great chessboard on the ground where men moved large pieces from square to square, stumbled and fell down a little flight of stairs—dropped his gun—and fetched up under a tree, gasping.

The red beam bounced as the assailant ran down the steps. The assassin was close, and the area underneath the beam became bigger as he aimed the weapon down the street. There was only one chance.

Jake pushed off on his good leg and dove low, reaching for his gun. He got it in his left hand, rolled, aimed at the red light and fired two shots. The beam stopped moving, then disappeared. Jake heard the crash of metal hitting cement followed by a thud.

He trained his gun on the heap lying on the staircase. As he inched closer he saw the bald head. Rolfe.

Why would Rolfe kill Walsing? Was he working for the Levant Group? If so, Walsing wasn't the leak. Then how did the Levant Group know everything?

Jake rummaged through Rolfe's pockets and found an I.D. pouch in the dead man's blazer. He opened it and saw the insignia emblazoned over Rolfe's picture. Another betrayal.

CHAPTER 33

Tel Aviv

Maya sat in a basement office at Mossad headquarters, reserved for field operatives who needed workspace in Tel Aviv. It contained the essentials: a desk, a secure line, a computer linked to Mossad's main frame and a chair.

As her fingers danced across the keyboard, she thought about Jake. Had he plugged the leak? Who was responsible? Did Jake think she was the sieve? He didn't know her well, and was tailing him before they teamed up. But he seemed to trust her.

She pulled up a data base on immigrants run by the Jewish Agency, the organization that provides documents, passage and housing for Jews moving to Israel. She typed in Professor Steiner's name and hit Enter. Seconds later the screen told her the data base did not identify a Dr. Joseph Steiner.

That's odd. She thought Dr. Steiner was an immigrant. She recalled the European accent when he lectured. Was he a *sabra*?

Maya closed the Jewish Agency data base and pulled up the Israeli Census. Again she typed in Professor Joseph Steiner and again learned there was no record for him. If he were Israeli, why wasn't he there?

The Israeli Defense Forces. Military service was compulsory. She'd find him there. A black screen blinked red letters that said access to Steiner's information was denied. She typed the name again and got the same message, but that time, she got a message: if she tried a third search of Professor Steiner, Mossad's information technology department would flag her computer. If that happened, security officers would be in her cubicle in minutes.

If access to Steiner was denied, it must be sensitive. But why? He was just a school teacher, wasn't he? If he were indeed sensitive, then chances were his biographical information would be part of a Special Access Program. And to retrieve information from a SAP, she needed to be cleared and read onto the program. And she knew someone who would surely have such clearance: Rafi Golan.

The elevator stopped on the eighth floor, and Maya went straight to Golan's office. He wasn't in but that worked to her benefit. She smiled at Dalit., who, for the first time Maya could recall, was dressed in civilian clothes.

"Maya, what a surprise," Dalit said before standing to hug Maya. "I had no idea you were back in town."

"I had to come back to do some research and check up on my mother." Maya pushed back from Dalit, took in her outfit, and complimented her. The secretary said Golan urged her to relax, thought regular clothes looked better than a uniform in a civilian agency.

"Listen, I know Rafi's not in, but I need to use the SAP room."

"Okay, that's not a problem. Let me get the key." Dalit opened a drawer.

"What's the name of the SAP for sensitive persons?" Maya asked. "It's been so long since I've used it."

"How can you access a program you don't know the name of?"

Maya giggled. "It's the strangest thing. I can remember all of my passwords, but the different SAPs escape me. If you ever do any of this type of research, you'll know what I'm talking about."

"I shouldn't tell you. It's a security violation"—Dalit looked around her—"but women here have to stick together, right?"

"Absolutely."

"The SAP is Shield of David."

"Thanks so much." Maya squeezed the assistant's forearm and winked.

Maya typed in SHIELD OF DAVID and waited. User name and password boxes appeared. The user name wasn't a problem, the same for all Mossad employees on any program. But figuring out Golan's password was different. She'd have only three chances before it locked her out and called the security office.

Maya leaned back and thought, then made a couple of educated guesses based on what she knew about Golan. The first three—cobbled together from information about his mother, a soccer team, his cigars—failed. "Think, dammit. Think." Then it hit. *She* was the most important thing in Golan's life. He had no children of his own and treated her like a daughter, better than her own father did. He always called her *Malcha Katan*. Little Queen. And the number was easy.

She typed in MK1975, hit Enter key and held her breath.

Five seconds later the screen went dark and the Mossad Logo appeared. TOP SECRET. SHIELD OF DAVID. She was in. She typed Joseph Steiner into a search box.

A picture appeared. The face was worn and weathered, but the warm eyes and soft smile were unmistakable. The expressions Maya saw in the photograph in Liz Reisz' study. The same expressions she remembered fondly from university days. It was Professor Steiner, sure enough.

Biographical data rolled onto the screen. As Maya read, her initial excitement faded. Were the pieces of the puzzle coming together, or had she run into a dead end? What would Jake think?

Thinking of Jake, Maya checked the time on the screen. She was late.

CHAPTER 34

Bern

A bear hug and a smile from the Regional Security Officer greeted Jake at Scott Bidwell's office at the U.S. Consulate in Bern. Of all the different greetings he imagined on the train from Zurich, that was not one.

"Damn, its good to see you. I'm glad you called," Bidwell said. "Have a seat. Do you want something to drink or eat?"

"Water would be great," Jake said from one of the two chairs in front of Bidwell's messy faux oak desk.

The RSO turned and tossed a bottle of Evian, then leaned against the desk, twisted the cap off a Perrier and took a sip. "So how have you been? What's new? It's been too long."

Jake wasn't sure how to respond to Bidwell's warmth. It was as if nothing had happened all that time ago. "I'm fine. I do P.I. and legal work in Philadelphia. Have time to read, write. I go to a lot of Eagles and Flyers games."

"Still a sports nut, huh? That's great."

"And what about you? I guess you still enjoy working with Diplomatic Security?" Jake referred to the State Department's version of the Secret Service.

Bidwell nodded and ran a hand through his thick brown hair. "Yeah, I still love the job. It's in my veins I guess. RSO took a while to get used to. Watching over security operations at the consulate and embassy is a lot less fun than protection details."

"I always figured you'd move up to management," Jake responded. "It was just a matter of how high."

"I think I'm finished climbing the Federal ladder."

"We'll see." Jake smiled for the first time.

The two had worked together when Jake was with Treasury and Bidwell was a senior Diplomatic Security agent, but they hadn't spoken since the Yassin affair, when two of Bidwell's men died. Jake wasn't sure where they stood after that.

"I don't blame you Jake. No one here does. We all know terrorist cases are risky. The enemy is smart."

"I lost my head, let down my guard. I shouldn't have let Anna get that close, and I certainly shouldn't have had your agents' contact information at home."

"Mistakes happen, Jake. Cut yourself some slack. You're old school Jake. You watched out for your people *and* mine. We miss you here."

Bidwell finished the mineral water and dropped the bottle in the garbage can. "Let's grab a beer and some dinner this evening and we'll finish catching up. But you didn't call about supper."

"Yeah," Jake said, "I need a favor."

"Okay, shoot."

"About a week ago I took a job for Henry Walsing and the Claims Resolution Tribunal. I was sure Walsing was leaking me to the Levant Group. But last night Walsing was murdered."

"Do you think it's the Herzog woman?"

"The thought occurred to me."

"Could the Levant Group have learned about you from anyone else?"

Jake didn't respond.

Bidwell nodded. "Okay, what's the plan? What do you need from me?"

Jake laid out his thoughts, down to the last detail. Bidwell removed his glasses and rubbed his eyes. "That's quite a request. You may be mad, Jake."

"I know it's crazy, but it's all I've got."

"It's risky. It's across the river from police headquarters. There'll be security. We'll have to get off the dime really fast."

"Yeah," Jake said softly.

"Could be a diplomatic and political disaster, even if things go as planned."

"I've thought about that, but it's risky for them too, and given what's at stake, I think everything will stay under the radar."

"Let's hope so." The RSO bit his lip. "We're going to have to be precise. I'm going to have to use seasoned agents. Vicki will probably want in."

"Are you sure that's a good idea?" Jake asked.

Victoria Hardey was a young DS agent when Jake was last in Switzerland. Though she was still green, Jake took a liking to her. She was smart, motivated—and could handle the men that dominated the office. She taught Jake all of the driving tricks that were so handy of late. After a while he began to suspect that she had a crush on him, but Yassin put a stop to all that.

"Like I said Jake, no one here, including Vicki, has any hard feelings about what happened. Besides, she's my best driver, and we're definitely going to need her."

"Okay. It's your team. You know what's best."

"When do you want to go?"

"Tomorrow night."

"We're on, then."

CHAPTER 35

Zurich

The Rheinfelder Bierhuas was a standard Swiss beer hall, cozy and loud, between Limmatquai and Marktplatz on the Niederdorf side of the Limmmat. Its clientele was a mix of students, working class types and businessmen who sat at long wooden tables drinking their favorite beers while trying to talk over the oompah band.

Jake stood in the entry, his eyes stinging from the smoky haze. A motherly waitress carrying a tray of eight steins above her head almost ran him down as she hurtled by. He took a step back and scanned the hall. Toward the back, a man raised a mug to him. Jake made his way across the puddled floor to Chief Inspector Albert Kessler.

"I ordered you a beer." Kessler said, handing Jake a mug.

"Thanks, I need it." Kessler had already emptied a mug and was on a second. The amount Kessler could drink despite his small frame was amazing.

"It's like old times," Kessler said. "The meetings, the parties when we shut down an operation."

After Kessler proposed a toast to "old friends", which Jake found ironic and insincere, the Chief Inspector started in. "I guess you wanted to meet to update me. Can we close the investigation soon? What's the latest?"

Jake looked at his watch. It was 8:08 P.M. *Timing.*

He told Kessler about the meeting with Elizabeth Reisz, her death and the narrow escape, though he left out Maya's revelation about Michael Freeman. "Whoever is behind this knows every move I make and has no intention of letting me make another."

"That's troubling. Have you been keeping Walsing informed?"

166

"Yep, just like you." Kessler's mouth twitched. "I hate to think it but Walsing could be playing you. I warned you about him. He's strange, like he has something to hide. He's never been very cooperative with the police. No one in Zurich trusts him."

Jake feigned pensive analysis of Kessler's statement. "Well, it's possible. But I suspected he might be the leak, so I didn't tell him I was going to visit Elizabeth Reisz." Jake ran the bluff out there and watched Kessler's face. "You were the only one who knew when I was going. I didn't even tell Maya until we got there."

Kessler didn't respond.

"I thought we were friends, Albert."

"Friends? Are you kidding me? We got along at work, but you always looked down on me, like I wasn't smart enough to be an investigator."

"That was just your perception Albert."

"Was it?" Kessler shrugged. "It doesn't really matter. You're the naïve one, you and your black and white world. With your Treasury Department credentials."

Jake stole a glance of Kessler's watch. It was 8:12 P.M. *Timing.*

"At least I know exactly where you stand now. You're no different from the vermin we fought."

"That's just your perception." Kessler enjoyed returning Jake's words. "The group I work with, stands for progress, growth, security and comfort."

"Progress for whom?"

"Eventually for everyone."

"And at what cost? So a few can benefit, while everyone else suffers. That's how I see the Levant Group's agenda."

Kessler's eyes narrowed. "You have no idea what you're dealing with."

"Perhaps, but since I've almost been killed a lot lately, I'm willing to find out." Jake took his gun from his waistband and pointed it at Kessler underneath the table. "Get up. We're going for a drive, and you're going to tell me what is going on here."

"You know, you never gave me enough credit. Look at the bar to your right. See the woman in the blue sweater? Plain looking isn't she? Guess what? She's one of my best."

Jake looked at the blonde and caught her gaze.

"And see the man standing by the post behind me? I guess you could say we're not going anywhere, at least not without them. And if you try anything, they'll deal with it."

"Albert, I said get up."

"You don't want to do this."

It was 8:18 P.M. *Timing*. He had to move.

"Oh, I'm pretty sure I do. Stand up."

Kessler frowned and stood. As he walked around the table, the man at the post began to move.

Jake grabbed Kessler's shoulder and shoved the gun into his left kidney. They headed for the door, and the woman in the blue sweater started toward them.

Jake pushed Kessler through the front door into the pouring rain and was stunned not to find his ride waiting. *Damn it, Bidwell, where the hell are you?*

"Cobra 2, this is Cobra 1. I'm red boarded on Waffenplatzstrasse." Victoria Hardey was stopped at a traffic light near the Reitberg Museum, on Zurich's right bank.

"Cobra 1, this is Cobra 2. I read you loud and clear. I'm en route and should be at the T.P. in ten minutes," Scott Bidwell replied.

"Roger that." Vicki looked at the clock on the console. Eight o'clock. Her boss would be at the transition point with twenty minutes to spare. She was getting worried, though, since the heavy traffic and rain did not seem to be lifting. The mission required precise timing.

"Cobra 2, this is Cobra 1 I'm headed to Selnaustrasse," Vicki said, just as brake lights glared and traffic slowed again.

Shit.

Five after eight. *Timing is the key*, she recalled telling Scott Bidwell eight hours earlier at the U.S. embassy in Bern. Now, as she made a slow left onto Selnaustrasse and traffic came to a stop she realized she was going to have to make some choices.

She looked at the clock. Eight after eight.

Timing.

"Cobra 2 this is Cobra 1. Change of plans. Heading northeast toward Langstrasse and then underneath the train station."

"Cobra 1, this is Cobra 2. Isn't that roundabout?"

"Yes, but there's too much stop and go. I need to pick up the pace."

"Roger."

Vicki crossed the Sihl River and veered right onto Staufacherstrasse, and the traffic was finally moving.

Red light at Staufacherstrasse and Langstrasse. She looked at the clock. Twelve after eight.

Timing.

She was late. "Cobra 2, this is Cobra 1. Making a right onto Limmatquai. ETA is two minutes."

"Roger that," Bidwell said. His voice told her the boss was worried.

Timing.

She flew through an intersection and barely missed getting rammed by the streetcar. To her right she glimpsed the flash of a muzzle. Then another flash from the left. Was she too late?

Jake was supposed to be on her right. What if his plans changed? If there was gunfire, somebody had made contact. She had to make a choice. She rolled down the window and veered to the right curb. She grabbed the Sigsauer holstered to her thigh and let off a few rounds. Someone went down.

Somebody piled into the back seat, then another. "Where the fuck were you?"

"Sorry, I got stuck in traffic!,"

Vicki drove and listened to the conversation in back. She finally let herself smile. Jake was okay.

CHAPTER 36

Zurich

Kessler grunted as Jake thrust him into the street. "You're making a mistake."

"Shut up." Jake pulled the Chief Inspector onto the narrow sidewalk just as the street lit up, and the Bierhaus door flew open. Jake spun Kessler around to find the man and the woman, weapons drawn, coming at him.

"They're crack shots. They won't hesitate. Trust me, I wont get hit," Kessler warned.

Jake kept Kessler in front, but he wasn't much shield. The woman fired, slicing Jake's outer thigh. He yelled but managed to keep a tight grip on Kessler. He looked high and low, but there was only the railing and the Limmat below. The man raised his weapon and aimed for the thigh. They were trying to cripple him, not kill him.

Then, like manna from heaven, a car screeched through the intersection to his left. The shooters turned their heads. Jake threw Kessler to ground, shoved his knee into his back and got off a shot that hit the man's arm, and he dropped his gun. Before the woman could turn back, the car skidded to a stop in front of Jake. He heard a gun pop, and the woman fell.

Jake threw Kessler, climbed in behind him and slammed the door. "Where the fuck were you?"

"Sorry, got stuck in traffic"

Jake punched Kessler hard in the gut. "I didn't think you were stupid, Albert, just predictable. I have a ride. And now you and I are going to have a chat."

"It'll have to be a short one because half the Stadtpolizei will be looking for this car in no time."

"That's my problem. Tell me more about the Levant Group."

"It doesn't matter. You can't do anything about them."

He slammed his elbow into Kessler's chest. "That's not what I asked."

"I don't know who they are exactly, only that they're rich and powerful beyond belief."

Jake heard sirens.

"I've got it" Vicki said and switched on the navigation system. They sped south on the Limmatquai and veered left, toward the Grossmünster. Two police cars came after them.

"Why is the Levant Group worried about old bank accounts?"

"I don't know, and if I did they'd probably want me dead too. You're in quite a mess, my friend."

"Why did you do it Albert?"

"The power and the money, of course. Civil service doesn't pay. They offered me a lifetime of comfort. They got me promoted."

Jake slapped Kessler's mouth.

"You won't get far." The Chief Inspector wiped blood from his lip.

A Stadtpolizei police car boiled out of a side street and barely missed sideswiping them. "How much further?"

"Kilometer and a half."

"Who gives you instructions?" Jake was back at Kessler.

"Josh Dempsey. He's in your State Department."

"I know him," Vicki said.

"Who is he?"

"Young guy, worked in Political Affairs on his first tour. He was around for a couple of years.."

Odd that someone so green was Kessler's contact. "Who's his boss?"

"I don't know," the Chief Inspector said.

Vicki made a left across oncoming traffic and into the garage of an apartment building.

"Good night, Albert." Jake kayoed Kessler with the butt of his gun, and he and Vicki got out and jumped into another vehicle.

"Thanks for the lift," Jake said as Vicki climbed into the back seat behind him.

"Not a problem."

The new driver, Scott Bidwell, hit the gas.

They raced back over the Quaibrucke headed north. Beyond city limits, Jake sat up. "I need to get to Klotten." He turned to Vicki. "I hate to ask, but I need another favor."

"No problem."

"Can you find out who Josh Dempsey works for and let me know ASAP?"

"I'll see what I can do. But you owe me dinner. We have a lot of catching up to do."

CHAPTER 37

East London

The Merchant cracked his eyes. His head was pounding, and his mouth was dry, full of cotton. The last thing he remembered was an attractive brunette trying to seduce him. He guessed she slipped him some sort of drug.

He moved his eyes back and forth, trying to get his bearings. He had no idea where he was, but the smell of cheap air freshener and smelly soap suggested a second rate hotel.

He was slouched in a chair. Music came from the television behind him. On the small round table in front of him he saw three blue gel caps and a glass of water.

"Take them, Herr Fuchs. They'll help with the headache."

The Merchant tried to make out who was sitting opposite him, but the light was too dim. He summoned what energy he had and stood up to leave.

Hands pressed his injured shoulders so hard he thought he'd pass out again. He fell back into the chair.

"The woman who shot you was good, wouldn't you say? I imagine that hurts. The pills will help that as well."

"No, thank you." He could still talk at least. "The last time someone gave me a pill I ended up here. Wherever this is."

"You don't trust me, Herr Fuchs?" Sarcastically.

The Merchant shook his head.

"Suit yourself."

The Merchant couldn't place the accent, a mix between German and some Middle Eastern language.

"What do you want?" The Merchant asked.

173

No answer. The Merchant tried to lean forward to see the person behind the voice but the hands pulled him back and hurt his shoulder again.

Quite calmly he said, "Do that again and I'll kill you."

"That's not a threat you're in a position to make." The man paused. "It seems you're having problems with Meyer and his female colleague. This should have been over by now. Perhaps you're not as good as they say."

"I'll finish the assignment. You'll get your money's worth."

"I haven't paid you anything."

That was strange. The Merchant had the assumption his Levant Group contact had orchestrated the little display to scare him. And the Levant Group had deposited the fee. "Who are you? Who do you work for?"

"I won't answer, but you'll know shortly."

The Merchant was confused.

"Let me ask *you* something, Herr Fuchs." The man finally leaned into the light. One hand stroked mutton chops that led to a black and silver goatee. "Did Chaim Herzog say anything before you killed him? Did he have any final words I might pass on to his family?"

"I don't know what you're talking about."

"A couple of months ago, you entered Israel with a false passport. The name was Simon Ackerman, I believe. You rented a car in Tel Aviv and drove to Netanya, where you went to Herzog's home and shot him in the head and chest."

"I didn't know that was his name. Since you know all about me, I guess you're Shin Bet or Mossad."

The man tilted his head left.

"I guess I wasn't careful enough." He had lost his edge.

"Or maybe we're that good."

"I suspect you have a thick dossier on me. Why haven't you killed me?"

"Because up to now, your work has mattered only tangentially. There was no need to risk taking you out. Better to watch and see who you're working for. At times you were beneficial to us. That nasty business with Mulberry, for example. He was funneling funds and weapons to Hamas."

"What do you want then?"

"We'll get to that, but first indulge me. What did you know about Herzog?" The man seemed angry.

"Not much. They gave me an address and a photograph. It's all I needed."

"Of course. Murder comes naturally to you."

He found Chaim Herzog in the living room reading a novel, listening to the sea through the open screen door. He looked up over his glasses but did not seem shocked or surprised. His eyes showed no fear. He finished the job quickly, but it took something out of him. Even killing Mulberry was draining. Maybe he didn't have much left.

"Killing was easier then."

"I imagine you don't know who hired you?"

"No, it was immaterial."

"There was nothing immaterial about Chaim Herzog. He was a good man, a hero, a friend." the man growled. "I should rip out your heart right now."

Blood from the reopened wound trickled down The Merchant's chest.

"But there are more important things we have to deal with. They hired you to follow Jake Meyer and the woman to learn more about withdrawals from old Swiss bank accounts."

"So, what do you want?"

"I want you to go ahead but with some changes."

"For example?"

"Meyer and his woman are in too deep. I want you to stop everything. Make everything go away."

The man gave him the bill of particulars. The Merchant pondered the terms. "How can you trust me?"

"Because you know what the alternative is, Herr Fuchs. All it would take is a few phone calls, and that's if I don't strangle you myself. For Chaim's sake." The man's voice softened slightly. "Against my better judgment I'm offering you freedom. Freedom to live as you please. You just do as I ask."

CHAPTER 38

Tel Aviv

El Al flight 36 from Zurich Klotten to Ben Gurion International greased the runway, and Jake navigated the terminal to the luggage carousels and customs. Maya waved, standing by the official in the last booth. As he approached the cubicle Maya said something in Hebrew to the passport agent and turned to Jake. "*Shalom, bruchim ha baim l'yisrael*. Know what that means?"

Jake grinned. "I accept your gracious welcome to Israel."

Maya kissed his cheek. "Give me your passport, and we'll expedite this."

The officer found him acceptable, and Maya said "Let's go. I have a car waiting outside."

A policeman stood by a black Mercedes-Benz waiting at the curb. He nodded to Maya and walked away. "Being in the Mossad has perks." Maya opened the driver's side.

"Like not having to park your car in the garage?" Jake watched her for a moment and was mesmerized. She was stunning. He wanted to tell her he'd missed her but he couldn't. The words would not come.

Jake threw his bag into the back, jumped in and they sped away from the airport. "So, what do we know about our professor friend?"

"Well, it seems as if Dr. Steiner appeared out of thin air."

"What are you talking about?"

"He fought with the IDF in the 1948 War, mostly driving supply trucks through the Mitla Pass. His leg was injured by a mortar exploded right in front of his vehicle. The truck rolled and pinned him underneath. He spent two months in rehab at a hospital in Tel Aviv."

"Sounds legit so far."

"Perhaps. But this is where things get a little weird. The records say that from 1941 to 1945 Steiner served as a logistics officer in the Jewish legion attached to the British Army. He fought the Nazis."

"Nothing strange in that. I expect able-bodied Jewish men were ready to fight the Germans."

"Here's the thing. Turns out there's no record of Joseph Steiner in the Jewish Legion."

"Well, the times were crazy. Could have been a clerical mistake. After all, the Legion came from Palestine, not from Britain. It could have been an oversight."

"Possible, but doubtful. The British were almost as obsessive about record keeping as the Germans."

"Point taken." As they drove, the drab, modern cement buildings gave way to green trees, farms and fields. "Okay, so some records from that part of his life are missing or non existent. What else did you find?"

"The problem is I can't seem to find anything about him prior to his military records. Nothing about where he came from or when; nothing about his parents or siblings. Like he just appeared out of nowhere."

"Well, what happened to him after the 1948 war?"

"From what I can find out, Joseph Steiner received a doctorate in history from Oxford in 1952 and returned to Israel and taught at Hebrew University in Jerusalem. He married Laura Simon in 1953, and she bore their only son in 1954. In 1965 he received tenure at the university. In 1973, he turned down a cabinet position and began working as a consultant."

"For the Israeli government?"

"Yes, and the Palestinians."

"I don't understand."

"Dr. Steiner had a good relationship with the moderate Arabs. He spoke Arabic, knew about their culture, and for some reason, they trusted him."

"How did he know so much about the Palestinians?"

"I don't know."

"What do you mean?"

"There wasn't anything in the records about studying or working with the Arabs."

"Now that is strange." Jake looked out the window as the highway weaved up through the hills and pondered.

"What are you thinking?" Maya asked.

"From what you tell me about Professor Steiner and from what's missing, the biography looks like somebody created it for him."

"I don't follow."

"It sounds like he was part of a witness protection program. You had to pull up an SAP just to find his bio. Some of the information seems contrived, like his service records. On the other hand, he couldn't fake being a university instructor or a government consultant. I don't know, just a gut instinct."

"A witness protection program might make sense."

"Is he still teaching and consulting?"

"Not exactly. He died five years ago."

"Then who the hell are we going to see?"

"His son. Nachum Steiner, Professor of History at Hebrew University."

"So the apple fell next to the tree."

"Maybe he can fill in some of the blanks for us."

"Does he know we're coming?"

"Yes, I set up an appointment. If we show up unannounced, he might get spooked."

CHAPTER 39

Zurich

It hurt to breathe.

Albert Kessler's ribs weren't broken, but every time he inhaled, pain seared his right side. He was in the living room of a suite at the Widder Hotel where Josh Dempsey told him to wait.

Meyer knew he was the leak. Inevitable, he supposed. The only other two possibilities were Walsing, dead thanks to the bodyguard Kessler placed with him, and Maya Herzog.

He took in the room's Baroque décor; an ornately carved wooden armoire, an equally impressive desk and a 16th century tapestry that hung on the wall. The only reminders of the twenty-first century were the direct fax machine, a high definition television and a Bang Olufson stereo on a sleek black entertainment stand.

Kessler sipped the brandy he helped himself to when he came in. Why didn't Meyer kill him? If he knew Kessler let Anna Constantine into the files that got a bunch of U.S. agents killed seven years earlier, he'd have shot him.

A card key clicked in the lock, and Josh Dempsey breezed in, followed by a man with a cane and a limp. The Chief Inspector had never seen Lance Piedmont. He thought he'd seen Lenin's ghost.

"Mr. Piedmont, this is Chief Inspector Albert Kessler," Dempsey said.

"How are your ribs?"

"They're fine. Thank you for asking." Kessler had not expected to see the head of the Levant Group.

Kessler met Piedmont's assistant at a U.S. consulate cocktail party. He contacted Kessler later with a very appealing proposal, including good pay and promotions. How Dempsey could make such promises Kessler wasn't sure, but ambition dictated that he agree to the deal. Ever since, he'd worked with the Levant Group and Josh Dempsey had been his only liaison.

Piedmont's presence indicated the gravity of the situation.

"It's a pleasure to meet you, sir," Kessler said.

"Josh, pour the Chief Inspector some more brandy, will you," Piedmont said as he lowered himself into a chair next to Kessler. "That is what you're drinking, correct?"

"Yes."

Dempsey passed Kessler the snifter and stood against the armoire.

"Ilse and the boys are well, I presume."

"They are well indeed."

"Your son Peter's graduating university this year, isn't he? You must be proud."

"You know a lot about my family."

"It's my business to know everything about everyone in whom the Levant Group puts its trust."

The Chief Inspector was uncomfortable. Did Piedmont doubt his loyalty?

"I trust you have found your relationship with us lucrative and beneficial?"

"Immensely. I'm proud to be associated with the organization."

"Good. Josh speaks highly of you. He says you're an asset."

"You handled the incident with Meyer as we discussed?" Dempsey asked.

"Yes. As far as the Stadtpolizei are concerned, my officers and I got hurt chasing suspects over the Lindenhoff. Our reports corroborate each other."

"Excellent. We need to keep this very quiet. There's too much at stake."

"How much does Meyer know?" Dempsey asked.

"From what I gathered, he knows about the Levant Group and the Dissenters."

"Did he mention anything about a pact?" Piedmont's voice was tense. "Think carefully, Chief Inspector. This is vital."

Kessler ran through all his conversations with Meyer the last couple of weeks. He'd reported as he promised when Kessler "deputized" him, but he didn't' say anything about a document or a pact.

"No, nothing about a pact." But obviously Piedmont was looking for one.

"Is there anything I can do to help find out about that?" the Chief Inspector asked.

"Tell me what you know about where Meyer is now?"

"Meyer flew to Israel. Why, I haven't a notion, though I suspect he'll join up with the Herzog woman again."

Piedmont turned back to Dempsey "Is it really possible? Might they actually find it?"

Dempsey shrugged. "It would be unbelievable."

After a moment's thought, Piedmont said, "Josh, get our people in Israel to locate Meyer and Herzog. Give instructions and anything else they need."

"Yes, sir."

"And what of our friend The Merchant?" Piedmont turned to Kessler.

"He was treated for his injury in Salisbury, but I haven't talked to him in a few days."

Piedmont frowned. "We're paying him good money. Chief Inspector, find The Merchant and bring him to me. The two of you could be very useful now."

"How can we help?"

"Information. I trust Meyer has humiliated you enough?"

Piedmont found his cane and stood. "I'll see you soon then. Josh will give you the details and directions."

Piedmont turned at the door. "By the way, you should be aware The Merchant killed Ms. Herzog's father. You might find that useful at some point, I don't know."

The Lenin clone grinned. "I recommend the jazz club downstairs. If you like that sort of music."

As they left, the pain in Kessler's side was not quite so intense.

CHAPTER 40

Jerusalem

Dr. Joseph Steiner made himself a tuna sandwich on wheat bread and took it, along with a bottle of beer and a copy of *The Jerusalem Post* to the dining room, newly remodeled at his wife's behest. Dr. Steiner was home alone. His wife was at the beach in Netanya visiting friends, and he could relax.

He twisted the cap off the beer and took a swig. He'd gotten a call from a Maya Herzog. The last name was familiar, but he couldn't place her at first. Then he remembered. A couple of months ago, the Prime Minister's chief of staff told him that Chaim Herzog was murdered the night before.

After he got the call from Maya Herzog, Steiner did some research and learned that she was Chaim Herzog's daughter. That was sad, but why did she call? She said she needed to speak with him urgently. She did not say what office or agency she was from.

Nor did she use the usual channels. She contacted him directly. That was strange.

Dr. Steiner thought about the clippings he read about the dead Dissenters. Could Maya Herzog be part of the Levant Group? They had their sources in every government. But how could the Levant Group know about *him*? He wasn't a Dissenter, and his only connection to them was through his father, who, as far as the Levant Group was concerned, died a long time ago. And even if they had figured out the truth about his father, his identity was a state secret.

No, there was no way they knew about him. Impossible. If Ms. Herzog was from the Levant Group she wouldn't have bothered phoning. She would just shown up at his doorstep and killed him.

At first he was ashamed of his father, figured he was partly responsible for the suffering of thousands, but as the story unfolded, shame turned to pride and admiration. Steiner's father was a learned teacher, consultant and advisor, and his son followed in his professional footsteps - not in response to parental pressure, but because he shared his father's principles.

When he finished eating, Dr. Steiner washed his plate and got another beer. He walked down the hallway to his study enjoying the family pictures on the walls. Weddings, births, holidays, the events that mark a life time. But there were no pictures of his father. They weren't permitted.

CHAPTER 41

Jerusalem

"We're almost there" Maya said as she shook Jake. He yawned and sat up. He'd catnapped only five minutes, but it felt like an hour. The cell phone in his pocket vibrated. "This is Jake."

After a short conversation, Jake said, "Thanks so much. I owe you another one. Yes, I'll follow through. Strangers no more, I promise." He snapped the phone shut.

"What was that about?" Maya asked.

Jake told her about Walsing's death and that Kessler had been the leak, how he asked a couple of friends to help him deal with Kessler and escape from Zurich.

"I asked Vicki to find something out for me."

"Well, did she?"

"Yes. We know who the head of the Levant Group is."

"Who?"

When Jake told her, she blurted, "Are you serious?"

Jake nodded. "We may be into something very big. We still don't know exactly what's going on. Let's see what the Professor can tell us. Which house is his?"

"That one, over there." Maya pointed right.

"Okay, drive around the block. Let's be sure we don't have any company."

Maya drove past the house and the Benz half a block away. They walked up a path lined with yellow and orange flowers, and Maya rapped on the front door.

"Dr. Nachum Steiner?" Maya asked the tall, lean man who answered.

"Yes, and you are Ms. Herzog, correct?"

Nachum Steiner's healthy appearance surprised her. His father always looked worn out.

"Yes, and this is Jake Meyer." Jake held out his hand and Dr. Steiner shook it.

"You have credentials, I presume?"

Dr. Steiner carefully examined their documents and handed them back. "What's the urgent matter you mentioned on the phone Ms. Herzog? At first I thought the Chief of Staff's office was sending you to brief me about some matters with the Prime Minister. But Mr. Meyer's presence indicates that I was wrong. What do you want from me?"

"We need a history lesson," Jake said.

Steiner often got requests for information from journalists and government officials but through the university. And if he agreed, the meetings happened on campus. "Why didn't you go through the university?"

"This is a very important matter, and we didn't have time to schedule an appointment with your assistant."

Dr. Steiner was getting suspicious. The clippings about dead or missing Dissenters danced through his mind.

"We need to talk to you about your father, Dr. Joseph Steiner. Or was that Michael Freeman?" Jake's question caught Steiner off guard.

Steiner's face went blank. If they were from the Levant Group he'd be dead already. "All right. Come in."

Jake and Maya followed down a corridor lined with family photos— but not a one of Joseph Steiner.

Dr. Nachum Steiner led them into his study and motioned them to sit down. "What do you want to know about my father? You obviously know who he was. How did you find out?"

Jake began by telling Dr. Steiner about Harold Burns, the dead CRT auditor and his investigation of the big 1936 bank withdrawals. He told him how Henry Walsing hired him and about his own investigation. He told him about Pincay, Reiner, Crowe and Elizabeth Boyles, all dead, as well as the fact that a former colleague and member of the Levant Group betrayed him and Maya.

When Jake finished, Professor Steiner leaned back in his chair and studied his guests. "I read about all that in the newspaper. I suspected they didn't die of natural causes, and you confirmed that. And the

Levant Group is behind the death or disappearance of other Dissenters a few years ago."

Steiner knew about the Levant Group and the Dissenters, Maya noted. "So the Levant Group has been eliminating its opposition for years?"

"Absolutely. Though the earlier murders had more to do with Dissenters threatening to expose the Levant Group. I have a feeling that the current mess has more to do with what you're really looking for."

"Do you know what that is?" Jake asked.

"Perhaps. But first, indulge me. How did you learn about my father?"

"I was your father's student once."

"All his students adored him," Steiner smiled.

"So did Elizabeth Boyles." Maya paused to let the statement register. The look on Steiner's face showed he knew nothing about Boyles.

"I noticed a photo Elizabeth Boyles had, a snap of her and a young, handsome man picnicking by a river. The man seemed familiar, the kind of face that stays with you. Then she made a gesture your father always used in class. She was talking about a man named Michael Freeman, and I was thinking Dr. Steiner. But she said Freeman died in 1936, and I took your father's course in the nineties."

"Surely you had more than a resemblance and a gesture to make the connection," Steiner said.

She told him what she learned from Mossad's data bases. "There were just too many holes in the information on Joseph Steiner."

"That makes sense. My father was part of an early identity protection program. I guess they never got around to redrafting his faux biography. But it worked for over fifty years."

"What was your father's real story?" Jake asked. "What was the Pact he and Weizmann got the Levant Group to agree to?"

Dr. Steiner took a deep breath and leaned forward. "What I'm about to say I did not hear from my father. As you may recall from my father's class, Ms. Herzog, though the British had a mandate over Palestine after World War I, they were in a bind. The Balfour Declaration promised the Zionists a home in Palestine, and the Hussein McMahon correspondence promised land to the Arabs for their help against the Ottomans. Throughout the twenties and thirties, both Jews and Arabs pressured the British government to find a solution to the conflicting claims. Britain did not want to lose its influence in the region, so the government vacillated.

"In the meantime, they restricted Jewish immigration to Palestine to appease the Arabs. Weizmann lobbied his British government contacts to increase the quotas, but got nowhere.

"When Hitler and the Nazis came to power, everything got a lot hotter. Anybody could see a storm was gathering."

"So Weizmann approached the Levant Group to help buy a home?" Jake asked.

"That would be a simplistic way of putting things, Mr. Meyer," Dr. Steiner said with a hint of irritation. "You see individual people and groups had been buying land from the Arabs for some time. But in a stroke of amazing fortune, a British diplomat named Philby approached Weizmann about the possibility of buying a lot of land from Prince Ibn Saud. The Saudis needed money to explore their oil reserves."

"How much was involved?" Jake asked.

"Twenty thousand pounds sterling. Not an insignificant amount at the time. So Weizmann began looking for investors. He knew lots of industrialists and financiers and worked with the utmost discretion. He learned about a new group with a vision of the future. They believed governments were incapable of dealing with people's needs. Only global capitalism and business could offer a safe, prosperous future. They wanted an end to European colonialism. The group planned to invest heavily around the world to create connections among people and blur national borders, all in the name of growth and security."

"All of which would keep them rich and powerful," Jake sneered.

"A byproduct of their altruism," Steiner sneered back.

"So Weizmann got in touch and offered them their first big investment opportunity," Jake posited. "They could get a permanent capitalist foothold in the Middle East by making a deal with Ibn Saud. That was the Pact."

"Precisely." Steiner got up and gazed out the window. "That's why they called it the Levant Group."

"Well. That confirms what Liz Boyles told us," Jake said.

"Not completely," Maya rejoined. "We still don't know exactly what territory was included in the Pact."

"All of present day Israel, including the West Bank and parts of Jordan," Dr. Steiner said without turning away from the window.

"My God, that means the Saudis sold the Palestinians out," Maya blurted. "But surely the Palestinians would not accept that."

"No, they wouldn't have. They were to be relocated."

"Excuse me, did you say relocated?" Jake wanted to make sure he heard right.

"I did, Mr. Meyer. The Levant Group people were very wealthy. They were also very shrewd. They knew the Palestinians would never buy it, so they would have to do something. So they got help."

"From whom?"

"The Americans."

"What?" Jake's head spun.

"It was all very complicated." Dr. Steiner turned back around. "I don't know the details but the Yanks in the Levant Group were tight with the government and thought the Pact would improve the United States' position as the next world power.

"And now since your government has taken a big hand in the Middle East, the Arabs would see the Pact as evidence of the West's bias against them and the cause of all their troubles—especially if they could prove it..

"In any event, when some of the Levant Group learned of the relocation plan, they were furious. They wanted to let the Palestinians stay if they chose and become part of the new state. But the rest wanted to move forward. The minority became known as Dissenters."

"What exactly happened to the Pact?" Maya asked.

"That's where my father comes in. He was Weizmann's aide. They met at Oxford. Weizmann gave a lecture, and they spent time talking about politics afterward. Weizmann asked my father to work for him, to make connections and contacts all over the British establishment.

"Weizmann saw my father as his protégé and let him help lobby the Levant Group investment. The members withdrew the money, and my father channeled the funds into a special account. When the Pact was fulfilled, Ibn Saud would get access to the account. Philby set up a clandestine meeting between Weizmann and Ibn Saud in old Jaffa. My father went with Weizmann, the Pact was executed, and my father gave the prince the account information. In return, Weizmann got a detailed map of the land they bought.

"Weizmann, my father and their bodyguards left the meeting and found themselves in the middle of an Arab riot. They tried to find a way out of Jaffa. They had to get the map and the Pact back to the Levant Group. The Arabs were all over them. My father stumbled and tore the ligaments in his foot and ankle."

"So that was why he limped? Not a war injury like the Mossad files say?" Maya asked.

Steiner nodded. "They kept moving, but my father got separated from them and ran into a mob. He hung onto the map and the Pact for dear life. He didn't know who, but somebody pulled him to safety. He tried to find Weizmann and the security detail, but they were gone.

"And he never returned to London," Maya said.

"He was badly injured from the beating, and the man who saved him—Yousef Jabril—took him home and nursed him back to health. Jabril was a good man. While he recovered, my father learned Arabic and a lot about Arab culture. They talked about everything from religion to politics to art.

"When he was well, he knew he could not return to London. The Levant Group would want the Pact, the map and their money. But my father had changed his mind. He knew it wouldn't work."

"So, Weizmann and the Levant Group presumed he was dead and the Pact was lost, and your father stayed in Palestine and created a new identity for himself," Jake said.

"He had help, but I don't know how it all happened. I only know that he went to the Jewish Agency's Tel Aviv office and told them he was British and wanted to live in Palestine. He told them he was an army deserter and knew things about Britain's Mandate forces that put him in danger. He told them he knew Arabic and Arab culture. Together they created Joseph Steiner, professor of history and politics—and secret advisor on Arab affairs to the new Israeli government."

"And you followed right in his path."

"I admired him greatly, Ms. Herzog."

"Let' get back to the Pact," Jake said. "The Levant Group never got its money back?"

"No. Ibn Saud withdrew it and used it to hire Western oil companies who had the technology to exploit his oil. Oddly enough, that benefited certain members of the Levant Group."

"Then why is the Levant Group so anxious to get its money back now?" Maya asked.

"It's not about those specific funds. That's a pittance in today's value."

"So why have we been chasing withdrawals from Levant Group accounts? What are we looking for?"

Silence filled the room. Then the epiphany bloomed.

"The Pact wasn't lost?" Jake asked.

Dr. Steiner nodded.

"Where is it?"

Steiner spoke in Hebrew, so Jake didn't have a clue what he said. But Maya's eyes went wide with shock, then narrowed with understanding. Finally, in English, "Ms. Herzog, Mr. Meyer, you must get to the Pact before the Levant Group does."

"We understand, Professor." Maya stood and took Dr. Steiner's hand. "Thank you so much for your time."

Dr. Steiner escorted them to the door. "I heard about your father, Ms. Herzog. I'm very sorry."

Maya turned around. How did he know?

CHAPTER 42

Jerusalem

Dr. Steiner turned on the television and tuned in a basketball game on ESPN. He loved basketball, played when he was young, but he was no longer in shape for that.

As he watched, his thoughts strayed to the conversation with Maya and Jake. He'd told them everything. Why? They weren't Levant Group operatives. He was sure. They didn't kill him. And he liked them.

If they got the Pact before the Levant Group, perhaps disaster could be avoided. He was certain the Levant Group would use the Pact to blackmail governments and competitors. Worse, they could hold onto it and use it to start a war that would benefit some of them immensely. The thought of another war led Dr. Steiner to conclude that he did the right thing. He only hoped Jake and Maya would get to the Pact first.

Suddenly someone knocked on his door. He stood and turned the television off. Perhaps Jake and Maya wanting to clarify something. He rushed to the door and opened it, expecting to see his guests. Instead he saw a nightmare. Before him stood two men in shirt sleeves and slacks. Dark skin, hefty physiques. The typical Shin Bet look, but Dr. Steiner knew better.

The men came inside unbidden and shut the door. One man grabbed Steiner's arm and pushed him toward the kitchen. The men had a purpose and would not leave until they got the information they wanted. Steiner knew he wouldn't last long. He hoped he'd die before he talked, but he doubted it. Perhaps he could hold out long enough to buy time for Jake and Maya.

CHAPTER 43

Jerusalem

Maya was in a fog. It couldn't be true. She sped off before Jake closed his door. "What's going on?" he yelled.

"The Pact. Steiner—I mean Freeman—he hid it!"

"That's what Steiner said in Hebrew?"

"Yes, its in Hezekiah's Tunnel. Brilliant!"

"Whose tunnel?"

"King Hezekiah. He built it in 701 B.C. to withstand a siege. It brought water from the Gihon spring outside the Old City to the pool of Siloam inside the wall."

"And what's so brilliant about hiding it there?"

"Because it's dark and narrow and three feet deep in water. Even if anyone knew the Pact existed, they'd never look for it there."

She drove east, away from the setting winter sun, made a right and headed south along the eastern wall of the Old City toward the Kidron valley—in the Palestinian sector. She thought about calling Golan for assistance but figured it was better to stay quiet until they had the Pact in hand.

"Where is it inside the tunnel?" Jake asked. Maybe it was at the mouth, and he wouldn't have to crawl around in the ancient city's intestines. Jake did not like tight places.

"At the midpoint. Two teams dug the tunnel, digging in both directions. They met in the middle, about three hundred yards feet in."

Jake's stomach sank. He wasn't even in the tunnel, and he wanted to get out. After a few deep breaths,, he settled down enough to wonder how Maya knew so much about the place.

192

She answered the unspoken question. "My father was a history buff, especially when it came to Biblical references. He took me to Hezekiah's Tunnel several times when I was a little girl."

She noticed a car following them. "We have company."

Jake turned and saw a green Opel not far behind. "There isn't a lot of room on these streets to maneuver."

Maya stepped on the accelerator and raced through the squalid neighborhood. She turned left down a hill, checked the mirror for the Opel's lights—and had an idea.

"Jake, when I tell you to, get out of the car. The entrance to the tunnel will be on your right. Find the Pact, and I'll meet you at the other end, once I shake whoever is tailing us."

Jake wasn't afraid of being chased, punched, kicked, or even shot at. But the prospect of getting stuck in the tunnel petrified him. He took five deep breaths to calm himself down.

"You look flushed. Are you all right?" Maya asked.

"I'm fine. Just prepping myself. Tell me exactly where the Pact is."

"Steiner said it was behind the third stone from the top of the right wall, exactly at the midpoint where the tunnel suddenly stops and veers off at a tight angle."

She braked to a stop. "Go now!"

Jake jumped out of the car and was about to close the door when Maya called, "Wait. You'll need this." She found a penlight in the glove compartment and tossed it to him.

He'd never been so grateful for a flashlight.

CHAPTER 44

Jerusalem

Jake was sweating.

Even the cool night air couldn't keep fear from pushing his body temperature up. He pointed the pen light at the entrance. Five steps down to a pool of water and an iron gate that appeared to be locked. He closed his eyes, and edged down the stairs and into the cool water. He pushed the gate which opened only slightly and stopped with a clang. Chained shut. He sucked it up and tried to squeeze through the slit but couldn't.

He flashed the penlight on the iron grate and saw that moisture had rusted the hinges. He shoved it, the hinges gave enough to open just wide enough for him to slide through. Inside he stumbled and fell forward, got up soaked and shivering and pointed the light forward. The beam barely lit the tunnel.

He splashed along noisily. He had to find the Pact and get out of this ancient bowel. The water was at his waist, and the tunnel grew smaller and bent this way and that. Was he to the middle yet? He felt like he'd walked the length of three football fields.

After another fifty feet he had to make a tight right turn. He stopped. *This must be it.* All he had to do was locate that Pact. He played the light over the smooth boulders. Third stone from the top of the right wall. But which was the right wall? The tunnel ran in both directions. He turned and searched the other wall.

Nothing. Green algae and water stains. He felt between the crevices. Nothing.

And then he saw it. A tiny *W* scratched into the rock, three stones from the ceiling. *Weizmann.* Jake stuck the light in his mouth and reached for the block. The fourth tug on the slimy surface pulled it free, and it splashed into the water.

He reached into the hole and fingered the surface. Nothing.

Jake shone the light into the hole. Nothing.

What if Steiner lied? Worse, had the Levant Group gotten there first? His head was spinning when he felt something brush his knee. He looked down and saw something floating in the water. A plastic tube.

He fished it up and opened it. Inside were sheets of damp parchment. He unrolled them, and there it was. He could hardly see, but it was there—Arabic, Hebrew and English. He started rolling them up but stopped cold when he heard a loud noise, the sound of metal striking rock. Someone was in the tunnel behind him.

He stuffed the Pact into his jacket, but as he turned the penlight fell out of his mouth into the water.

Fuck.

Terrified and panicky, Jake dropped to his knees, then all fours, in the water and felt around him for the light, sloshing water this way and that and fighting panic. And he heard someone, maybe more than one, splashing toward him. He stood up.

Get it together. Breathe. In and out. In and out. Slow and deep.

He could see the light from his pursuers' flashlights and hear men yelling. He placed his hands on the walls and headed for the tunnel's other entrance. He was moving. He was back in control.

Suddenly the shouting got very loud. They must have found the Pact's empty tomb.

A rush of air on his face told him the exit was not too far ahead. He heard a woman's voice but couldn't make out what she was saying. The water was only ankle deep again, the tunnel wider, and he saw moonlight reflected in the water just ahead.

The voice called again. Maya. He stumbled out of the tunnel and into the pool of Siloam. In the light of the moon, he saw Maya on the steps, reaching for him. He lunged toward her, but then came sharp pain in his jaw and a mighty blow on the nape of his neck. He splashed forward onto the stone steps. The last thing he saw before the lights went out was a man holding a gun to Maya's head.

CHAPTER 45

Davos

Jake was scared. He saw bright white. Was it the shining light people who "come back" from death described as the tunnel to the afterlife? His eyes opened and closed slowly. His ears rang, and the base of his skull throbbed. He could barely move. Was he paralyzed? He must be alive. The pain was intense.

He opened his eyes and focused. He could see clearly through only one eye. He'd lost a contact lens. But his good eye saw white. White, indeed. An incredible vista of snow-covered mountains. In the distance. But much nearer was a man sitting on a couch, wearing a gray suit, palming a cane and looking like the reincarnation of V.I. Lenin. "Hello, Mr. Meyer, how do you feel?"

Is that some sort of joke? Jake didn't respond.

"It's mostly the drugs. We kept you sedated during the trip. They'll wear off in a few hours."

"Who are you?"

"My name is Lance Piedmont, but you already knew that, didn't you?"

"I had a suspicion. How did you get me here? And where are we?"

Piedmont smiled. "Davos. Via extraordinary rendition. We gave you a sleeping drug, put you in a diaper, and flew you out of Israel on a private jet. One of our security companies devised the process for the CIA."

"Nothing is a problem for the Levant Group, is it?"

"Not usually. Though *you* have been rather difficult."

"Sorry."

Piedmont rubbed his goatee. "Where is the Pact?"

196

"I don't know what you're talking about."

"Don't be coy. Is this how it's going to be. Mr. Meyer?"

"How what's going to be?"

Piedmont stood and smoothed his jacket. "Why were you in Hezekiah's Tunnel?"

"Its historical significance interests me."

"That's not what Ms. Herzog said."

Jake's stomach dropped at Maya's name. He vaguely remembered her calling to him just before he was knocked unconscious. "Really. What did she say?"

"At first, she denied everything. You know, the meeting with Professor Steiner and the Weizmann-Abdullah Pact. Oh, Steiner's dead by the way. Just thought you'd like to know."

Jake wasn't surprised.

"But then Ms. Herzog met Herr Kessler. I believe you know him, correct?"

"If Kessler hurt her . . . "

"So I ask again, what did you do with the Pact?"

Jake had no aces in the hole. "I don't have it."

"Really?"

"I've seen it. It's explosive. It could cause real problems for the West, especially the U.S. I can understand why you want to get hold of it."

"Why is that, Mr. Meyer?" Piedmont seemed amused.

"So you and your friends in Washington can use it as blackmail."

"Which is what?"

"I'm not sure, but I figure it's all about more American aggression and all sugar for the Levant Group."

Piedmont nodded his head like a professor pondering a student's response to a tricky question. "So you think it's all about imperialism?"

"Yes, I do."

"Let me ask you something, Mr. Meyer. Does the U.S. have any significant overseas settler populations?"

Jake thought a moment. "No."

"Good. Does America exercise direct rule outside its borders?"

"No."

"And finally, assuming America does control some foreign populations to a degree, does the United States offer the people it controls citizenship?"

Piedmont's questions reminded Jake of law school. "No."

"Well, since those are the hallmarks of colonial rule, you can hardly accuse your government of imperialism."

"What about the string of military bases across the globe and the soldiers and other people who run them? Or the aircraft carriers prowling the oceans and the spy satellites? That's a lot of control."

Piedmont deposited himself back on the couch. "Control, yes; imperialism, no."

"So the Weizmann-Abdullah Pact, the Levant Group, it's about control?"

"Exactly, though not the way you think. Not by nations or governments."

"I've heard it all before. Business can do a better job of meeting people's needs than governments. And make the handful at the top richer than God in the meantime. It all comes down to the same thing: slavery. One kind's the same as another."

"Have governments produced much freedom? Look at the Middle East. Everybody there is a slave to terror. The Levant Group tried to avoid that. We had a better plan. If things had gone our way, the Middle East today would look a lot more like Singapore than the murderous morass it is."

"But things *didn't* go your way. Tell me, what happened when the Pact was lost?"

"Not much. Some were upset that they could not recoup their investment, but in the grand scheme of things the amount was trivial. And the Levant Group was too busy making deals to buffer itself against World War II. The end of that conflict opened up amazing opportunities. The world needed rebuilding, literally. Science and technology exploded, and we were into everything. In fact, the Marshall Plan was the Levant Group's doing. And the United Nations gave the Jews a home. The Weizmann-Abdullah Pact was no longer important.

"Until now." Jake said.

"Until now."

Piedmont stood and poured himself a glass of Scotch from the bar.

"Well," Jake said, "I don't have it."

"Even if I believed you I still would want it."

"So you could destroy it?"

"No. As insurance. The Pact would help us remind certain parties of their place in the order of things."

Jake looked puzzled.

"Let me put it this way. While constant chaos is bad for business and human well-being, so is continuous stability. An occasional conflict here and there is like a social high colonic. It cleans the world's bowels and reminds people of what they need. An insurrection in Namibia and our security companies advise the military. A terrorist attack in Egypt or a natural disaster in Asia and our construction companies rebuild. A civil war somewhere in South America and our textile and food companies provide clothing and food. The Levant Group, not governments, meets basic human needs best. Conflicts create jobs in the war zone and all over the world for people who would otherwise be without work. Do you have any idea how many Filipinos, Indians and Sri Lankans found work as a result of the war in Iraq? There were more private contractors than soldiers during that war. Conflicts generate job almost any industry. In fact, Mr. Meyer, war *is* an industry."

"And think what a new war in the Middle East would do for the Levant Group! Never mind if it escalated into an apocalypse," Jake snarled.

"Don't be silly, Mr. Meyer, we wouldn't let it come to that. It really is about control, isn't it?"

"When it's necessary, the Levant Group creates 'controlled chaos' to assert its power. Then the Levant Group gets rich taking care of basic human needs—shelter, clothing, work, food."

"By George, I think he's got it." Piedmont sipped the golden liquid. "Think of it this way. We have a symbiotic relationship with global society."

Piedmont hobbled over to Jake, took a pocket watch from his vest, popped it open, then snapped it shut. "Mr. Meyer, our time is up. Now. Please. Tell me where the Pact is."

Jake tried to stand but couldn't quite do it. "I don't have it. I don't know where it is," Jake said.

"I'm really sorry to hear that. Do you know what really drives a man, Mr. Meyer?"

"Megalomania?"

"Humiliation. A man detests being embarrassed and will do anything to avoid it or to remedy the slight. Isn't that right, Herr Kessler?"

Jake's good eye saw Albert Kessler, his face swollen from the beating Jake gave him. "Very true, Herr Piedmont," he sneered, "very true."

"Well then, I have a meeting, but I have complete faith that Kessler here will help you remember where the Pact is. Goodbye, Mr. Meyer."

Jake was about to respond, but Kessler's fist slammed into his mouth. Darkness descended, and Jake tasted blood. When the light returned Jake saw Kessler at the bar, pouring a drink. Outside a helicopter lifted off.

After Maya dropped Jake at Hezekiah's Tunnel she tried to get out of the Kidron Valley and get to Ha-ofel road, the street that rings the Old City. She figured she could just circle the walls and then pick Jake up. But on Ma'alot Ir David she saw the flashing blue lights of a Shin Bet vehicle in the mirror. She stopped and got out of the car. The Shin Bet car stopped too, and men in uniform got out. But before she spoke, one of them kicked her in the stomach. Another shoved his gun into her face. *Dammit!* Of course, the Levant Group had moles inside Shin Bet.

The men asked where Jake was, and when she did not answer, they broke two fingers on her right hand. One radioed someone that Jake was probably in Hezekiah's Tunnel. She wondered how they knew that. *They probably got to Professor Steiner.*

The men threw her in their car and drove her to place where she meant to meet Jake. They made her stand on the steps and call him. She remembered seeing him when he splashed into the pool. She remembered reaching for him as he fell. After that, she remembered nothing.

She woke up tied to a chair somewhere in Switzerland. At least that's where Kessler said she was.

"Tell me about Professor Steiner and what you know of the Weizmann-Abdullah Pact," He barked.

When Maya didn't respond he slapped her face. She turned her head back to Kessler and held his gaze.

"Where is the Pact?"

"I don't know."

"I don't like beating women, but I will if I have to." Kessler slapped her again.

Her ear rang. "I just told you, I don't have any idea where it is."

He ripped her blouse open and slipped bra straps off her shoulders. "Well, if I can't get any information out of you, then I might as well get some pleasure." He fondled her breasts and bit her neck. He shoved his hand between her legs.

Maya wasn't worried. Kessler was awkward. It was all for show. He was ruthless, even sadistic, but she had a hunch that when it came down to it, Kessler couldn't rape her.

He groped some more, then pulled away, his breathing even and controlled. The wheels in his head spun. "Very well. You don't know where the Pact is, but I'll bet Meyer does. Before I kill him, I'll bring him down here and let you have one last look. Though I hardly think you'll recognize him."

Kessler was about to say something when another man came in and whispered in his ear. "Good. I'll be up in a minute."

The man left and Kessler hit Maya one more time before he turned off the light and locked the door behind him.

CHAPTER 46

Davos

The Merchant felt a new resolve. No more failures. He was going to finish things once and for all and disappear with Sophie. When he got back to Brown's Hotel he phoned his Levant Group contact, Albert Kessler, who berated him. "Where have you been?"

"In Salisbury. The woman with Meyer got lucky and shot me in the shoulder. I had to get to a doctor."

"I know that. Remember we spoke right after you were fixed up? But what's happened since then? We haven't heard from you."

"The doctor gave me Vicodin, and I've been out for a couple of days."

There was silence.

"Where are Meyer and the girl?" The Merchant asked. I'll take care of them."

"Interesting you should ask. They're with us. No thanks to you. I'm inclined to recommend that you not get paid." Kessler paused. "But if you can get over here quickly and get something out of them, I imagine all will be forgiven."

"Very well. Where is here?"

"Mr. Piedmont's chalet in Davos."

The Merchant caught a night train to Zurich, rented a car and drove the hundred miles to Davos. Piedmont's chalet was in the mountains above Davos, and though one could ski in and out, vehicles got access only via a private road.

After ten minutes, he spotted a small guard house on the right and turned in. He stopped at the gate, and a uniformed guard stepped out of the booth, a machine gun slung over his shoulder. The Merchant touched the Makharov tucked between his seat and the gear shift.

"I'm here to see Piedmont and Kessler. They're expecting me."

"And who are you?"

"Dieter Fuchs."

"I'll check. Wait here."

The guard went into the booth and lifted the phone. The Merchant got out of his car and slipped around the cement hut. When the guard came back, the car was empty. When he swung around to sound an alarm, The Merchant was in front of him, gun at eye level. Before the guard could make a sound, a round blew through his forehead. The Merchant did not want any hassles on the way out. He dragged the cadaver back into the booth and propped it up in the chair.

He sped up the serpentine road, slick from a recent snow plowing. At its end loomed Piedmont's magnificent chalet. He stopped in the parking circle in front of the guest house, and two more guards came out of the building to greet him.

"Hello, Herr Fuchs," the taller one said. "You can head up those stairs to the main house. Herr Piedmont and Herr Kessler are in the living room."

"Thank you." The Merchant raised the Makharov and eliminated two more impediments.

Instead of taking the steps to the front door on the second level, The Merchant went in on the ground floor. He wanted to surprise Piedmont and Kessler from inside. He walked lightly down a hall to a staircase. He took them slowly and at the landing found himself in a gymnasium with the usual equipment. He saw another entrance across the room and went through it into another hallway. He followed it to a corner, peeked around and saw two more guards. Neither seemed aware of him.

No problem.

The Merchant pulled his head back, checked his weapon and then stepped into the corridor. The guards turned their heads, but it was all over.

He moved like a cat, ready for anything. When he got to the door where the guards were, he stopped. Someone was inside.

A sliver of light came under the door. Maya's eyes adjusted and she made out a bed, a dresser and a vanity. She was tied up in a chair. She tried to move her hands, but the rope burned her skin. She recalled her father telling her that when you can't see, you can still smell and hear. She closed her eyes and inhaled gently. Cigarette smoke. She made her ears block out the thumping noise in her chest, and in seconds she heard voices, muffled but she recognized the language as German. She strained to make out specific words, but it was no use.

There were at least two people, probably guards. Suddenly she heard four soft, quick pops. Then two more. The talking stopped. Maya knew her guards were dead.

The light under the door disappeared just before the door flew open. The bright light blinded her, but she could make out the silhouette of someone in the doorway. "Are you all right?" Perfect English.

"Yes."

"Where's Meyer?"

She still could not see the man's face. "I don't know."

"Does he have the Weizmann-Abdullah Pact?"

"I don't know that either."

Maya squinted and saw the shape approaching with an arm stretched toward her. She heard a click and saw something pointed in his hand. A knife. Not a savior but another torturer.

The man got behind Maya and cut the ropes. "I need to find Jake Meyer. Grab a gun from one of the men outside and be careful. There are more guards."

The man ran out of the room before Maya's eyes adjusted. She never saw his face.

CHAPTER 47

Davos

The second blow made his lips balloon like an overdose of collagen. He spit blood and saliva and wiggled his jaw. Not broken. Jake trained his good eye on Kessler. "Having fun Albert?"

"All of this could have been avoided. You got *too* curious."

"It's what I do."

"Not for much longer. Where is the Pact?"

"I told Piedmont, I don't have it."

Kessler punched Jake again, and the remaining contact lens flew out.

Two of Kessler's goons came in. They looked like black blobs to near-sighted Jake. They pinned him to the chair. Jake heard somebody opening and closing cabinets and recognized Kessler's shape back at the bar.

"During our drive a few days ago, you asked me why I did it. Let me elaborate," the shape said. "The Stadtpolizei doesn't pay very well. My wife uses a lot of money. My boys need tuition for school But most of all, the payoffs are . . . unfair." He pulled a chair up and sat in front of Jake. "You were always so condescending and pious. I would have thought all that with Anna Constantine would have humbled you. Apparently not. But don't judge me now. You don't know me. You never knew me."

Kessler was right. He didn't *know* the *man*. Until now.

"The Levant Group got me promoted and offered other benefits. There really wasn't much choice."

"There's always a choice. You didn't have to kill Harold Burns."

Kessler raised a brow. "One of our Arab friends did that, a little too much sodium pentothal. On the other hand, it brought you and

205

me together again." From somewhere he came up with a Mark 1 knife, the kind the U.S. Navy issued during World War II and sliced Jake's forearm. "Tell me something. After all you've learned, are you really that stupid?"

Blood ran from the wound. Kessler opened a green bottle and poured lemon juice over the cut. "The terror attacks, the drug smuggling, the payoffs, the tips, the arrests. It's all up to the Levant Group. They control everything. We're all just puppets, and I'd rather be a puppeteer."

Kessler twisted Jake's left palm up and cut diagonally across the hand from the index finger. He held up the lemon juice. "So, where is the Pact?"

"I don't know where it is, Albert."

"What a pity." Kessler poured lemon juice and then a red liquid onto the wound. "The pepper sauce really enhances the affect."

Kessler spoke to one of the Stern operatives. "Take his shoes off and hold his leg up." He turned to Jake. "The sole is very sensitive. Cuts take a long time to heal and make walking very painful." He grabbed Jake's foot. "But severing the Achilles tendon leaves a permanent limp." He looked up at Jake. "I'm losing patience. You were in Hezekiah's Tunnel. Maya Herzog told us you were there to get the Pact. What did you do with it?"

Jake could not respond.

"Wait a minute," Kessler said. "She got that same look when I said your name to her. You're in love with her, aren't you?" He dropped Jake's foot and stood. "Fool. Let your guard down again, didn't you." He turned to the goons. "Fetch that woman here."

CHAPTER 48

Davos

Meyer had to be with Piedmont and Kessler but where? The Merchant was lost in the bowels of the chalet.

He heard someone was bounding down the stairs at the end of the hall and ducked into a bedroom. He held the door cracked and watched as another guard came up and found his colleagues on the floor. He unholstered his weapon and went into a room across the hall, then ran back out and down the hall. The Merchant followed.

When he reached the steps, he heard a helicopter turbine roar to life and lift off. Up the stairs, he heard more voices and recognized his contact Albert Kessler. At the same moment, a short uniformed man appeared in the stairwell, and The Merchant instinctively disposed of him. At the top of the stairs he found himself in a large salon. A big man on a couch got up. One shot and the man fell through a glass cocktail table.

Then The Merchant saw Kessler, a knife in his hand, and Meyer sitting in a chair, blood all over his face.

Kessler enjoyed cutting Jakes' face up. "Let's see how much your girlfriend likes a man whose face looks like a pizza." He stood back to get a better look, and while he studied his work, the shorter Stern man returned. "There's a problem." He whispered to Kessler.

The Chief Inspector did not whisper. "She couldn't be far. Find her. Use the Davos police if you have to. Tell them she's mentally unstable."

Thank god. Maya had escaped.

"Looks like you messed up again," Jake said. Kessler wheeled and slapped Jake hard as the Stern operative headed back out. Kessler was about to say something when Jake heard two soft pops and a thud.

The blob on the couch jumped up and reached for his weapon. He never had a chance. Two more bursts, louder, and the big man crashed through the glass cocktail table.

Jake saw another blurry figure emerge from the staircase.

"What the hell are you doing?" Kessler asked in Schweizerdeutsch.

The shape came toward them. "Cleaning up."

"Where have you been?" Kessler demanded. "You haven't lived up to your end of the deal. Piedmont is furious. You'll get no more money. You haven't delivered."

"I was tied up with another problem," the figure answered. "Is Piedmont here?"

"No, he left about thirty minutes ago in the helicopter."

"Thank you, Mr. Meyer," the figure said, in English.

"What do you want with Herr Piedmont?" Kessler asked.

The man did not answer. Rather he raised his weapon and shot Kessler in the right shoulder. "Do you have the Pact?" Again in Swiss German.

"Meyer has it," Kessler replied.

"Do you?" In English.

"No," Jake answered.

"Can you get it?"

"I don't have it."

"He's lying. He took it from Hezekiah's Tunnel and hid it somewhere else," Kessler blurted.

"He may be lying, he may be telling the truth, but you'll never know." Another pop and the inspector dropped to the floor.

The man pulled a knife from somewhere. "I never cared much for the Chief Inspector." He man bent and cutting Jake's bindings. "Ms. Herzog is either downstairs or has left the chalet."

Jake could not make the man's face out. "Is she okay?"

"Yes." The man cut the last restraint. "I figure you know what to do with the Pact?" Jake looked up at the man, caught a glimpse of his profile. He seemed familiar, but he ran from the room.

Jake headed for the stairs and took them two at a time. He could hardly see. As he staggered around looking for a way out, his mind flipped through his memory. Then it came to him. Was it possible? The Merchant had rescued them.

CHAPTER 49

Davos

Seize the opportunity! Maya learned it from her father, from her Mossad trainers. So despite her bewilderment and curiosity about the apparition that set her free, Maya wasted no time dwelling on it. She raced through the door and grabbed a weapon from one of the fallen guards down the hall. She walked along the hallway, looking for a way out, or Jake, or both. She opened a couple of doors but found only empty, elegant bedrooms. At length she ended up in a garage full of snow equipment— skis, ski suits, and a lot of mechanical gear for maintaining snowmobiles. She knew there was an exit and soon found the control button next to a workbench. She pressed it, the airlock hissed, and she was outside.

Her eye picked up a trail of crimson staining the snow and followed it to a body propped against the wall, eyes glazed with horror, blood trickling from an armpit. Her rescuer was clearly a professional. The knife severed a major artery from the heart.

Suddenly an engine roared to life. Maya ducked into a corner and peered out at a man speeding down the driveway in a blue BMW. When the car disappeared, Maya raced to the front of the chalet and found another dead guard, his neck broken.

She started back into the chalet through the front door and suddenly felt the cool steel of a muzzle against her temple. She turned and saw Albert Kessler, his face clammy and his white shirt was stained with blood.

"Drop the gun, Ms. Herzog."

Maya complied and turned to face the Chief Inspector, his weapon inches from her nose. She raised her hands to shoulder level. "Where's Jake?"

"I'd like to know that too," Kessler grunted. "He's probably somewhere in the chalet looking for you."

The Chief Inspector closed the door and walked backwards, beckoning Maya to follow. "But now that you're here, we can find him together."

Maya followed him through the vaulted foyer into a den to the right. As Kessler led her to the intercom on the far wall he asked, "Why didn't you shoot him?"

"Who?"

"The man who drove away. The Merchant."

"I would have missed."

The man who released her from the basement room was the same size and build as The Merchant. Was it possible? Why would The Merchant save her?

"Would you have tried if you knew The Merchant killed your father?"

"Nice try, Chief Inspector. You don't know anything about my father's death."

"On the contrary. The Levant Group referred The Merchant to an Iranian who said he had a delicate situation and needed someone crafty. A couple of weeks later Mr. Herzog was dead. In his home, no less."

Was Kessler telling the truth? Did the Iranians hire The Merchant to kill her father? If so, did Rafi Golan know it? He promised to keep her informed.

Maya noticed that Kessler was out of her reach. She needed to close the distance if she wanted it to work.

He was by the intercom, his smile gone. "Press that button and call for Mr. Meyer."

Maya moved to the intercom and closer to Kessler, her hands at shoulder level. "What if he doesn't respond?"

"Tell him I'll kill you. That should do the trick."

Sweat fell from Kessler's temple. He was in shock and weak. Maya figured she was now close enough. With the speed of a cobra she twisted the gun away from him, took three quick steps backward, aimed and shot him in the head.

As the inspector fell to the ground, she sensed another presence in the room. Swinging to her left she was about to pull the trigger again when she saw Jake Meyer.

CHAPTER 50

Davos

Even with his hazy vision Jake knew Maya was pointing a weapon at him. The fact that she was a millisecond away from blowing a hole in his chest was immaterial. She was alive.

He took her in his arms. "Are you okay?"

"Yes, yes," she said, "but look at you!" His face was a swollen mess.

"It stings, but I'll be fine. What about you?"

Maya raised her bent fingers. "I'll have them re-set, no big deal."

"Did you find the Pact in Hezekiah's Tunnel?" Maya now asked, leading Jake out of the den.

"Yes, just where Steiner said it would be."

"What did you do with it?"

"Funny, that's what Kessler and Piedmont wanted to know."

Maya looked at him quizzically.

"I took care of it."

Maya was about to ask, but Jake cut her off. "Trust me. Right now we have to get out of here. Kessler probably called the police before you ran into him."

"Do you know where *here* is exactly?"

"Davos."

Maya nodded. "That makes sense."

"What do you mean?"

"I saw the town from the garage. It didn't have the *Heidi* aura."

"Garage? Any cars?"

"Nope. It's more like a repair shop for snowmobiles. And before you ask, there aren't any of those either."

211

"Great. Any idea how to get down to the town?"

"Do you ski?"

"I did, a long time ago, until I got hurt. I haven't skied since that."

"Well, it's the only way out of here. It'll come back to you." Maya led Jake to the ski garage.

"The Merchant gave us a hand," Jake said.

Maya said nothing, her face as tight as a drum.

"I agree, its puzzling," was all Jake could think to say.

"Kessler said The Merchant murdered my father."

"Do you believe him?"

"His explanation sounded plausible, but . . . "

"But what?"

"Nothing."

Jake figured she would tell him when she was ready.

In garage Maya collected ski clothes and boots off the wall. "These look about your size. Try them on."

Jake sat down, shucked his clothes, and got into a makeshift ski rig which more or less fit. He figured it would do.

After Maya rigged up and found skis that suited her, she carried them outside into the snow. The sky had lost its orange glow. Dark in thirty minutes. Jake's blurred vision and the dusky haze left him all but blind. "There is one other thing," he said.

"What?"

"They knocked out my lenses. I can barely see."

Maya looked down to the town, then back at Jake. "It's not that far but since we don't have a trail map we may not make it before nightfall." She went back into the garage and found a flashlight, slid it under her belt and pushed it around to the small of her back. "Now you have a beacon. Just follow it. I won't ski too fast."

Jake clicked into his bindings, inched forward and turned on the light on Maya's back. "Okay, let's go."

Maya was off. Jake watched the yellow light arc through a couple of turns and followed, praying his muscles remembered how to maneuver the skis.

Jake pointed the tips of his skis downhill and thought he was going to be a human snowball and roll right into town. But then, his first ski instructor's voice rang in his ear. *It's all about shifting weight to your downhill ski. It doesn't feel natural but that's how you turn.* Jake pushed hard on his right foot—and turned left. A second later he shifted weight to his left foot and turned right. It was coming back.

Maya looked over her shoulder from time to time to be sure Jake was behind her. In the fading light she saw his black form and a storm of snow ever time he turned. *Not pretty*, she thought, *but he'll be fine.*

She worried more about where they were heading. The town lay before them, its lights a lone star in deep space. But she knew nothing about the run. A sharp turn and they might ski right off a cliff or into the trees. She wished she had a map.

Then she heard sirens. Jake was right. Kessler called the police. Once they saw the mess at Piedmont's chalet they'd seal Davos off. They had to get out of town.

At a fork in the trail she came to a stop. A wooden directional sign read *Davos-Platz*. An arrow pointed to the right. At least she knew which way to go.

Maya waited until Jake came up and stopped just he crashed into her.

"Well done," Maya said, strapping the flashlight back onto her belt.

"I almost bought it when I landed."

"It's good you didn't. The police are on their way to the chalet."

Two more labored breaths. "I know."

"Can you speed things up?"

"I think so."

"The sign says Davos is to the right. I don't think it's much farther."

"Good. The town is small. There should be a train station. If we can get there before the police close things down, we might make it out." Jake leaned on his poles to take some of the strain off his legs and feet. "The only question is where do we go?"

"Mossad has a safe house in Rome. We're near the border. We just take the train to Italy."

Jake doubted any place was safe from the Levant Group. "All right, after you."

They were at the base of the mountain in seven minutes. They found a lodge and went in. Après skiers sat in the bar, enjoying the crackling fire and strong drinks. No one noticed them as they sat on a bench and got out of the ski garb.

As they changed, Maya scanned the lodge. "No police."

"That won't last," Jake said. "We have to get out of here."

Maya reached behind her head and yanked her ponytail and fetched up with a handful of hair, as if she had scalped herself. One second she had a long silky mane, the next she tossed short, tussled hair. "Extensions. They come in handy at times like this."

"Well if the police have pictures, there's no way they'll recognize you. I'm not sure I do."

Maya grabbed his hand, and they walked out of the lodge. "But they might identify you." She said hailed a cab.

"Yeah, there's the rub." He followed her into the cab and shut the door. *"Hauptbahnhof, bitte."*

Jake ran the scenarios in his mind. The train station would be crawling with Stadtpolizei looking for them. If they were stopped they needed a story, something convincing. *Pretend. That's it.* He turned to Maya. "I've got an idea."

"What?"

"They don't know my contact lenses are gone."

"So?"

"I'm an attorney."

"I don't see the connection."

"It also means I'm an actor."

CHAPTER 51

Davos

In the Hauptbahnhof at half past six in the evening, pandemonium reigned. Travelers jostled one other, luggage and ski gear in tow. Announcements in German, French and English pierced the din. To make matters worse, the Stadtpolizei were all over the place.

"Looks like we are a little late," Maya said.

"How many and where?"

"About twenty in teams of two on the platforms and at the exits."

"Are they checking papers?"

"No, they're just eyeballing. They know what they're looking for."

"That should help us."

"So should this." Maya knelt down to tie her boot and shoved a couple of coins into Jake's shoe. "It's an old trick but it works. The coins will make you walk funny."

"You know what to do?" Jake asked.

"Yes. Don't flinch."

"Let's get tickets."

Maya looked at the schedule board. "The next train to Rome leaves in ten minutes."

"Perfect."

After they bought tickets, Maya headed for pay phones. "I need to make arrangements." He stood against the wall while she called, staring into the distance, trying not to blink.

Maya hung up the phone and took Jake's hand into the crook of her elbow. "This way, Dear." They made for the platforms.

Maya picked out the youngest looking Stadtpolizei officer. When she stopped, Jake reached out to stop himself.

"Excuse me, officer, which platform for the train to Rome?" Maya asked in English. The policeman's partner studied the faces of other commuters.

"It's on the board. Number four."

The young officer's patronizing grin for the foolish woman hardened when he saw Jake. Jake didn't blink and focused on a point beyond the other man's shoulder.

"This is my brother." Maya kissed Jake's cheek. "He lost most of his vision a few years back. We've been here for a few days of relaxation, and we're going to visit family in Italy. Trying to keep life normal, you know?"

"What happened to his face?"

"Oh, he slipped on the ice and fell into the shrubbery along the Promenade. Things happen."

"Bet it stings."

"Sure does." Jake looked past the policeman.

"What is your name?"

Jake didn't respond. How did he know who the cop asked?

"Lisa," Maya said.

The young man looked at Maya as if to say *not you*. He waved his hand back and forth in front of Jake's face.

"That is extremely offensive," Maya snapped. "Do you think this is a joke? He can't see and you are playing games? Is this how you treat people in Switzerland?"

The officer waved them through.

They boarded the train and found their seats.

Jake turned toward the window and studied his eyes in the reflection. He turned and looked at Maya. Even without his contacts, he was beginning to see clearly again.

CHAPTER 52

Davos

The Merchant sped down the serpentine roads, his left index finger tapping the steering wheel like a metronome. Getting into Piedmont's chalet was not easy, and leaving without finishing up frustrated him. The Merchant had looked forward to a relaxing flight from Klotten airport to a quiet Caribbean island with Sophie by his side. That would have to wait.

Meyer said he did not have the Pact, and The Merchant believed him. It helped that Kessler and Piedmont did not have it either. But then again, the Pact was never his primary objective. It would have been a nice insurance policy, though.

From Davos-Platz, he followed the signs to the train station and parked the car. Early evening passengers trooped in and out like ants. Inside, The Merchant headed to a kiosk to survey the scene and buy a bottle of water and a newspaper. No signs of danger so he went to the ticket window and bought an entire compartment, six first class tickets, to Vienna. He didn't want to be bothered by strangers.

The Merchant settled into his seat, snapped the paper and was reading when he noticed a number of Stadtpolizei taking up inspection positions on the platforms. He had little doubt they were looking for him.

A few seconds later there was a knock. "Ticket please."

The Merchant handed his ticket to the young but bespectacled man. "What is the commotion out side?"

The conductor scanned the bar code on the ticket and handed it back. "Just a security check. They're more common around the time

217

of the World Economic Forum. There shouldn't be much delay. The Stadtpolizei are thorough but quick."

"Any idea how much longer? I have a meeting in Vienna."

"A few minutes. I believe they are almost finished searching this train."

The conductor left and The Merchant sat back down, his mind calculating the possibilities. He killed Kessler in the chalet, so Herzog and Meyer must have alerted the authorities. *Ingrates*. He saved their lives, and that's how they return the favor. He should have killed them. But that would have nullified the deal.

The new deal that is. Had it been broken? Did Golan set him up? It wouldn't be the first time he'd been betrayed, but, he fumed, it would be the last.

Another knock. The Merchant slid the door open. The officer in blue fatigues with an MP-5 across his chest was about to say something when a look of recognition crossed his face. Shock replaced it when The Merchant kicked his knee cap and buckled his leg, grabbed the machine gun and shoved it into the man's chin. Before the officer could yell, The Merchant cupped his mouth and yanked him into the compartment and closed the door.

A small, razor sharp knife slid from his sleeve into The Merchant's free hand, and he held it to the cop's throat. "Life or death is your choice."

The policeman struggled but stopped when The Merchant broke skin with the knife and blood streamed down his neck.

"Call your superiors. Tell them all is clear and the train can leave." The Merchant's voice was soft and soothing. He lifted his hand from the officer's mouth so he could speak into the Motorola walky-talky on his vest. The policeman pushed the button and relayed the message in German. Then his eyes rolled up to look at the person cradling him, like a child expecting praise from a parent. It was the last thing the cop ever did. The Merchant covered the officer's mouth, twisted hard to the left and shoved the knife into the base of the man's skull.

As The Merchant forced the corpse underneath the bench seat, the train lurched forward. He took a seat and a deep breath. He spotted blood on his fingers and felt slightly ill. He never enjoyed killing, and recently it was difficult, even distasteful. Well, he was retiring, he was finished killing.

Almost.

On his cell phone he dialed the number for a bank account in the Cayman Islands. No money deposited. *Not surprising.* Golan said he wanted confirmation the job was done. On the other hand, even with proof, Golan might never have intended to pay up, especially if The Merchant got caught or killed.

It would not end that way. He dialed Golan.

"Have you finished?" the Israeli asked.

"No. But you tried to fuck me."

"What are you talking about?"

"Someone called the police. The train station was full of Stadtpolizei looking for me."

"I had nothing to do with that. Maybe you were compromised?"

"Yes, by Herzog and Meyer."

"Are they still alive?"

"Yes, for the time being."

"I hope that wasn't a threat. I can make the Stadtpolizei seem like a bunch of eunuchs. I honor my deals. You should do the same."

The Merchant thought about it. Golan needed him. "Very well, but I want an act of good faith, half the fee in the account in twenty minutes."

"How do I know *you* will finish things?"

"You haven't got a lot of choices."

Golan hesitated. "Done. Where are you going now?"

"I don't know. You tell me."

"Try Washington D.C."

The Merchant flipped the phone closed and dozed for twenty minutes. When he awoke, he called the Cayman number again. Ten million new dollars were in the account.

CHAPTER 53

Tel Aviv

Rafi Golan, veteran of the Yom Kippur war and the 1982 Lebanon campaign, skilled commander of covert operations in the Middle East and Europe, sat in his office, the pits of his shirtsleeves stained with sweat. Despite his experience with stress, the visible manifestations remained a part of his physiological makeup. So it was not surprising that the phone call from Dieter Fuchs, *a.k.a.* The Merchant, got such a reaction.

Somebody tipped law enforcement off *before* The Merchant finished. A search after he finished was predictable, factored into the arrangement. But with the police looking for him already, the chances he'd finish shrank. But Golan had to put all his chips on The Merchant.

The Merchant had gotten away from a good many intelligence services, including some with close ties to the Mossad. Rather than tell the CIA or MI-6 about Dieter Fuchs, Golan would help him disappear forever. Engaging The Merchant was necessary. So was silence.

But he'd have to tell Maya who killed her father, wouldn't he? He promised to keep her informed. Maya would be furious with him for making a deal with The Merchant. She might not ever speak to him again.

Someone knocked on the door

"Who is it?"

"Sir, we just received a message from Maya Herzog," the cadaverous communications officer said. "She's on her way to the safe house in Rome."

Golan stood from his chair. "Where's the contact from?"

"A phone in Davos."

"Did she say anything else?"

"No."

Golan grabbed his coat, a few cigars and a Desert Eagle handgun from a drawer. "Tell her to stay put. I'm going to Italy."

"Yes, Sir!"

"I'll be out of touch for a few days."

CHAPTER 54

Georgetown, Washington D.C.

Despite the incident in Davos and the likelihood there was an international alert out for him, The Merchant got through customs at Dulles without a hassle, partly because of the blond toupée, fake moustache and colored contact lenses, partly from the false documents he got from some old Cold War contacts in Vienna.

As the cab drove through the maze of Washington, The Merchant reflected how odd it was he'd never been to the American capital, the spy capital of the world. Too bad he couldn't tour, because once he finished the job, he'd never get to visit Washington or any other city, for that matter. It was part of the deal.

"When it's over, you'll be *persona non grata* around the globe," Golan told him in London.

"I don't see the upside for me."

"Well, how about this? You get to live. Beside your fee, we'll make sure you spend the rest of your days in comfort and peace." Word would spread that Israeli agents had eliminated The Merchant. He'd get a new identity and a home A witness protection program. The catch was that if Merchant even tried to leave the "designated area," they'd kill him. Fuchs recalled the look on Golan's face: *Please, try leaving.*

It wasn't the way The Merchant hoped things would work out, but it was better than having one of Golan's agents put a bullet in his head right then. At least he wouldn't have to look over his shoulder all the time. He relished the idea of settling down to relax his soul with books, paint and wine… and Sophie Foucard.

On Wisconsin Avenue, a couple in dark overcoats and scarves walked more slowly than the throngs newly released from a day at the office. They studied a tourist guide, and The Merchant was close enough to overhear them.

"Do you know what those are?" The man pointed to a staircase to his right.

"Stone steps in an alley?" The woman must have thought her companion was making a lame joke.

"Not just any steps. The ones the priest fell down in *The Exorcist.*"

"Really?" She admired them as if she were looking at a Hollywood star. "Pretty cool."

The rush hour traffic slacked off as The Merchant made his way to 34th Street in the West Village. Gas lamps flickered by the front doors of the charming colonial row houses. After five minutes The Merchant found the address he was looking for.

He knocked on the door. "Please show your identification."

The Merchant flipped open the badge and lifted it toward the camera. Only the photograph had been replaced.

"Thank you, Inspector Kessler. One moment please."

A man with dark hair opened the door. "You weren't expected so soon." He invited The Merchant inside.

"I suppose it's the superior interrogation techniques. I finished quickly." The Merchant didn't have to fake the German accent.

"Please raise your arms." The man frisked him. "Just a precaution, old habit from my days with the FBI."

"I understand completely. No doubt your concern for safety earned you big bucks."

The man smiled, nodded and leaned over to pat down The Merchant's legs. When he stood back up, The Merchant slammed a knee into his groin and chopped the sides of his neck. The man keeled over gasping for air.

The Merchant found his silenced gun and shoved it into the man's mouth. "Where is he?"

The man's eyes shifted right.

"And the surveillance room and tapes?"

The eyes shifted down.

"In the basement?"

A nod.

"Thank you." The Merchant shot him in the head.

Down the hallway he saw light underneath double doors, turned the brass handle and went in. An elderly gentleman sat reading a book in front of a fire.

"I suppose you have the Pact, Herr Kessler?" Lance Piedmont did not bother looking up.

"Not exactly." The Merchant inched closer.

"What does that mean?" Piedmont shut the book and looked up.

"I don't have the Pact."

"Who are you?" Piedmont demanded.

"Dieter Fuchs. You call me The Merchant. You hired me. Actually, Herr Kessler hired me."

"Where is Kessler?"

"Dead."

Piedmont didn't seem upset. "Okay, where is the Pact?"

"I don't know. Meyer said he didn't have it either." The Merchant came closer.

"And you believed him? What about Meyer and Herzog. Where are they?"

"Somewhere in Europe I suppose. But that's not my concern anymore." The Merchant's tone was matter-of-fact.

"It should be, Herr Fuchs," Piedmont snapped. "We paid you a lot of money. Finish the job."

The Merchant raised the weapon and Piedmont fell silent. A hint of concern on his face turned to curiosity. "Who turned you?"

The Merchant didn't answer.

"Meyer and Herzog couldn't afford you unless . . . " Piedmont's voice trailed off. He seemed to understand. "Do you think killing me will change anything?"

"Doesn't much matter. It's just a job."

"You'll be hunted, probably dead within days," Piedmont stammered.

The Merchant didn't respond. He simply watched the Lenin clone's face go from angry red to frightened white and shot Piedmont twice in the chest. Then he stood over the man and fired one more bullet into his head.

Now he was finished.

CHAPTER 55

Rome

From a window in the kitchen corner, Jake gazed at the spires of Trinità dei Monti, the church at the head of the Spanish Steps. He sipped potent though tepid coffee while Maya made ham, salami and cheese sandwiches.

"When is Golan going to get here?" A message from Tel Aviv awaited at the safe house on Via del Babuino.

"Shortly, I suppose. The flight from Tel Aviv doesn't take long." Maya handed Jake a plate. Her face was blank.

He knew she was angry. She hardly spoke on the train from Davos. She had questions about The Merchant. Jake wanted to know *why* The Merchant saved them.

They ate in silence until Maya asked, "What did you do with the Pact?"

Jake stopped chewing. "I tore it up."

"When?"

"While I was stumbling through Hezekiah's Tunnel to find you, it occurred to me that I was holding something as dangerous as a nuclear weapon. No good could have come from anyone with the Pact. It was too tempting. Somebody—the Levant Group, the Israelis, the United States—somebody would have used it for blackmail. The world is complicated enough as is. That Pact would just make things worse."

"That makes sense. But why didn't you tell Piedmont or Kessler that back in Davos?"

"They wouldn't have believed the truth. Piedmont wanted to hear that the Pact existed and that he could get it. Would have been his crown jewel." Jake looked down. "And frankly, I didn't know where you were, and I was hoping to buy time if you needed it."

Maya blushed and took Jake's hand. "What will you tell Golan?"

"Just what I told you."

"He might not believe it."

"Then you can back me up."

Maya nodded. "Sure."

A sound from inside the apartment startled them. "Does Golan have a key?"

Maya whispered, "I don't know."

Jake took the gun from the table and Maya headed to the bedroom.

Jake tiptoed down the hall, arms extended. In the living room he found a bull of a man sitting on a couch, unfazed by the muzzle pointed at his chest.

"Mr. Meyer, it's nice to meet you at last. I'm Rafi Golan."

"You should have knocked."

"Why? It's my house."

"It's Mossad's house," Maya corrected him.

Golan hugged Maya, who responded desultorily.

"Are you all right?" he asked her.

Maya crossed her arms. " I'm fine."

Golan returned to the couch and lit a cigar. Maya sat down. "Let's get on with the debriefing."

"Where did Steiner hide the Pact?"

"In Hezekiah's Tunnel," Jake said.

"Do you have it?"

"No. I tore it up."

Golan looked perplexed.

"It's true," Maya said.

"How do you know? Were you there?"

"No. A couple of Shin Bet agents were breaking my fingers to get information about Jake and the Pact." Her voice was not pleasant.

"The Levant Group has infiltrated Shin Bet?" Golan was not shocked.

Maya nodded.

Golan turned his mistrustful gaze to Jake. "The Levant Group would have paid a mega-fortune. Why didn't you sell it to them?"

"I might have avoided a whole lot of pain if Piedmont had put *that* option on the table," Jake retorted.

"And why should I believe you, Mr. Meyer?"

Jake thought about it. "Because I swear on Maya's life that the Pact is gone."

Jake's choice of words surprised them. Golan studied the pair and backed down.

After a moment, Maya asked, "What about The Merchant?"

Golan pursed his lips. "What about him?"

"He's the reason we're alive." Maya described the events in Davos, though she didn't mention Kessler's revelation about her father. "Why did he help us?"

"It was part of the deal. What I can tell you is that even without the Pact the Levant Group is a threat. It lives on chaos. We decided to cut the hydra's head off."

It took Jake only seconds. "Piedmont?"

Golan nodded. "And because of Piedmont's position and contacts, you had to give yourself deniability."

"Correct," Golan said. "But Piedmont left the chalet before The Merchant got to him." He looked at his watch. "But it should be over soon. It'll be big news. CNN and the BBC will report it."

Maya's face was red and her eyes full. "What did you give The Merchant?"

"I can't say." Golan's eyes went to the floor again. "National security, you understand."

Maya got up and slapped Golan. "Kessler told me The Merchant murdered my father. And you knew. You knew it all the time and you didn't tell me. You promised." And the tears fell.

Golan's face was red with shame. "Maya, there wasn't a choice."

"Sure there was. You could have told me."

"And what would you have done?"

She didn't respond.

"I'll tell you. You would have dropped everything to kill him. You would've put everything in jeopardy, including Mr. Meyer. We had to make sure Piedmont didn't get hold of the Pact and we had to hit the Levant Group. The Merchant was the best option."

More tears dropped. "I suppose your word had its limits."

"I didn't want to hide things from you, but what could I do? Do you think I didn't want to shoot him myself? Chaim was your father, but he was also my best friend, my brother." He touched Maya's head. "Can you forgive me?"

Maya walked back to the kitchen, but Golan did not follow her.

"She'll be okay," Jake said. "She just needs time."

"Perhaps," Golan said, pulling on his jacket and scarf. He walked to the door and looked back, the steel blue eyes a bit softer. He loved Maya too.

In the kitchen, Maya was staring out the window, knees in her chest. "Is he gone?"

"Yes." Jake wanted to hold and comfort her, but decided against it. "He didn't mean to hurt you."

"I know." She ran a hand through her hair. "And in time I'll know he was right. He did what he had to." Her eyes were red, but the tears had stopped. "Anyway, it's over now. When are you going home?"

He hadn't thought about leaving her. "Tomorrow, but I'll keep you company tonight." It had nothing to do with sex. He pulled a chair over, and they sat together in a comfortable silence. He looked into her eyes and for the first time in a long time did not want to be alone.

EPILOGUE

Jerusalem—Two Weeks Later

The guide put on the sunglasses dangling around his neck and waited for the group to emerge from Hezekiah's Tunnel. It was his fifth tour in five days, a real dilly. Fifty teenagers from Miami whose adolescent dramas competed fiercely with Holy Land's ancient wonders.

As he waited on the steps, one of boys came up with something in his hand. "Hey, look what I found." He held a piece of torn paper up. "Do you think it is an ancient text? How much can I get for it?"

The guide glared at him. He took the paper and turned it this way and that, trying to read it. The writing was blurred. He saw both Hebrew and Arabic, but the ink had run. He could make out some numbers and the names of Jericho, Hebron and what looked like Bethlehem.

"It's nothing. Maybe some kind of purchase order. Somebody dropped it in the water."

The teen rejoined his friends.

The guide was tired of waiting. He wadded the paper up, raised his hand and shouted,"Ah, people, move over here. We have to get going." On the way to the Eged tour bus he tossed it into a trash receptacle.

Maya trudged up the tallest hill in Jerusalem looking for the site. The headstone would not be in place for another three months so she had to find her father's grave from memory. As she searched, Maya passed others paying their respects to the dead, leaving stones on the graves and reciting the Kaddish.

Soon she found her father's final resting place. He could have been buried at Mount Herzel, Jerusalem's military cemetery, with Israel's presidents, prime ministers and other dignitaries, but he chose a plot on the Mount of Olives. According to the Old Testament, that's where the redemption of the dead will begin at the end of days. Jews have long sought to be buried there.

For Chaim Herzog, the hill had a personal significance. He was part of the unit that stormed the mountain just before the Old City fell in 1967. He told Maya that when he marched through the Lions Gate of the Old City, he felt complete and knew he would spend the rest of his life protecting the city for future generations. And he wanted to be buried on the Mount of Olives to watch over the city for eternity.

Maya turned and looked at the ancient stone walls, the glittering golden Dome of the Rock and beyond. For the first time since her father's death she let herself cry for him, not just one or two tears but a torrent. When the convulsions calmed, she realized she'd shed tears not only of grief but also of relief, of joy. She would miss her *abba*, but she knew he was proud of her. She was proud of herself.

Soon the sobbing subsided and Maya wiped her tears. She noticed an Eged tour bus driving in the Kidron valley below just as her cell phone vibrated. She answered it and smiled. "Shalom. How are you?"

The fifties retro diner in Arlington was empty except for two patrons. An old woman at the counter complained that her bowl of oatmeal was too hot and asked for a cup of cream to cool it. Jake sat in a corner booth finishing off a plate of scrambled eggs and sausage, reading *The Washington Post*.

His external injuries were healing, and Jake's inner demons had fled. He felt lighter and more energetic.

A waitress refilled his cup. "Anything else, Honey?"

"No, thanks, just the check."

Jake checked his watch. He didn't have to be in court until eight, which gave him just over an hour. He put away the sports section and started the front page.

AP-Washington D.C.-----Information gleaned during the investigation of the death of Lance Piedmont has led House Minority leader Thomas Richardson (D-Wisconsin) to call for Congressional hearings into alleged connections between Piedmont, the White House and certain members of the federal legislature. Richardson, a member of the Foreign Relations Committee claims that there is evidence that

Piedmont headed a cabal of business and industry that had dictated U.S. and global politics for decades.

"It is clear that through various means, from subtle threats to bribes to blackmail, this consortium has exerted influence over certain members of the executive and legislative branches of our government," Richardson said. "This influence has created an agenda that harms our national and international interests. It is frightening."

Another member of Congress, Vanessa Brown (R-Florida) echoed Richardson's sentiments and further stated that she "has heard rumors that this 'organization' goes back over fifty years" and that if this were true "the ramifications could be mind boggling."

He didn't bother to finish the article. He read on for a few pages and looked at his watch again. He thought about it for a moment and wondered if he should. There was a seven hour time difference. He went back and forth, then decided to trust his instincts. He got his cell phone and dialed the number.

"Hi, Maya."

ABOUT THE AUTHOR

Ethan Paritzky currently works as a Policy and Security Officer for the United States Department of Defense dealing with international security issues. He has been published in the *International Journal of Intelligence and Counterintelligence*. Prior to his present position, he acted as in-house counsel for international legal issues to two multi-million dollar corporations and was also a litigation attorney. Mr. Paritzky earned his B.A. in communications from the University of Pennsylvania, his J.D. and M.A. in International Relations from the University of Southern California, and his Masters in Strategic Intelligence from American Military University. *The Weizmann Protocol* is his first novel.

LaVergne, TN USA
12 May 2010
182448LV00007B/64/P